Every Mile a Memory

Grea Warner

Every Mile a Memory
Copyright © 2019 Grea Warner
All rights reserved.

ISBN: (ebook) 978-1-949931-27-3
(print) 978-1-949931-28-0

Inkspell Publishing
5764 Woodbine Ave.
Pinckney, MI 48169

Edited By Rie Langdon
Cover art By Najla Qamber

DEDICATION

For my road-trip, girls-getaway friends – SW, KC, PJ, MS. We don't get to see one another often, but every time it is full of wild and wonderful memories.

And with love to my family for supporting me on my writing journey and in life.

CHAPTER ONE

The empty, faux-wood bucket swung loosely in my hand. I was on a mission to find the hotel's ice machine, located inconveniently, of course, in an obscure location on an opposing floor. But my real mission wasn't ice. In fact, I rarely put the cold cubes in my beverages. My real reason for the late-afternoon search was to have a moment to myself.

We had been in the Keys for a little more than twenty-four hours. Although I loved the warmth and the relaxing, beachy pace, we had been together practically non-stop. But the thing was, I had become used to solitude and realized now I even kind of craved it.

A tall, built man, most likely around my age, was approaching in the otherwise empty hall. He was flanked by two children—a boy, maybe four years old, and a little girl who did more of a waddle than a toddle. I internally cringed, thinking that now I had to acknowledge them with either a generic stranger "hello" or one of those quick, fake-smile deals. At least my peace and quiet wouldn't be interrupted that long.

And then it was…in the most violent kind of way. The popping sound was quite recognizable and one that haunted my dreams on a regular basis. It was loud. It was deadly. And it was definitely near.

Just as startled as I was, the man, still many feet in front of me, grabbed the little girl in one of his well-defined arms and started at a quicker pace in my direction. But the boy didn't follow. He stopped mid-stream and turned toward the obvious gunfire.

"Chance!" The man yelled urgently to the young boy.

Passing the man and little girl, I instinctively went to the startled preschooler. Quickly bending down to his level, I said, "No. No. We need to go this way, all right?"

He looked at me with round, gray, doe-eyes but didn't move, even when the man again yelled out what I was guessing was his name. Forgetting everything else, I scooped him up in both of my arms and scurried back in the direction I had come. Opening up a room door, the man, with closely cropped, dark auburn hair and significant matching scruff, ushered the little girl inside and turned to me. But as he did, another round went off, even louder it seemed, and I found myself being physically tossed into the hotel room. The door slammed behind us, and I momentarily struggled for breath as the brawny man lay protectively on top of both me and the little boy still snuggled in my arms.

"You okay?" he asked, lifting himself up and looking from me to the kids. "Chance, you all right?"

"I scared." And he appeared as if he was going to absolutely bawl.

Before the man could respond, we heard another round. Although that time, it was, thankfully, a little more muffled because of the closed quarters. But it threw the tall stranger into an even more protective mode. He went for the loveseat and started to move it toward the door as a blockade.

Getting the children out of the way, I directed them to the wall near the bathroom. "Can you stay here? It's all right. You can play something called the quiet game." I encouraged the kids, while trying to get them to sit. "You—"

"I know quiet game." The little boy's silent tears seemed to slow as he displayed his pride. "I beat Arinn all the time."

Assuming every version of the quiet game, something I had been relishing myself just moments before, was similar, I played referee. "Okay. Ready…Set…Go."

On the word "go," Chance put one index finger up to his mouth. Had I not been so terrified, I would have laughed. But instead, on the word "go," I jumped into action, pulling a chair over to contribute in the building of the barrier against the door.

"Your belt," I said to the guy, who started assisting me with the chair. "Take off your belt."

"What?"

"Tie it around the hinge. It won't open." I watched as, without questioning, he obeyed and unleashed his belt from his black cargo pants. Then a thought erupted in my mind— maybe it was the guy next to me that the shooter was after. "Are they going to try to get in here?"

Strapping the belt around the hinge as told, he said, "I hope not. I have no idea what's going on. You know as much as I do. It's better to be prepared." The genuine tone in his voice and the look in his hazel eyes made me know he was telling the truth.

"Is there anything we can use as a weapon?" I began to look around. "Can you get that curtain rod? I can look for things to throw."

"If someone gets through this, I've got it covered," he claimed.

I couldn't help but wonder how much of his statement was machoism, as I actually verbalized, "Well, that's all good and—"

"Believe me, I got—" He started to interrupt but was cut short by another blast of gunfire.

"I don't want to play game no more," Chance immediately whined and, in essence, gave the win to the girl next to him, who was too young to even understand how to play.

"Hey. Hey." I tried a soothing voice, knowing it was those two little ones who were actually keeping me from freaking out.

When a loud broadcast announcement soared through the hallways warning everyone to stay in their rooms, the guy, who had thrown me into one, approached the kids. "Maybe we should all just get in the bathroom. It's central, there's no windows… Who knows where they are and how long it will—"

"I'll be fine here." I sat up against the wall with the kids.

"I don't know…" He crouched down in front of us.

I looked in the direction of the barricaded door. "If they get through that, they'll get into the bathroom. You do what you want, though."

"You're right."

"Mousey," the little girl, who I assumed to be Chance's sister, cried out.

Like dominoes, she looked at me, I looked at the man, and he looked at the boy. "What's Arinn saying?" he asked Chance.

"Mousey." The brown-haired boy pointed to the sofa a few feet or so away.

I looked across the room, only then realizing how expansive it really was. It must have been a mini-suite. There was a definite living area separate from the bed. We already had a loveseat and chair up against the door, and there was still a sofa. And, sure enough, sitting on top of it was a white and gray stuffed animal—a mouse. I got up and brought the toy over to the girl, who instantly looked better in its embrace.

When the guy stood up again, like he was on guard, Chance began to whimper, and I broke into Plan B. "You know what we're gonna do? We're gonna build a fort—a pillow fort."

"There no pillow fort!" the little boy exclaimed, as if I'd

said the most ridiculous thing.

"Yes, sir," I claimed. "A pillow and blanket fort. We're gonna drape it around the sofa and sit under it." I started to gather the comforter and blanket off the bed. "All of us. You get the pillows," I directed to Chance, who was happy to be distracted...just as I was.

Only as we began to build the soft structure did I have a second to think. What the hell had just happened? How did I end up in there, and who was I with? As if trying to read my mind, I saw the man staring at me.

"You got good kids," I offered in exchange, because that was the one thing I knew for sure.

"They're not mine," he replied.

"Oh?" I asked slowly.

Crawling underneath the arched covers of the makeshift tent, Chance asked on cue, "Where Daddy?"

"Dada," Arinn called out as she crawled under, too.

"I'm calling Daddy right now, big guy." Taking out his phone, the man sat down at the entrance of the tent after I sat partially in, partially out.

Trying to piece together another part of the puzzle called that afternoon, I wondered what the relationship was between the man and the kids. After all, the two little ones seemed so comfortable around their elder. Relatives, perhaps?

"Hey, where are you at?" He spoke into his phone, causing me to listen... as if I had any other choice, being captive in the room. "That close?" he questioned, and then, "Yeah, that's what I'm—" He listened as the person on the other end was obviously trying to figure out what was going on in the hotel. "Yeah. I'm sure they're not going to let you through." Pause. "I don't know. We're in my room. Whatever is happening is happening here—close. But we're all right." Another break as he listened. "I don't know. There's guns and alarms, and they're telling us to stay in the room." The guy looked at the kids, who were cuddled up and watching him just as intently as I was. "Of course." He spoke back into the phone. "They're fine. We're just trying to keep them quiet." And another pause. "Yeah, there was some lady—" He stopped mid-conversation and looked at me in a way where the question was understood.

"Maya," I offered.

"Maya," he continued back into the phone. "She was walking down the hall when all of this happened. She helped get Chance in the room. She's kinda stuck here with us." He looked back at me, and Chance started to squirm in his direction. "Yeah." There was another pause and then he said, "Can you talk with Chance?" As the little boy scurried onto the guy's lap, he passed him the phone. "Here you go, big guy. Talk with your dad."

"Hi, Daddy. Where Mommy?" Chance asked, and then, after a pause, said, "Hi, Mommy. I all right." He listened some more. "Arinn all right. I good big brother." And with that response, one of my questions was put to rest—the two were definitely siblings. "I play quiet game and built a big pillow and blankie fort." He looked at me then with pride. "Yeah, it loud." He looked at the man, who seemed to flash a surge of sadness for the kids' suffering. "Uh-huh. Daddy, you sing me dat song?"

I watched as the little boy swayed a little in the man's lap, and Arinn cuddled next to me with the stuffed mouse. Chance was obviously listening to some song because there were occasional words in lyric form coming from his mouth. It was a song I thought I recognized, but there weren't enough continuous words to make a clear identification.

"I love you, too," he said into the phone as the swaying stopped. "I love you, too, Mommy." There was another pause and then he concluded with an "okay" before handing the phone back to its owner.

"Finn?" Speaking into the phone, the man identified the person on the other end. "No, I don't think it has anything to do with you. Just wrong place, wrong—"

He was still talking, but I was mentally backtracking. He

had called the daddy by the name Finn, and the song Chance had been singing…I knew the country singer was in town. That had to be it. Those were Finn Murphy's kids.

When I regained focus, I heard him say, "Stay put. When it's clear—all clear—I'll wait for you to come to us. Tell your wife they are fine." He listened for a second and then said, "I know. I hear her crying, man." There was another pause before he said, "I know. You know I got this. Nothing's gonna happen." He nodded toward the kids when he said it. "All right. Holler back if you hear something." After he hung up, he looked at me soothing Arinn's hair. "You're good with kids. You must have some?"

"No." I swallowed and felt like I should give maybe a little more explanation. But all I said was, "Just like them."

"Hmmm," was his even shorter response, followed by, "They said there are police cars in front of the hotel. So whatever is going on, it's being handled."

"Hawk?" Still in his lap, Chance helped me finally identify the man's name.

"Yeah?" Hawk answered.

"Daddy say I his brave little man."

"That you are, buddy."

Arinn started to amuse herself by belly flopping up and down on one of the pillows on the floor. So Chance decided simultaneously to do the same thing next to his sister. It provided giggles not only from the kids but from us adults as well. So much for quiet.

As the kids continued to play, Hawk said to me, "You're also good with crisis management."

"My husband was a cop." I breathed in. "We actually met when he came to teach a safety class at my work."

"Oh, that explains it." He followed with, "Is he here? Do you need to call him?" He then paused, obviously thinking of our immediate situation. "Do you think he's helping out with this?"

"No." My one-word response essentially answered all three questions. And then came the explanation, which had gotten easier over those past months but still always caught my breath. "He died last year."

Hawk looked first at my bare left hand and then at my right, where I had moved my wedding band about nine months after Jeff's death. I hadn't wanted to remove it completely. But leaving it on "the" ring finger seemed like a lie—a lie to myself—like I thought there was still some kind of hope that everything had been a horrific nightmare and he was coming back. I could get away with wearing that simple gold band engraved with a heart symbol and our initials. But the raised diamond engagement ring, I could not. That was tucked away safely with some of my grandmother's jewelry I never wore.

I found myself playing with the ring as Hawk, obviously recognizing what it was, said, "Sorry."

I had been hearing that for twelve plus months. No one ever knew what to say. And it seemed even harder when the deceased was so young and in a noble career such as Jeff's. I had thought it had slowed down—the condolences, the sad looks—until the one-year anniversary of his death happened. And then the department organized a candlelight vigil where people could pray for and share stories of Jeff all over again. His family and I appreciated all the support, but I also had been finding my way out in more positive than somber ways. The vacation to the Keys was actually one of them.

I bailed my fellow captee out. "I should call my friends, though. We're on a girls getaway."

When he nodded in agreement, I realized I didn't have my cell phone. Why would I have needed it? I was going on a little walk a floor away. I certainly hadn't brought my phone. I had stuck the room key in my shorts pocket, thrown on flip-flops which matched my T-shirt, and had been off. I should have known…nothing was ever easy.

I used the hotel phone to call directly to Juanita and Sophia in our room. We didn't talk long. I just wanted to let them know where I was and to make sure they we were both safe and secure. When I got off the phone, I saw that Hawk was busy on his cell phone, texting. I sat back down with the kids and tried to alleviate some of the excessive pillow-bouncing energy by making up a story. There were superheroes and mice and little boys and little girls in it. Hawk tried jumping in every so often, but he was actually more of a third child listening, which was kind of amusing in itself.

And then the story came to an abrupt halt. It had been a little while since the last loud crackle of gunfire. But there it was again…at least three pops. And that time, admittedly, I jumped. Probably because, for the tiniest of seconds, I had actually let myself slightly relax.

Noticing, Hawk confirmed my name. "Maya, is it?"

"Yeah."

"You good?" he asked, but immediately followed up with a confident, "We're all right."

"Yeah. I just…I wish it wasn't gunfire and police," I admitted.

"Crap, yeah. Did he die…"

Again, it was something even harder for others to say to me than for me to actually articulate. "In the line of duty," I finished for him. "I'm good. Let's concentrate on these cute kids." I tried to change the subject for all four of our sakes. "Talk about being good with kids," I said, referring to his easy demeanor with Chance and Arinn.

His right eye narrowed slightly as if he was trying to figure me out…trying to figure out if I really was all right after that latest round of gunfire. When I didn't speak again, he decided to go with my kid topic. "Yeah, because I'm like a grandparent. I give them back after a little bit," he joked.

"Not my grandma," I replied.

And while we got Chance to play on Hawk's tablet and I rocked Arinn a little bit, I somehow ended up telling the story of my life. I started with the fact that my father died in a car crash when I was four, which Hawk confirmed was also Chance's age…and that Arinn was one-and-a-half. I then explained that my mother died suddenly just about a year after my father. It was technically an aneurysm, although most people claimed it was a broken heart. She never recovered from the loss of my dad. Both sets of grandparents fought over my custody—as if being a freshly minted orphan wasn't bad enough. My dad's parents lived in Canada, which was just too much upheaval. So my mom's mom, who lived near us in Maryland, got me. And she never let me go until she, herself, died when I was twenty-six.

"God, you've lived it, huh?" was Hawk's response to my tale.

"And only in my mid-thirties." I looked down at a soft-murmuring Arinn in my arms.

"No brothers or sisters, then?"

"No." I paused, but then thought, why not? We needed to talk about something. It helped distract me from being entombed in the closed-off room. "My mom was pregnant when my dad died. They had just found out. But the grief of him leaving…forever…was too much. She miscarried."

"Mmmm," he murmured, and then redirected with another question. "Still live in Maryland?"

And I wondered if he, too, was doing it to keep both of our minds off what was happening down the hall, which, thankfully, had not involved any more gunshots.

Regardless, I answered. "Yeah."

"What do you do there?" was his next question.

I went on to explain my career choice. I had worked in small-press publishing doing promo work for authors. It was a lot of getting the word out through blogging, hosting online parties, and the like. But when Jeff died, there was so much litigation to deal with—the trial that ended in a plea, the press, the money, the remembrances—I had to quit. It wasn't fair to the authors.

"I'm doing general secretarial temp jobs now but would like to get back into doing something like that again. And you…?" I prompted, still trying to figure out his connection to Finn Murphy.

But just as I did, another hallway announcement boomed from the speakers. However, that time, it was a much more positive one. The hotel management was thanking the guests for their patience and letting us know we were free to exit our rooms.

Hawk immediately got off the floor and started moving the furniture away from the doorway. I offered to help, but he insisted I stay, since Arinn was slumbering so peacefully in my arms. Plus, he didn't seem to need the help. No sooner was everything back in semi-order then there was a knock at the door. I watched as, still showing caution, he peered through the peep hole and then opened the door to whoever was on the other side.

There was no mistaking him. Sure enough, it was Finn Murphy who scurried through the door alongside a strawberry blond woman with turquoise eyes. Because of the circumstances and a few online articles, I recognized her as Finn's wife. Although, I could not immediately remember her name.

Finn did the briefest of looks around the room and patted Hawk's shoulder in that man kind of way before Chance yelled out, "Mommy, Daddy!" He ran into his mom's hug before bounding into Finn's arms.

I stood up and carefully handed Arinn to her mom. "She went to sleep about ten minutes ago."

Eyes damp, she held on tight to the toddler. "Oh. Okay. Thanks."

"You guys all right?" Finn, who had a comparable hold on Chance, took another look around the room while ruffling his little boy's similarly-hued brown hair. "Everybody okay?"

"Yeah," Hawk answered. "Pretty much unscathed."

Extending his hand out to me, the country music star said, "Hi. Sorry you got caught up in all of this."

Reciprocating the handshake, I tried to make light of the horrific situation. "Last time I go searching for the ice machine."

"Well, you couldn't have been in safer hands." He bro-punched Hawk on the chest.

"The gal does pretty good for herself." Hawk looked over at me and then back to Finn. "And she was a big help with the kids."

"Thanks. I'm Lara, by the way." Mrs. Murphy smiled my direction but didn't let go even the slightest bit of her child.

"Maya," I offered. "And no problem. They're sweet."

"Whatcha hear?" Hawk nodded his chin up to Finn.

Finn set down his mini-me son and spoke slightly lower. "Some nutcase went loco and started shooting up the place."

"Casualties?" Hawk's blunt question made me cringe.

But Finn's answer surprised me. "No."

"Really?" The word burst out of my mouth before I realized I was interrupting a sort of private conversation.

Neither guy seemed to mind, though. Finn turned slightly and answered me. "He was literally shooting up the room, the hall, but not anyone. The cops got him detained."

"No one was hurt?" I needed that double-check. When Finn shook his head to confirm, I blew out some air I hadn't realized I had been holding in. I knew it was a reflection of everything I had been through with Jeff...even before his death, but I couldn't help it.

"Maya—" Hawk started.

But I didn't want to hear him say what I was sure he was going to. Even though we had only known each other for a short period of time, he knew what my exhale meant. There was no need to relive it.

"I should probably get back to my friends," I interrupted.

"Yeah. Sure," Finn replied. "Thanks for your help with whatever."

I brought my attention down to the main star of the afternoon. "Bye, Chance." I bent down to his level and stuck out my hand for a shake. "You are the best fort builder I've ever seen."

"I is not! You are!" he exclaimed and gave me a high five instead of a handshake—even cooler.

Laughing, I turned toward the door where Hawk seemed to still be standing guard. "Thanks," I said as he opened it.

"Not sure which way you're going," Finn interjected, causing me to turn his direction again. "But making a right out of here is off limits. It really was just down the hall a bit."

Hopefully my shudder was undetectable, but I guess not because Hawk said to Finn, "You be here? I'll just make sure she gets back."

"Absolutely," was the answer.

"You don't need to. I can manage."

The only response I got was Hawk extending his arm out in the sign for me to lead the way out the door. I did so, and we both continued left out of the hall. Luckily, it was the direction of the stairwell to my room, anyway.

After a minute or so, Hawk said, "Some girls' getaway, huh?"

"Yeah, and here I thought the main event would be the concert," I joked.

"You're here for the concert?" He stopped in his tracks.

"Yeah," I answered plainly.

"You know who that was in there, right?"

Sure. It was Finn Murphy. He was the main reason we had chosen the late March dates and the Keys as our destination.

But my response was again, "Yeah."

"Hmmm."

What did he expect? Did he think I was going to be one of those women in the whatever era Elvis was in and swoon? Even though the authors I dealt with were nowhere near Finn Murphy's celebrity status, I was used to famous people and—

Juanita's screeching voice interrupted my inner one right there in the middle of the hall. "Maya! Holy shit! Are you okay?"

"We heard it was on this floor!" Sophia, Jeff's sister, joined in.

"Everything's fine," I answered, while giving them both a hug. "You guys?"

"Yeah. Yeah," they seemed to say simultaneously. In that moment, the two women acted like twins with their over-the-top expressions and demeanor. But physically, they couldn't have looked more different. Juanita was taller, with silky straight black hair, and Sophia, who had the same palest of blue eyes as her brother had, was topped with the curliest of red hair.

I turned to my temporary escort. "I think I'm good from here."

"Yep. Guess so." Hawk slid his hands into his pockets and said, "See ya around, Maya."

"I guess you never know." I crinkled my nose and gave a little smile.

I had just gone through a life-and-death scenario with basically only that guy. And I most likely—well, for sure—would never see him again. How strange. I felt like I should have said something more, but the opportunity was taken away as my two closest friends pulled at my arms and started leading me back to our room.

CHAPTER TWO

After swapping tales of the chaos in the Keys, Sophia, Juanita, and I ventured down to the hotel bar. We enjoyed drinks and appetizers, over a formal dinner, and listened to the bartenders and fellow patrons abuzz from the previous police activity. I didn't offer my story and the girls knew not to, either. While not specifically being instructed to, I wanted to respect the Murphy family's privacy.

Shortly after we came back to the room, there was a knock at the door. Juanita, who had been reading a book, jumped up from her bed to answer it. I couldn't hear what she was saying, though, because it was a little bit of a distance from the sofa, where I was sitting and mentally backtracking my day.

"Maya!" Juanita said as the door closed behind her and she came closer. "The card is addressed to you."

I slowly got up and met her at the desk, where she was putting down an ice bucket. Oh, God—our ice bucket! I must have dropped it when I had scooped up Chance in the hallway. That was the last time I remembered seeing it. And, clearly, it was ours. The room number was inscribed on the side. Inside, however, it was not only filled with ice, but there was a bottle of champagne. Sophia, standing on the open balcony, quickly wrapped up her phone conversation with her husband in Maryland and joined us.

I took the card from Juanita, opened it up, and read out loud. "Think one of these things is yours. The other is in appreciation for helping keep my family safe today. I can't thank you enough. I would also be quite honored if you and your friends would accept backstage passes to the show tomorrow. Just call Hawk and let him know how many. Finn Murphy."

Sophia and Juanita had obviously heard about my close encounter with the country music king. But the note, with phone number attached, brought on a whole new level of excitement. There they were, grown adults, screaming like teeny boppers. While it was fun watching their faces light up in excitement, I was glad I didn't act that way.

"Maya, God, that's awesome!" Juanita let out a light squeal.

And although it really was, practical Maya spoke. "That's ridiculous. I got caught up in gunfire and am being rewarded."

"You helped his kids," Sophia explained.

"Yeah, but who wouldn't? Who—" I started.

"Who"—Juanita emphasized the first word—"cares? Get the passes. One." She pointed to herself. "Two." She pointed to Sophia. "Three." Finally, to me. "Tell him three passes. Yes, absolutely."

"Well, I'm glad I made the cut," I joked. "Okay. Okay."

"Now, Maya!" Juanita started walking me toward my cell phone. "So when do we want to indulge in this lovely?" She held up the champagne bottle.

"Let's drink it before the concert tomorrow," Sophia suggested.

"Yeah, all right. Sounds like a plan," Juanita agreed and looked at me.

I had the card in one hand and my phone in the other. I dialed the number. I supposed I would, after all, see, or at least talk with, Hawk again.

But I didn't. I got an extremely brief voicemail, to which I left an embarrassingly disorganized message about receiving the bottle and the offer. I hated asking people for things. It was like a pet peeve of mine. I think it was because everybody gave me so much after Jeff died. And that was another circumstance where I most certainly didn't deserve it. But while food and donations were their compensation for a husband lost, I guess backstage passes were for a family saved. At least this time it was a happy occasion.

***

And before we knew it, it was the next evening and there we were…three women in our mid-thirties with star-struck eyes, taking in the behind-the-scenes of a major recording artist. Per Hawk's text message, we met a security guard who directed us backstage right before Finn was set to perform. There was so much action, commotion, and noise as people were moving things and yelling out directives, it was a little overwhelming.

I spotted Hawk just as the security guard went to help someone else. He was dressed similarly to when we had been holed up in the hotel room—a T-shirt and a lighter shade of cargos. In contrast, I, hopefully, looked a little better than I had before, wearing black capris and a sleeveless, fuchsia slouchy top. Anything would have been an improvement over my lazy, beyond casual, roaming-the-hallway-for-ice attire.

"Maya. Everything all right? Do you need anything?" he asked upon approach.

"No. This is great. Just don't want to get in anyone's way."

"You ladies are fine here. Finn will be up in a minute. I gotta bolt. Have someone flag me down if you need something." And he was off. Just like everything else backstage, Hawk was moving at super-speed.

Fiddling with the long necklace she had bought at a local

shop that day, Sophia started to say something but stopped mid-sentence. When I followed her gaze, it was obvious why. Finn was making his way toward us.

"I think I'm going to faint," Juanita whispered.

"Oh, God," I groaned. "Please don't." But I was sure any guy in the near vicinity would have jumped to do mouth-to-mouth on my friend, considering how her spaghetti-strap, black floral dress hugged her curves. And even though she was in a pretty serious relationship back home, I'm sure Juanita wouldn't have minded.

Standing next to us, Finn spoke. "Hi. Hawk just told me you girls made it. I'm so glad. Everything good?"

Still trying to figure out Hawk's role, I said, "More than. Uh, these are my friends…Sophia and Juanita."

"Hi, friends." Finn smiled a full set of teeth and, from the corner of my eye, I think I saw Juanita sway. "So, listen, they're going to bring out some seats for you here on the edge of the stage if that is okay. Or if you prefer your other…I know it's kind of a side point of view."

"God, no." Juanita managed some words. "Our seats are crap. We'll take these."

Finn laughed. "These you will have, then."

"Thanks…" I started and, oh geez, I was stumbling on his name.

I mean, I remembered it. But should I call him by his first or his formal? Yikes!

"Finn," I settled with. After all, I thought, he wasn't my elder. We were the same age.

"Thank *you*, Maya," he said, and then there were lights going down and even more flurry backstage. "I'm sorry. We're ready to do this thing. We'll talk after, yes?" He looked at all three of us.

"Sure." Sophia had her turn.

"Enjoy the show, ladies." And with that, he rushed onto the stage and began singing one of his top hits from a few years back. He had so many, I'm sure there wasn't enough time to pack all of them into a single show.

I had been to a couple Finn Murphy concerts before with Jeff. They were fantastically produced, and Finn always gave his all. Each time we had attended one of them, both my husband and I had felt reenergized and younger.

And Finn did not let down that night, either. His energy level had all three of us not using our seats for even a second of the ninety-minute set. We saw Hawk a few times, meandering through like he was a programmed machine, and then Lara appeared during the encore. I only saw her at the last moment, though, as I was completely into the booming bass of one of my personal favorite tunes.

"Hey." She sidled up next to me.

"Hi." I acknowledged the superstar's wife. "He puts on a fantastic show."

"He does." She beamed with pride. We listened as Finn completed the song. And then when he started taking bows and signing a few front-row autographs, Lara said, "Chance can't stop talking about that fort."

"Sorry." I chuckled. "Hope you don't mind a lot of messy pillows and blankets in your future."

"No." She laughed right back. "He's a good cleaner-upper, too. I'm glad he wasn't too scared. From what I understand, you were a big help with that."

"Thanks, but I think he's just a brave little dude," I replied, while Hawk joined our group of women.

"Not always," she said as her husband, drenched in sweat like he had been in a wet T-shirt contest, made his way off stage and wrapped his arms around her from behind. They looked like the ideal couple. It was not only in their coordinating outfits—he in jeans and a black T-shirt with white guitar graphic and she in an all-black tank top and jeans—but in the way they melded naturally into one another.

"Hi, Beauty," I heard him coo into her ear.

"Chief…water?" Hawk handed a bottle to Finn, who took it and swallowed a few hearty gulps.

"Whatcha think, ladies?" Finn turned to Sophia, Juanita,

and me.

"The best," was Sophia's response.

"Awesome," was Juanita's.

"I'm afraid any concert after this is going to be anticlimactic," I concluded.

Finn laughed and started fist-pumping and high-fiving the band as they made their way off the stage, after finishing the instrumentals to lead the concert-goers out of the venue. "There's some complimentary merch on the table over there if you want to grab it on your way out."

"Thanks. Awesome." Juanita's word again. "Can we get a pic first?"

"Uh, sure." Finn obliged, wiping his brow with a white hand towel that had somehow taken occupancy in his hand.

"Here, I'll take the pictures." I reached for both Juanita and Sophia's cell phones.

"Maya, join us," Sophia said as she flanked the side of Finn that Juanita wasn't already occupying.

"I can—" Lara started to offer, which I thought was incredibly thoughtful, considering there were two women almost getting handsy with her husband.

"It's all right. I got it." And I clicked the photo button a number of times on each of the ladies' phones.

"Thanks!" Almost as if they were participating in a cheerleading competition, they bounced, giving their joint appreciation to Finn.

"No problem," he countered with the slightest of eye rolls.

As my friends started toward the merchandise table, I told them I would join them in a minute. I wanted to extend my gratitude in a more subdued manner. Although, admittedly, the concert had been terribly thrilling.

"Well, thanks." I tried to look at Finn, Lara, and Hawk simultaneously. "If you can't tell, we had a really great time."

"I could tell," the singer concurred with a chuckle. "*You* don't want a picture or anything?"

"Uh, not much of a picture person. Besides, you didn't

ask to take a picture of me." As soon as I got my sarcastic remark out, Lara, who was once again wrapped onto her husband's side, busted out in a genuine laugh. "Sorry. Did I offend you?" I asked.

Finn's laugh was as robust as his wife's. "No."

"Finn's not an ego guy." Hawk jumped in to the conversation. "Believe me. He's just used to people celebritizing."

Sarcasm aside, I spoke honestly. "I don't know. We're all the same, right? We just chose different paths in life. You make a lot—well, a heck of a lot—more money than I do. But I wouldn't want to be on stage like you. And if you heard me singing in the shower, you wouldn't want me to be, either."

"Sorta like my dancing." Lara's eyes lifted to her husband's green ones, which made me think they weren't that color in the hotel room—they were a cool gray, like Chance's.

"Totally agree about being all the same." Finn made a point of dragging out the first word. After the slightest of pauses, he added, "And agree about her dancing." When his wife playfully hit him, Finn did a quick wink in the direction of Hawk and me. "It was very nice meeting you, Maya. Enjoy the rest of your trip."

"Yeah, just tomorrow. Then back to colder weather on Monday," I lamented.

"Hopefully there will be another concert in your future," the entertainer said.

"For sure." I smiled one last smile and said goodbye, not only to the three people standing in front of me but to the magical evening that had taken place through a series of unlikely and unfortunate events.

***

Of course, we didn't—couldn't—go right to sleep once we made our way back to the hotel room. All three of us ladies were wound up. There was the retelling of the night…step by step. There was watching the concert videos on cell phones. There was looking at their photos with Finn and mooning over how handsome he was. There was examining our backstage passes like we had never seen them before. There was looking through the merchandise bags, which each included a poster and a towel.

And, finally, there was Sophia's comment—the one I had been thinking before she even said it. "Jeff would have loved this. All of it. The entire trip."

I took a slow, cleansing breath from the sofa. I had let Sophia and Juanita take the two regular beds because I had been used to sofas. After all, I had slept on mine at home for months after Jeff died. I had not been able to be in our bed alone and needed to feel the snugness of something against me, even if it was just a cushioned sofa back. It had been my new year's resolution to once again sleep in our bed. And, with much initial sadness, I had managed to do it.

I tried to keep things light. "Jeff would have been making fun of you with your idol-screaming routine."

Laughing, my sister-in-law admitted, "He would have!" And then she said, with more seriousness, "Of course, he would have never let you be in any danger. He would have been up there in that room yesterday getting you out."

"But immediately afterward, he would have been right in the middle of it," I amended, and noticed I had subconsciously been twirling my wedding band.

All three of us took pause. There were no truer words. There had been no truer words the night he was killed. Yes, it was in the line of duty, but he also took the lead and initiative. It was just like him. One of the things everyone loved about him. But also the very thing that made me an early widow.

"To Jeff." Juanita picked up the nearly empty bottle of champagne and took a sip.

Sophia stood up and took a hearty gulp before handing it to me. I finished the effervescent, bubbly liquid and let that be the final word. Curling under the blanket, I hugged my pillow and, with the influence of alcohol and an exciting, exhausting evening, fell asleep.

***

"But this is the one with the narrow, dark tunnel," I whined. "I'm not going to like it."

"It's just for the tiniest of moments in the beginning-middle-ish part. Come on, you know I'll be with you," he said.

That somewhat reassured me. So I carefully climbed into the empty car of the roller coaster. As soon as I did, the protective bar practically slammed down on top of me, locking me securely in place. He was right behind me because each seat only held one person. And then, we started to move.

The first part was fine. We were winding around some bends but in open air. But then, *swoosh*, it came on so sudden and with a loud, terrifying bang. We were definitely in the suffocating tunnel.

"Jeff!" I yelled out.

"Maya, it's okay…just hold on." His voice was soothing…more so than I ever recalled. "I'm looking out for you. See, it's getting light." I tried to focus on his voice because I couldn't see him. "There's a little uphill and then there are so many people waiting for you…who love you."

I did as I was told, and it was true. As we neared the top of the hill and it started to level, I could see Sophia and Juanita. And there were children. Who were they? The faces were blurry because of the speed. Oh, Chance and Arinn, I thought, and possibly more, and some other people who were starting to come in a little more clearly.

"Jeff," I yelled.

"You're on the right track, Mai Tai." He used his loving nickname for me, and then his roller coaster car separated from mine and went skyward.

"Jeff!" I called out again.

I woke up in a semi-sweat. It had been a dream. Of course it was. Jeff was dead. I was holding on to a sofa, not a roller coaster. Jeff was dead. But I didn't feel so alone. The frightening nightmare had startled me. Yet in the center had been my husband and his reassuring words. He was with me, and I was on the right track, even though I had no idea which direction I was going.

***

I wasn't able to get back to sleep. So I surrendered by sitting on the balcony and watching the sunrise. The dream about Jeff stayed with me. I ran through it over and over again in my mind. It seemed, somehow, so prolific and final.

When I knew replaying it was doing more harm than good, I reentered the room. Both Sophia and Juanita were starting to stir from their slumbers. But I still needed some alone time. So, after much friendly teasing that we didn't need any ice, I got dressed and headed out for a walk along the beach. I told them I would be back so we could all go for brunch together.

It was toward the end of my hour-long stroll when my phone buzzed a text. Thinking the girls were hungry and wanted me to hustle, I almost didn't look. After all, I was nearly back to the room. But the vibrating was going to drive me crazy. So I swiped my phone and looked. It wasn't Sophia or Juanita at all. It was a message from Hawk. He was texting on Finn and Lara's behalf. They wanted to know if I would join them for drinks that night.

What? What! A second look at the message turned into a third and fourth. Yes, I had read it correctly.

I plopped down right there on the uneven, sandy surface. I didn't care that the bottom of my shorts was going to be covered with tiny beach remnants. I didn't care that I was pretty much in the middle of a natural walkway near the water. I *did* care what that message read and, more importantly, what it meant. Why would they want to meet with me? The concert and champagne were far and beyond enough thanks, especially when I felt like I hadn't done anything.

The only way I was going to find out, though, was by responding to the text. *Me? Drinks? Tonight?* And I signed my name, just in case he had sent the message to the wrong number.

The text from Hawk came back immediately. *Yeah. & food. They want to talk w/ U about something. 7ish?*

I guess.

My hesitation, speculation, and curiosity must have come across in my two-little-word reply because Hawk's text back to me was equally as short but reassuring. *It's all good.*

Still in a semi state of shock, I confirmed. *OK.*

I'll pick U up @ 7.

The questions were compounding in my head. *Where R we going?*

Their suite in the other hotel.

The other hotel? I thought they were staying at the same hotel as we were. What hotel? I didn't even really know this Hawk guy, and he was going to drive me to another hotel? I mean, ninety-some percent of me knew it was legit. But being the wife of a police officer for seven years made the other percent just a little cautious.

Before I could question or reply, though, Hawk sent a follow-up text. It was almost as if he was reading my mind. *It's 2 blocks away. We'll walk.*

Ah, yes, I knew the hotel. Fine. Whatever. There's not much more that could surprise me on this trip, anyway, I thought.

Boy, was I wrong.

CHAPTER THREE

I whined and stared. But, no matter how long I did either, I couldn't come to a conclusion. The debate on what to wear to the mystery meeting was on. It wasn't like I was at home and had my entire closet to pick from. We were leaving the next morning, and I had already worn most of my packed clothes. And then there was the fact that it was going to take place in someone's hotel suite. Geez, that could mean anything from sweats to formalwear. It was a silly thing to stress over, but I was. I wished I would have asked Hawk, but what good would that have done? He was a guy, and guys, well… But the girls weren't any help, either. They were partially pissed because they weren't included and partially crazed with their celebrity connection once again.

I finally decided on my blue bandana halter maxi dress. It was casual enough in style with its loose buttons and exposed arms but long enough to say it was not beachwear. I had just finished spritzing my shoulder-length, layered golden-brown hair into beachy waves when the knock on the door came. Since Sophia and Juanita had already left for their own dinner out, it was up to me to answer it. Wringing my hands through my hair, I did one last scrunch, grabbed my wristlet and room key, and opened the door. Scanning Hawk's black slacks and tan colored button-down, I determined I had chosen my attire appropriately.

"You look nice," he offered.

"Thanks," I said as I double-checked the door to make sure it had locked behind me. "I wasn't sure. I'm not really s—"

"Anything would have been fine," he interjected, and it made me confirm my original assessment of not asking a guy about clothing options.

I tried not to laugh outwardly as we made our way down the hall and just a flight of steps to the ground floor. While we were discussing general things like the weather and what I thought of the concert—both I answered with enthusiastic, positive, honest responses—I noted how easy it was talking with him. He didn't say much, which I had observed during our previous two encounters, but I could tell he was legitimately listening and interested.

As we entered the other resort, I asked one of the questions that had been rolling around in my mind. "Why two different hotels?"

He understood without further explanation and pretty much revealed a trade secret. "It's kind of a distraction tactic. We're, actually, all scattered among three hotels. Finn is registered under his name in our hotel but uses a fake name at the one they are actually staying at, in hopes it will deter some of the crazies."

"Like my friends?" I laughed.

"Uh…"

"Don't choke," I teased.

"No. Your friends are fine." He laughed as we entered the elevator. "You haven't seen crazy."

We were thankfully, remarkably up to their floor before I could verbalize the major question I had—what was I doing there? Hawk braced his solid arm against the elevator doors to allow both myself and the only other two people who were on the lift to exit first. I then waited for him to direct us to the Murphy suite.

Lara greeted us at the door in a classic yet casual little black dress with a colorful wrap tied around her waist. Her long hair was pulled back in a ponytail. Good, I'm good, I thought. She would really be the one to compare myself to.

"Hi, Maya. We're so glad you could make it."

Unfortunately, I'd answered as nonverbally as possible. "Uh-huh." I wasn't nervous. I was just so confused.

As we officially entered the ginormous hotel room, Hawk asked, "Where's the man?"

"C'mon, Hawk, you know him, never on time. He had to fit in a workout and then showered. He's just about—"

"I'm here." Finn entered from a side room, dressed in similar pants as Hawk but with a white polo shirt and tan belt. "Hi, Maya."

One could tell he worked out. He had a body similar to Jeff's—lean and fit—although Finn was taller. When I'd worn heels, Jeff and I had been the same height, but Finn and Hawk were still inches above—both a little over six feet. Finn most likely had to work out in order to keep up the energy he needed on stage where, in contrast, Jeff had worked out to release stress. Those last few months or so of my husband's life had been like he was training for the Ironman, with all of his running, biking, and swimming.

"Hi." I managed one actual, sort-of word that time.

"Did anyone offer you something to drink?"

"Uh—" I started, but my empty hands probably gave away the answer.

"What do you prefer?" the country music star questioned.

"It doesn't matter. Do you have something open?" What was stocked in a bar in one of these elite rooms?

"Bourbon," was the Kentucky native's answer.

"Uh, no," was mine.

Lara smiled at my response. "I have a bottle of sangria. That good?"

"Sure." Much better.

"Hawk?" Finn turned to the broader, yet still very fit, of the two of them.

"No thanks, chief." It was the second time I had heard Hawk call Finn by an obvious nickname. "I think I'm gonna go."

"No. Part of this is to thank you *both* for the other day," he replied.

Hawk started to protest at the same time I did but then gallantly let me speak. "I think the bottle of champagne, never mind those passes, more than covered it."

When Finn handed Hawk a tumbler, which looked identical to his bourbon, I knew Hawk was staying. He took a swig of the brown liquid as Lara handed me a glass of wine. I brought it to my lips, readily relishing its fruity sweetness.

"Have a seat. Please," Finn requested.

He led Lara to the table, which was just big enough for each person to have a side of their own. I ended up across from Lara and the guys across from one another. There was a near smorgasbord in front of us.

"We just ordered like every appetizer and dessert on the hotel menu. Is that all right?" Lara was already passing the plate of fried zucchini around.

I was in foodie heaven. "Did someone tell you that's what I do? I am not an entrée fan."

"Seriously? Me, either." My hostess' eyes lit up.

"Oh, my God, yeah," I replied honestly.

"Must be a chick thing." Hawk nodded across the table to Finn.

"Must be a smart thing." The honest and sarcastic response came out of my mouth, causing Lara to laugh and Hawk, lips pressed shut, to raise his glass to me. "Where are the kids?" I asked, changing the subject.

I saw Lara look at Finn and smile. The natural love between them was so beautiful to see. A relationship like that was hard to come by for anyone, but especially, I was sure, in the world of celebrity.

"They're in the other room," Lara answered. "They already ate."

"Oh. I was hoping to see them." I dipped a tortilla chip into the white cheese sauce.

"Believe me, you will." Lara's voice was light. "One of them will make their presence known, followed almost immediately by the other. I give it maybe fifteen minutes."

"You're being generous." Finn shook his head in a knowing kind of way. "I'm surprised it hasn't happened already."

"They are so good and so darn cute." I flashbacked to the fort in Hawk's room.

Finn looked at Lara, who nodded a serious-looking affirmation to her husband, and then spoke. "Maya..." He put his fork down and looked directly at me. "Listen, there's another reason we asked you to join us tonight." He shifted his gaze momentarily to Hawk and then back to me. "Hawk told us about your husband." He paused.

I waited. Obviously, everyone in the room knew Finn was referring to Jeff's death, and there wasn't much more to say. I had learned over the year since his passing to just let there be an honorary moment or so of silence. That spoke more than the "sorrys" and "thank yous" ever could.

Recognizing my silent nod as acknowledgement, Finn continued. "Hawk also mentioned what you used to do for a living and how good you were with the kids."

I looked at the man, my personal escort that evening, to my right. He squinted his eyes extremely quickly at me. He wasn't much for words, but he obviously had relayed most, or all, of mine from the afternoon a couple days before.

"I'm just glad I could help," I reiterated, for what seemed to be the hundredth time.

"It was more than help." Lara politely contradicted my statement. "You don't understand. Chance can feel very anxious. He's particularly apprehensive around loud noises and when he knows things aren't right. He was good when we got to the hotel room. He really took to you, and that is so rare."

"Maya, listen, I'm gonna throw this out there, and there are a lot of factors, but would you be interested in coming to work for us...being a part of my team on the road this summer?"

The glass I had just started to raise to my lips went back to the table with lightning speed as I looked at Finn to make sure I had heard him correctly. "I'm sorry, what?"

What? What! Why? Doing what? Professional fan? What? Thankfully, I was given a moment to let my brain bounce around my skull. Because if Finn or anyone had begun to talk, I'm sure I wouldn't have heard or comprehended any of it.

After that second or so, Finn continued. And although he had a friendly voice and soft eyes, I could tell he was very serious about the subject matter. "It's kind of a dual job. We need someone to occasionally watch the kids so Hawk here or someone else isn't pulled from their regular duties."

My gaze followed Finn's to Hawk. Hawk smirked at Finn first and then squinted at me in that invested, observing way. It was a little more of the left eye than the right that time. He reminded me of someone when he did that. But who? A young Clint Eastwood, I decided. He was in those old movies my grandmother used to watch. But Hawk had a tint of red to his shorter, dark hair and, while probably as tall as Clint, had a broader chest.

"It wouldn't be a lot." Lara made me swing my attention back to her and the what...babysitting gig? "Not even every day. Just some nights, maybe, when I want to be at the concert, or we get an occasional trip into town."

"But mostly," Finn piggy-backed to the dual part of the job offer. "I'm looking to hire someone to assist my publicist Reese. She wants to cut back a little and will need help with anything that is out there media-wise with my name on it and updating my social media sites. Her newest idea is to have someone, not me, do a blog a couple days a week this summer...sort of 'a day in the life of a concert tour' kind of deal. That's the type of work you did for authors, right?"

I looked at Hawk once more. Yeah, he hadn't missed a beat when we were harbored down in his hotel room and I had told him my life story. And he certainly had relayed it to the Murphys. Hawk's response to my quizzical look was to take another drink of his bourbon.

"Yeah. It's exactly what I did," I answered, first looking at the man with dark hair touched with red, then to the one with lighter brown locks.

"Can you send Reese some examples of your work and references? That is, if you are interested. It would mean being on the road pretty much twenty-four-seven—from May until mid-September—living on the busses, seeing the country, writing, being with our two little ones, and maybe some decent music thrown in there." He smiled in jest.

"Ha." I was trying like mad to catch up to what was being said and adding a little bit of humor while I did. "I'd say a little more than decent, except for that 'Dark and Dusty' song. That's too depressing."

"I'll keep that in mind." Finn smiled in a friendly way and then turned serious again. "Of course, you would need to get all of your clearances."

"I was a cop's wife. It will check out." Clearances were the least of my concerns or questions. My main one was still, *what?!*

"I told him that." Hawk backed me up.

"I can get them. It's not a problem. I just never…this might have been the very last thing I expected you to say," I said.

"I know it's a lot to think about. But how real and natural you are, makes me think you will be a good fit. It's not a guarantee. I do want to see those examples and references, but…"

"Just so I don't have to sing." As Lara laughed, I continued. "Please let me think about it. It's such a big…. I am overwhelmed…and honored." I spoke with pure honesty. "I know I could do it and would love to. Can you give me a day or two?"

"Sure," Finn answered. "I'll give you Reese's card and, if it's all right, I'll let her know to expect to hear from you."

"Yeah." Finally, I took that sip, and then gulp, of wine.

"And as far as salary, we can negotiate. Until then, let's eat. I'll get more wine." He stood up from the table.

"So I'm guessing you do like country music?" Lara asked, touching Finn's hand as it brushed her shoulder.

"Want to know the truth?" I asked.

"Oh, say it." Hawk's hazel eyes seemed to open a little more. "I couldn't stand this hillbilly crap when I first started."

"You're out," Finn joked in his friend's direction, while refilling my wine glass. "I knew I never liked you."

"You're right," I admitted to Hawk, after thanking Finn. "I didn't like it. I was listening to pop and rock. And then I met Jeff. He was the one into country music. I started listening to it with him, and on the side, so I could impress him."

"*That* is a chick thing." Finn returned the bro nod back to Hawk.

"Shut up." Lara shook her head at her husband.

"Love you, Beauty." Finn spoke in a sing-song voice as he refilled Lara's glass and kissed the top of her head.

"You, too," she bounced back as Finn reclaimed his seat.

When they both turned to me, I decided I better continue my story. "I ended up loving it more than Jeff did."

"Is that why you did this girls' vacay—for the concert?" Lara was nibbling on another of the numerous appetizers.

"Well, sort of. Jeff and I..." While I wasn't shy about anything that happened in my life, I didn't know how much my hosts, although kind-hearted and friendly, would want to know. "We had a rough time right before he died. He was stressed getting set to make detective and I...well..." Yeah, I had said enough. "Anyway, he and I were talking about getting away someplace warm. We picked here. We were ready to book and then…he died." I charged right on, trying to ignore the need to touch my band the way I usually did when sad conversations about Jeff occurred. "So my friends—the one, Sophia,"—I said, knowing they had all met her— "is Jeff's sister. When they saw you were playing here, they thought it would be perfect. You know, to honor him and God, yeah, just to get away and unwind and escape."

"Huh. We kinda needed that, too." Finn looked at his wife, and it made me remember hearing the news coverage about Arinn being kidnapped for a few days right before Christmas.

Suddenly, it made me appreciate the job offer that much more, which I thought was already amazing. They were trusting me with their children…obviously the most precious things in their world. And, on top of that, knowing how much I knew through the press about the career side of Finn Murphy, made me understand how important the other part of the job offer was, too.

"This gig in the Keys was last-minute"—Finn was explaining— "as I'm sure you're aware. I wanted to thank all the staff, crew, and band for supporting my family. So we came up with this retreat and then threw in a concert to thank the fans, too. Wouldn't have been able to get through without all of them." After hoisting his bourbon in Hawk's direction, he reached out his hand to Lara, who softly stroked it.

Before anyone else could speak, Chance came running into the room. "Daddy, I—" Upon seeing me, he literally stopped and said with pure enthusiasm, "Maya!"

"Hi, Chance. How you doing?" It was hard not to just brighten when seeing his innocent little face.

"I good." The four-year-old's eyes grew round as he looked directly at me. "Are you here to build another fort with me? I have pillows!"

Finn intercepted his son's request. "Not today, Little Man."

"Hey, Chance, bud, what about me?" Hawk tilted his head to the side. "Or are you just all about the pretty girls now?"

Chance's feet, adorned by the sweetest little red Converse shoes, took off in Hawk's direction. When the elder stood up and flipped the boy upside-down, Chance's immediate response was, "Again!"

And then, as predicted, Arinn came toddling in. "Mama. Uppy."

When Lara brought Arinn into her arms, Finn looked at his watch. I knew it wasn't about him needing to be somewhere. I knew it also wasn't about wanting something to be done.

"I'd call it a tie," I said, making Finn give a slightly puzzled look in my direction. "Lara said fifteen minutes. You thought they would have been in here almost immediately. Ten minutes even for Chance. And Arinn, what? Less than a minute behind?"

"That was a little Hawk-like." Finn laughed.

"Hey, wait…" Hawk brought Chance back to the ground, whereupon he immediately went to his dad. "Should I be offended?"

"No. She's just observant." Finn settled Chance onto his lap.

"Guilty as charged," I said. "I'm a people-watcher. It's the writer in me."

"Well, hopefully, you'll be able to use those skills to our advantage this summer."

"That would be something," I admitted.

"I know you have a lot of questions…some you probably haven't even thought of yet," Finn said. "Think about it, write them down, and get a hold of Reese."

"I will," I promised.

"Here's to escaping to the Keys." Finn lifted his glass, as did the other adults.

***

Hawk walked me back to the hotel. I had attempted to protest but was cut short by both men who insisted, as would have my husband, that I be safe. Besides, Hawk was going back to his room, anyway.

In reality, I didn't mind at all. I was feeling a little light from more alcohol than food and, of course, the surprising offer. It all seemed as much of a dream as the roller coaster one. I used our stroll back to the hotel to soak in some of the crisp air and ask Hawk a few questions. They were mostly about what it was like being on tour. He said their days were extremes—hectic concert days and leisurely traveling ones. There were schedules, but each day and venue were different. I'm not sure my questions were answered completely, but I had, maybe, a little better understanding.

When we reached my door, I said, "Well, I guess I have you to thank for the offer in the first place."

He shrugged. "I just told them what the situation was. Everything else was Finn and Lara. And I agree with them—it was just you being you. You would be a good fit. Think about it."

I had been looking in my wristlet for my room key, but midway through his dialogue, I felt a need to stop and tilt my head up to him. He was a good four or five inches taller than me, which was the perfect height for his neck to bend down and do what I suddenly knew was coming. I hadn't felt the pull until really that moment. Before, I had been too wrapped up in the initial danger of the gunfire, then the excitement of the concert, and, finally, the offer. But listening to some of his words and knowing he had been listening to mine, when he kissed me, I kissed him back.

Even though it was quick, it was soft and delicious. It felt good. And, yet, it felt strange.

"That wasn't meant to influence your decision, by the way." Hawk broke the proverbial ice.

"Uh, yeah." I managed a breathy laugh and brought my

hand immediately down to the door handle. "I guess I better go, then. Good night, Hawk."

His eyes blinked in the slightest way. "Good night, Maya."

I inserted the key card into the slot and watched as he walked to the stairwell. But I didn't go inside. I removed the key and leaned up against the wall next to the door, trying to clear my mind. The whole night had thrown me, and that kiss was the icing on the top. But that was the thing—it was like icing. It was sweet. And I hadn't reacted that way to it. In fact, I was pretty sure I'd come off dismissive.

Sophia, in pajamas, opened the door just as I was set to leave. "Maya, everything okay?"

"Yeah," I said. "I...I'm sorry. I'll be right back."

"Where are you going?" You could see the worry on her face. After all, it was late, we were in a strange town, and we were leaving early the next morning.

"I just forgot to tell Hawk thanks for walking me back. It will be two minutes." It was mostly the truth, after all.

I left for the floor above us as Sophia, I'm sure puzzled, shut the door behind me. I took a hearty breath and knocked on Hawk's door. It was a room I probably would never forget, nor what happened there on that previous scary afternoon.

"Maya?" He sounded surprised upon opening the door, but I was pretty sure he had checked the peep-hole. He was that type of guy.

"I'm sorry about..." I said, with the presumption he knew what I was referring to. "It's just...I haven't kissed anyone since Jeff." A gust of air left my lungs.

"I only thought of that after I left. Sorry."

"No. No. Don't be," I tried to explain. I most certainly didn't want an apology. "I just needed to appreciate it and let it sink in for a moment. I wanted you to know that before I went into my room."

"Okay."

I couldn't tell for sure, but I think there might have been

the smallest of smiles. "*Did* you want it to influence me?" I was feeling more myself.

After a beat, he said, "Maybe." And that time, I knew if the smile wasn't on his lips, it was definitely in his eyes. When I smiled back, he said, "C'mon."

"What? Where?" I asked in rapid succession.

"Maya." He leaned in to his room to grab the key and then shut the door behind us. "It may have only been a couple days, but I'm pretty sure you know I'm the type of guy who walks a woman to the door."

"Sometimes you even throw them in!" I jested, feeling better since the twinge of awkwardness from before had dissipated.

"Would prefer not to have to do that again." His body shook with a silent laugh as we made our way down the stairwell.

When we returned once again to my room, I actually said what I had told Sophia I was going to. "Thanks for walking me back...twice." I added.

"You are quite welcome," he said. "I'm glad I got a chance to."

And then, after the slightest of pauses, as if he was silently asking permission, he kissed me again. While it was still quick, our lip-lock was a little longer than the one just moments before. And when we broke, I could tell each of us felt a little better about the result.

"Call Reese," he commanded kindly. Hawk squinted his eyes at me as if he were taking a picture and then strolled back to the stairwell.

When I opened the door, Sophia was standing directly in the entrance. My hand up to my mouth, I stifled a scream. It was her quiet words, though, which stung the most.

"You kissed him," she said, and I knew it wasn't a question. She had been looking through the door's glass eye.

"Sophia..." I didn't know what else to say. I didn't really even know how I felt.

"She kissed who?" Juanita asked, pulling earbuds from

her ears and rising from her bed. "You didn't kiss Finn Murphy, did you?" she practically screamed.

"No!" I retorted, stepping past Sophia but watching her hurt eyes as I did. "He's married—very happily, mind you."

"Who did you kiss?"

I looked at Sophia. "Do you want me to say 'I'm sorry'?" When she didn't reply, I tried again. "Sophia…" I think Juanita then understood how me finally feeling something again had ramifications on my sister-in-law. As Juanita sat back on her bed, I said to Sophia, "Please don't make me feel bad about this. It was just a kiss goodnight, and I might never see him again. God, Sophia, you know I loved Jeff. But he's gone. I can't… I can't…"

And then I bawled. I should have been so happy, but I couldn't be. The night was so mixed up emotionally.

Juanita got up and gave me a hug until my sobbing slowed. I was crying for Jeff, for Sophia, and probably, finally, from hearing those gunshots in the hall a few days before. It was a good release.

When my tears finally stopped, Juanita looked at Sophia and then, obviously not giving a hang, said, "It was the one with just the right amount of facial hair, huh? Mr. Protector?"

"It's not a big deal," I tried, even though in my head, any first kiss after my husband's was going to be. "Wait until you hear what the night was really about." I made my voice appear perky again and looked at Sophia.

"Go ahead," she said, "I want to hear. Tell us about it."

"Good." I breathed out. "Because, God, girls, do I need some advice."

CHAPTER FOUR

Decisions. Decisions. It was a big one. But after talking with my friends, both that night and in the airport the following day, I was closer to making up my mind.

Sophia and Juanita both thought I would be crazy not to take the job if offered it. There was really no reason not to. A: I didn't have a permanent job in Maryland. B: Sophia and her family would look after my house while I would be away. And C: It was an opportunity to see the country and do something I really enjoyed. The only downfall would be missing my friends for a few months or so. The topic of Hawk was not brought up as part of the consideration or, for that matter, at all.

After an exhausting day of flying, I ordered a pizza on the way home and gobbled up part of it before falling fast asleep that night. It was waking up the following morning in my own bed that made me ask myself if any of it had really happened. The pile of laundry and the few days of unopened mail told me the vacation definitely had. The saved text from Hawk, inviting me to Finn Murphy's suite, confirmed the rest.

Over the next couple of days, after temping at the local television station—basically just answering calls, delivering mail, and running errands—I would come home and get some of the requested items together. The list of references wasn't difficult, since I had recently done that for the temp agency. I was more careful, though, about looking through and selecting examples of my blogging and social media work to forward to Reese. After all, this job was more important than any I had ever gone for before.

By Thursday evening, I needed a little break. While I was great at working on deadline, I didn't like to feel rushed. I preferred getting something accomplished, removing myself from it, and then reviewing. And I wanted to do that before contacting Reese in any fashion. Besides, maybe I was blowing the job offer out of proportion. Maybe it was just a kind gesture, being grateful for keeping Finn's kids safe. Was I getting myself all worked up for nothing?

I needed a release. So I strapped on my Nike trainers, grabbed Allante's leash, and headed outside. Allante was Jeff's dog when we had gotten married. Jeff had named him after the classic Cadillac his father owned because he insisted the dog, despite being a light-haired rescue mutt, was a purebred classic. And with how sweet he was, I believed it, too. When Jeff passed away, it took Allante a while not to sit at the window and poke his nose through the curtains, waiting for his master to return. But he had rebounded and, despite his age of eleven years old, made sure to be, ever more so, my guardian and pal. I had missed him those few days in the Keys, but I knew Sophia's sons had been spoiling the heck out of him.

Our Maya-doggy outing was more of a walk than a jog. Allante's arthritis wouldn't put up with the exertion, and I didn't need the exercise, as such. I was fortunate to have inherited my father's side of the gene pool—naturally tall and slender. It drove people like Juanita, who had to watch and measure every calorie that went into her body, crazy.

The spring-like air was invigorating and refreshing. But the buzzing of an incoming text on my cell, later that evening, made me feel even better. I took my dinner plate off my lap and exchanged it for the phone. Seeing it was from Hawk, I muted the television, knowing I needed full concentration on whatever his message might say. I took a deep breath. The more I doubted everything that happened—from the job offer to the kiss—the more I wanted it. And pressing one button might tell my fate.

His text read, *Hope U had a safe trip back.*

Hmmm, I thought, well, that was kind of generic...but concerned? I decided to play a little cute. *Yep—uneventful compared to the 3 days B4 that.* I tacked on a smile emoji.

Good thing. There is something to say about eventful, tho.

I couldn't help but smile, knowing we were both reflecting on those days. And I was glad he hadn't hesitated with his response. I was going to type back "for sure" when a follow-up text came through.

Finn wants to know Y U haven't contacted Reese yet.

His query made me stop some of my self-doubt. The offer was legit. And I needed to act on it.

Getting everything together, I replied. *I'll do it tomorrow.*

Glad to hear it. I'll let him know.

Because I didn't know what else to say, I typed, *Thanks* and added another smiley to suffice.

His concluding text said, *U got it.*

Feeling more secure, I took the time to write out an introductory letter to Reese that evening. And then, purposefully waking up early the next morning, I typed it into an email and attached all of the material requested before pressing send. It was weird how nervous I was. I'm not, in general, that type of person. But the job with Finn suddenly meant so much to me.

Knowing she wasn't going to pick it up that early in the morning or, for that matter, maybe even that day, I busied myself with getting ready and going into the television station. When I checked my email at lunch, there was a response. Well, it was more like a receipt, simply telling me she'd received my email and would get back to me soon.

My heart sank. To me, it was the equivalent of "I'll call

you" after the first date. Even though it had been years since being in the dating world, I could sense a brush-off a mile away. I sent the obligatory thank-you and look-forward-to-hearing-from-you response back and tried not to cry, especially knowing the whole idea of the job was fairytale-ish, anyway. And just when I had started to believe.

I didn't even want to check my email any more that day. I knew when I did, it would most likely be vacant of any response from Reese. I wondered if she would be the type to actually send a rejection letter or just let it go into the hopeless abyss of no return. I had dealt with enough authors to understand that pain.

But before starting my car at the end of work, I checked. I did. I thought if there wasn't anything there, I would swing by the liquor store for good measure on my way home.

There it was, though—another email from Reese. Was it just as generic? Was it the end? I could picture the neon light of the state store. I could picture the long aisles of wine and hard liquor. Which to pick? Maybe both.

But getting wasted wasn't in the cards. Instead, I blasted my car stereo all the way home, listening to a Finn Murphy shuffle. Reese's email was short, but it was also promising. She had a very busy schedule and was wondering if she could call me the next day. She realized it was a Saturday and she didn't want to interfere with any previous plans, but she would rather discuss everything verbally. Um…yeah! And, plans? Like I had any. Alcohol was even out of the question.

Of course, I emailed her straight back and, without trying to sound desperate said, *Mrs. Byrd, thank you for your reply. I will make myself available for your phone call at any time tomorrow. Let me know. Looking forward to speaking with you.*

Her email came back almost immediately that time. *First of all, it's Reese. The running joke is: it took my husband and I years to actually marry because of that horrible last name! So Reese, please. And how does 1ish sound?*

One o'clock sounds great until you wake up too early

and then either just sit around or start cleaning your house while waiting for the clock to tick to that hour. Thank goodness Reese was prompt with her time-telling. My furniture, floors, and appliances could not have gotten any cleaner.

Reese was very natural, although a little hurried. I instantly felt at ease with her. She seemed impressed with the examples I had provided, and she had done her own Maya research online, of course, meant articles about Jeff. So she added the obligatory "sorry for your loss." Then she described what the job would entail and how I would be working with her long distance—she lived in New York City. But, she reinforced, Finn always had the final say. She also said privacy regarding his family was absolutely non-negotiable. I told her I had understood that even before it was to be understood. She noted that Finn had picked up on that and many other positive characteristics. After speaking with her, I felt more confident about my capabilities of doing the job and told her so. She concluded by telling me she was going to pass on all the information to Finn and she would let me know.

***

Well, that next morning, I was either going to start cleaning my neighbor's house or hit the liquor store. As the latter wasn't open and I didn't like my neighbors that much, I decided to sit down and blog—just for the fun of it…put some words onto paper and let things flow. I hadn't done any writing since leaving my job with the publishing house, and, until I started again, I hadn't realized how much I needed to.

What came out was basically the dream I had in the Keys—being on the roller coaster with Jeff. By doing a writing recall, I remembered something at the end I hadn't initially. When I yelled out his name the final time and he wasn't there, I had let go. I let my arms release from the constraints of the heavy bar, and I was fine.

I printed out the piece, folded it up, and laid it on the living room shelf clustered with photos of Jeff and me. There was the selfie when we had just gotten engaged, a picture of us kissing on our honeymoon, a Halloween photo where I was the hot cop and he the convict, and the one at the amusement park for the Shriver family reunion. We were in a bumper car waiting for it to start. Jeff, whose tan accentuated his pale blue eyes and chiseled smooth face, had just said it was going to be an extra bumpy ride since he was going after his sister's car. Sophia, ironically, had taken the photo of us smiling, not knowing what we were talking about.

That was the summer before Jeff was killed. He—we— were naturally happy. My one hand lay on top of his on the steering wheel. His black hair was cut as short as possible for the summer, making him look younger and even more fit, somehow. Right after the picture was taken, he had yelled "Game on!" to his sister. And then we were bumped and spun around hundreds of times—just like my life shortly after.

I stared at the photo, thinking about the dream and him telling me I was on the right track when, suddenly, my phone began to ring. I refocused my attention and walked over to the table to retrieve it. Seeing Reese's name on the screen, I took one last look at Jeff's photo across the room and answered.

After the initial greeting and making sure it was an all right time to talk, Reese informed me that Finn was connected on the other line. It was a conference call. Finn and I did the standard "how are yous" and "good trip" comments before he got down to the actual business at hand.

"So Maya…" he said. "'Dark and Dusty' is going to remain in the lineup. I hope that's not a deal-breaker with you."

"Good grief." Reese exhaled.

"You sound like Charlie Brown," he teased his publicist.

"Would you just tell her?" Reese finished the banter.

"Maya, on the unanimous advice of five of my greatest advisors, one of them being Charlie Brown…"

"Ha. Ha." Reese's laugh was pure mockery.

"I'd like to formally offer you the job of…" He hesitated. "Well, I guess we don't have a title. Reese, do we—"

"I don't care about titles," I interjected, and my body felt like it had jumping beans inside of it over the excitement of the moment. "I accept."

"Great," the recording artist replied.

"Welcome aboard," Reese said. "I can tell we are going to work well together."

"Thanks," I replied. "I appreciate your support. Can I…can I ask who your other advisors are? I might need to thank them, too."

"Well, Hawk, you know, told us about your background and vouched for you initially."

Finn paused, but I didn't react. I wondered how much he knew. Did he know about the kiss…kisses? Did it even matter?

"And, of course, my wife," he continued.

"Of course. Tell them thanks."

"But you wouldn't have gotten anywhere without the final two," he said.

"Oh. Okay. Who?"

I was completely puzzled. Couldn't have been my references. They were not *his* advisors.

"Chance gave you a 'yay' and two thumbs up, and Arinn, well, she tried to say your name."

"Oh…God." I brought my free hand up to my face and admitted, "That just made my eyes water."

"Oh, boy," Finn lamented. "It was supposed to be a smile kind of thing. No tears allowed on tour."

"Then you better not play the 'Dark and Dusty' song!"

"Touché." He laughed. "Listen, I'm glad this is all

working out. I'm gonna go and let you and Reese hash some stuff out."

"Thanks," I said and quickly added, "Thanks for everything."

"I guess it was serendipitous that you were looking for ice—"

"I wasn't even doing that," I admitted, interrupting my new boss.

"Well, whatever. I know this is going to be good for all of us," he said. "Just don't pull the football out from good ole Chuck."

"Finn!" Reese screeched at the *Peanuts* reference. "Say goodbye. Let us talk."

"Bye, Maya. See you in May."

Reese and I talked even more logistics—from my start date, to signing papers, to meeting with her in Nashville, to what would be expected on a daily and weekly basis, to dealing with Finn. And when I got off the phone, I screamed out my excitement. Poor Allante came hobbling as fast as he could and tried to lick me as a nervous protective kind of thing. I gave him a hug and a kiss and then called Sophia and then Juanita, who both screamed, too. It had only been a week since I sat down to dinner in Finn and Lara's suite and, God, how my life had changed. But then I wasn't a stranger to that occurrence, either.

***

The next week flew by so quickly. I was trying to plan out every last detail of what my new job would involve. I practically had lists for my lists. I wanted to do everything—shopping, scheduling, correspondence—all at once, but I couldn't. I had plenty of time to get it all done. I was just excited for something like I hadn't been for so long.

It was that following Sunday when the ACM Awards were broadcast live. I had always been a music fan and, since Jeff, specifically a country music fan. But I never really got into the award shows. First of all, there were a lot of them. And second, a plaque or trophy didn't influence who I liked to listen to. But, boy, was I paying close attention to the ACM ceremonies. Literally on the edge of the sofa, I even took notes. I also monitored Finn's social media sites to see what fans were posting during the show. And I knew the likes, comments, and retweets would get even higher if he won something...which he did—Single Record of the Year. His emotional acceptance speech was about it being a particularly rough year for him, so it was nice to have the honor of the award.

I was so excited for him. It was as if I actually knew him. But...I did! The reality of my life was still not completely registering.

Not only did I want to extend my congratulations, but I also felt as an employee—a new one at that—I should. It would be good for him to know I was paying attention to those things, especially in the position I would be holding. But what to do? And how to do it?

I didn't have any direct contact information for the country superstar. Any time I had corresponded with him, it had been through Reese or Hawk. I had liked his fan page on social media and had occasionally done some internet searches. But that was before...before my whirlwind of a vacation turned job. And, somehow, it didn't seem right to contact him via social media because I knew Reese was the one manipulating those accounts, for the most part.

Hawk. I decided on Hawk. Hawk was always with him. I could say a quick congratulations to Finn via Hawk. And, yes, admittedly, it put me back in contact with the man whose lips I swore I could still feel on mine.

Knowing the awards show was live and there had to be a million things going on with Finn and his crew at that moment, I decided on text format. *Please tell Finn I said CONGRATS! I don't have his contact info.*

Surprisingly, Hawk's text back came promptly...just as the show was returning from commercial break. I looked at the television screen and tried to imagine where Hawk might be and what was going on. Then I looked at his text.

Will do. & U will get his info when U arrive in TN. As I was thinking I probably didn't have any direct contact information due to the confidentiality clause I had to sign when I arrived in Tennessee, another text came in from Hawk. *Congrats to U too.*

A broad smile spread across my face before I added a similar emoji next to my text. *Thanks.* I then followed up with, *& thanks for my endorsement.* I was glad for the opening to say something to him that was not a relay message to Finn.

I'm telling U, it was all U.

I didn't believe that. Nobody, especially someone as protective of his private life as Finn Murphy, just hired someone through a resume, work samples, and personality, even though I was confident in my capabilities. Finn had said it himself—he relied on those around him to help.

I texted back, *Just…thanks.*

U got it. C U soon.

Yep. I debated about another smiley emoji and at the last minute added it. After all, I *was* happy.

***

Less than two weeks before my big adventure was set to begin, Reese called with some final details, including my flight information and where she would meet me before all of us took off on tour. Then Lara called a few days later to help me know how much and what to pack. As much as I liked Reese, I liked Lara even more. Lara was so at ease. I admired that, especially considering all she and her family had been through. And because we were pretty much the same age, I felt like I could relate to her as much as a friend as an employee.

Mrs. Murphy did the best she could, trying to explain the tour bus facilities. Because of the closed-in quarters and her personal allergy to strongly scented things, she suggested not bringing a lot of perfumes. I was more than happy to oblige since, besides lotion and hairspray, I kept scents pretty low-key. The closed-in part, I thought, was what I was going to be allergic to.

Partway through our conversation, I heard Finn say something to her, but I couldn't make it out. Lara's end of the conversation was much clearer, though. "I'm talking with Maya." She paused, obviously listening to her husband. "Girl talk." There was another bit of silence on her end. "Telling her what to bring...pack."

When Lara started laughing, I had to question. "What?"

"Finn and Hawk said you don't need to bring an ice bucket!"

"Oh, geesh." I exhaled and went along with the joke. "I'd probably lose it, anyway," I said. "I'll figure it out. It sounds like you have a lot going on there."

"Always." She sounded both exhausted and exhilarated at the same time. "There's just a few of them over here ironing out the details."

"Oh." I pictured the two she mentioned standing next to her and thinking of me.

"We'll see you in a week, then?" Lara's voice interrupted my mental image of both men.

"Yeah. Tell the kids I said 'hi.'"

My brain tried to refocus on what it was supposed to. But how could it? A week. A week. In a week, my world was going to change.

CHAPTER FIVE

And in an instant, there I was—in the baggage claim of the Nashville International Airport. It may as well have been the Statue of Liberty welcoming a foreigner to a new land. It felt so surreal...so overwhelming...yet so right.

I watched as the luggage began circling the belt. I tried to concentrate only on it—not who was going to pick me up, not meeting Reese, not signing all the agreements, not my leap-of-faith career choice. But I must have been thinking of all those things because my navy-blue suitcase with its fluorescent pink label almost passed me by. I reached out my hand to lasso it to me as, at the same time, a muscular arm stretched across mine and grabbed for it as well. I was ready to defend my possessions forthright when I looked up at the perpetrator. Then my arm went lax, allowing him to remove my suitcase from the moving belt.

"Hi." I managed the word and a soft smile at Hawk. At least I looked nice—a blue top to match my royal blue eyes, and my makeup freshly updated on the plane. I'd wanted to make a good impression for whoever was picking me up. I hadn't anticipated it being Hawk but so much the better.

A slow blink was his response followed by, "This it?"

"Besides what's on my shoulder, yeah." I readjusted my

laptop messenger bag on said shoulder and went for my suitcase, propped up between the two of us.

"I got it." He grasped the handle almost like he was a little offended I would carry it. We locked eyes for a moment, and an intensity I couldn't quite identify vibrated through my body.

"Come on," he said. "Lots to do in little time."

We started walking stride for stride, with him taking the mini-lead. Dressed in a light blue button-down and khakis, he was quietly weaving us in and around the mass of people, making me think how he was the strong-and-silent type. But it was more than that. He seemed so serious—not quite as much as when we were first barricaded in the hotel room, but still. I didn't know what I had expected when I'd thought about first seeing him again. I wasn't naïve, and I was far from a Disney princess. But even if those kisses meant nothing, a partial smile would have been at least expected, right? Had I really misinterpreted the whole thing? Had we both only been caught up in the danger and proximity of being in that room together? Or maybe that was just the way it was in the music business. After all, the vacation in the Keys had been a month and a half before. He'd probably moved on…maybe many times.

Well, I figured, I can't keep torturing myself. I needed to get my mind in the game. I needed to make conversation. So, wanting a legit answer, I started with a casual question. "How'd you get roped in to picking me up?"

"Part of the job," he answered plainly. "At least I didn't need to hold up one of those cheesy name signs. I knew you."

He stuttered in his step and flashed me the briefest of smiles—the kind if you blinked you would have missed altogether. He was hard to read, but me not reciprocating didn't help. So, after a few more steps of silent semi-awkwardness, I forged forward again.

"Besides human shield during hotel standoffs, you are also a driver?" I tried to make light of our previous encounter.

"No." He half-chuckled out the word. "I don't do most of the driving. Airports, though, for special people." And he did that pause thing to look at me again with his intense hazel eyes.

"I hardly think that is me."

"Maya, you're going to be working with his kids. There's nothing more important to them than those two." His feet were slowing down since we were entering the parking lot. "And you are part of the team. Finn is extremely good to his team. You'll see. It's a family. Well, probably better than most." He stopped at the back of an SUV and opened the trunk. After placing both of my bags inside, he went to the passenger side and opened the door for me.

"Thanks," I acknowledged, and then it was silent again as he sent a text and we made our way out of the lot and onto the main road. The combination of silence, stillness, and no fresh air bothered me in the closed space. But instead of asking if I could open the window in someone else's car, I opted for the make-some-conversation option. "This is so foreign to me." Hawk glanced in my direction as I explained. "I have no concept how any of this works—this on-the-road thing."

"It's a different world." He stated what I had pretty much already figured.

"Any pointers?" I asked.

"Be yourself. That's what got you here." I saw the slightest shake of his head, and I was unsure if it was in relation to the car next to us thinking of cutting him off or at me just being me. "But..." he continued as I silently admired the smooth way he drove. "I will tell you this...what you saw in March is different than what you are going to see the next couple days and then a lot different than this summer once we start to roll."

Was that cryptic or hopeful? What did he mean? I asked it internally, but it must have started to come out verbally, too.

"Finn gets very stressed at the start of a tour," Hawk explained. "Cagey-like. And then it calms down…more like it was in the Keys. Well, except for the obvious hotel standoff." He looked at me for a second and then focused back on the road. "After the first concert venue or so, it's really a party. But right now, he has us going in fifty million directions. And one of my jobs is to keep him sane."

"Well, that didn't make me nervous at all," I said with pure sarcasm.

It got another partial chuckle from Hawk. "No need," he said and then continued. "I'm gonna drop you off at the studio. Meet with Reese and whoever you are supposed to. In the meantime, I'll bring your stuff to the hotel. You have my number, right?"

"Yeah." I looked over at him, trying to figure out the sequence of my day.

"Text me when you're done, and we'll get you to the hotel. I gotta get some of this other crap done."

I could see the truth in what he had just revealed—we were no longer at a beachy resort. It was the beginning of a massive, headlining production, and they were all feeling the pressure. And, surely, adding little ole me into the mix was more of a hindrance than a help.

"I'm sorry to be such a pain," I offered.

"You're not." His reply was short but distinct. He looked over at me before turning the car into a parking lot and an open spot. "We're here."

"That was quick." I acknowledged the under-twenty-minute ride.

"Yeah." His shoulders dropped as he pointed in the direction of a woman exiting the building in front of us. "That's Reese."

Medium to slightly plump in build, Reese looked to be in her forties, but then who could tell nowadays, especially with hair coloring and wrinkle serums. Regardless, her shoulder-length, red hair took on the shine of the beginning-of-May Nashville sun as she first greeted Hawk and then me as we made our way out of the vehicle. While Reese was asking me if everything had gone smoothly with my travels, Hawk quickly touched my shoulder and nodded the direction of the driver's seat. He was leaving. I nodded back but realized, as he pulled away, that I didn't want him to go. I felt more secure when he was around. Whether it was the presence he portrayed or the fact that I just knew him more than the person in front of me, I didn't know. But it didn't matter. He had to leave, and I had to dive in to my future.

***

Everything with Reese and the lawyers went well. All of my clearances were in order and the papers they had me sign regarding employment, as well as privacy, were more than understandable and generous. After being married to a cop and being sworn to secrecy about the tales he would bring home as a way to debrief, not giving out addresses or phone numbers or personal stories of a rock star was a piece of cake.

When we were done and all hands were shaken, I turned to Reese. "I just need to call Hawk so he can pick me up to go to the hotel."

"What?" she queried. "Did he tell you that? I'll take you. That would be ridiculous for him to come back. I'm staying at the hotel, too, and this way we can chat a little longer without all the fuddy-duddies around."

"Oh. Um, all right."

Really, what Reese proposed did make much more sense. And I would enjoy hearing more about…well, about everything. And, God knows, I didn't want to bother Hawk any more.

But I did need to send him a text. *Reese is taking me to the hotel.*

It was more than five minutes or so later, once we were already in her rental and heading out, when I got the reply back from him. *I could have done that.*

Already on our way. Get done what U need 2. Thx tho. Appreciated the ride & advice. I didn't add a smiley that time. I thought it and wanted to but wasn't quite sure about anything right then.

His return text said, *Best part of my day.*

Well, sheez, that threw me for a loop. Had I been in my own car or, for that matter, anywhere by myself, I probably would have screamed or at least said something out loud to question the meaning of his text after our shaky interaction earlier. I would have never been able to tell in person that it had been the best part of his day. But, also, in relation to what? Geez, how shitty of a day had he had? And, now, how would I reply? On top of that, I felt like Reese was staring at me and/or reading our texts, which I knew she wasn't. But I could sense the curiosity from her driver's seat since she had stopped talking while I was texting.

"Everything good?" she questioned.

"Uh, yeah. Sure. Sorry." I was able to reply to Reese but not to Hawk before another of his texts came through.

Rest up. Tomorrow's even crazier.

Somehow, that made me smile and want to try to make him do it, too. So I typed back. *U & these encouraging words. Hallmark needs your talent.*

Ha. Ha, he wrote and then followed up with a quick second text. *It was good to C U Maya.*

Although I was confused about what was between us, I wholeheartedly agreed. *U 2,* I replied and then directed my attention back to what I did know about—publicity and country music.

***

I knew I should have slept more. I should have slept more the night before I flew to Nashville, but I didn't. I should have slept more the night I stayed in the hotel in Nashville, but I didn't. I had been too nervous, excited, curious…everything. And, now, there I was—on one of, I think, eight buses, never mind the multiple semis hauling equipment—rolling down the open highway and wondering if I would ever sleep again.

The first day, I was in the bus with Finn, Lara, the kids, and Reese. Reese was traveling the fourteen-hour overnight adventure to the first concert stop so she, Finn, and I could meet in person and talk everything through. After that concert, though, she was flying back to New York to be with her husband.

Even without the previous pseudo-warning from Hawk, I could tell Finn was a little jittery and tense. But who wouldn't be? Who could handle that kind of pressure on their shoulders? I felt stressed just leaving my house for a few months, never mind leaving and being in charge of a magic carpet rolling down the road. Finn was periodically texting and on the phone while we met and chatted. But he also remained focused on what we were doing. And Lara and the kids provided the needed breaks for all of us, whether it was just to eat, talk cartoons, or play games.

When the subject of Chance and Arinn was brought up, Finn was absolute about having nothing about them get out to the media—no names, no references, no pictures. Reese brought up the whole Arinn kidnapping incident in December, which I acknowledged. That led Lara to talk about the other part of my job—watching their two simply adorable offspring.

"Maya, the kids will almost always be with me or their father. But there will be some times when I want to be backstage or we want some time alone. Knowing there is someone consistent for them on site is so nice. Everybody has enough of their own stuff to do. The work for Reese, though, that's your main thing," she said.

"But when they're with me," I punctuated. "There's nothing more important."

"Thanks." Lara smiled. "It's hard for me to, you know, leave them, after what happened."

"I completely get that." I looked at her straight-on to emphasize my understanding of the situation.

"Do you want to help me put them to sleep? It might give you some idea of their routine."

"Sure," I agreed, and walked a matter of steps to the main bedroom on the bus.

Amazingly, not that much later—probably out of pure exhaustion—I managed to fall asleep on one of the skinny bunks outside of Finn and Lara's bedroom. Reese took the other bunk across from mine. My nighttime lullaby that night was running through all the ideas and blog topics I had.

***

I had to remember I wasn't a fan. I was an employee. Okay, I was both. And I was pretty sure my first blog about opening night portrayed that. I was to blog as myself, showing the true backstage, on-the-road experience. I sat alone, behind the buses, and wrote, wrote, wrote. Having gotten Finn's approval the next morning, we linked the post to Finn's numerous social media sites. And it blew up—in the best way—almost immediately. It received a ton of likes and comments and, best of all, made both Reese and Finn happy.

It made *me* even more energized and confident. I immersed myself into my work full-force—prewriting, following up, and researching. I didn't go to the show or post-show with the rest of the crew the following night because I was watching the kids for Lara during the concert. She didn't stay long and was texting me constantly. I kept reassuring her that the kiddos and I were having a great time and all was well. But I could tell when she made her way back to their trailer, there was genuine relief on her face. Even though we got along great, I knew I had to completely win her and Finn's trust when it came to their children.

Afterward, I found a few moments to catch up with my

personal correspondence. There had been so many of my friends and family calling and messaging the night before—including a video sent by Sophia's sons, happily playing with and taking care of Allante. It was nice to finally have a chance to respond.

We were on the road completely for the fourth day—traveling a greater distance. It gave me more of an opportunity to get to know my bus mates. I was on the all-female bus, which was kind of fortunate because the guys by far outnumbered the ladies on the traveling lyrical circus. There were only five of us gals, which wasn't bad…until it came to shower time. Then it was like my old sorority house with the waiting and squeezing in front of mirrors.

I was ready to get out and mix and mingle during the dinner break that evening. All the buses stopped for a mandatory break. We got fresh air and a chance to really stretch. From afar, I saw Finn and Hawk talking. Finn, as projected, did seem much more at ease, having a couple days under his belt. He looked in my direction and nodded to Hawk who, in turn, made his way over to me. It was the first time we were really going to have a chance to talk since wheels had gone up four days before.

"Hey," said Hawk.

"Hi."

"Where've you been hiding yourself?"

"Ha." I kinda breathed out more than laughed. "I haven't. Just been busy trying to get acclimated to my new job."

"And? Everything going all right?"

"I think." I dared not say more in case Finn had said something to the contrary to Hawk.

"I'm *sure*," he amended before saying, "You need to join us post-show. You'll get a whole other side of this phenomenon."

"I will. I just need to get a hang of…" Of being with all these people all the time, trying to fit in, trying to remember what I was there for—

"Tomorrow." He bowed a little to meet my gaze.

And I couldn't resist. I was actually appreciative of the invitation...especially from him. "Sure."

"C'mon." Carter, Finn's drummer with the floppy dark hair, seemingly came out of nowhere and slammed Hawk in the shoulder. "Let's go hit the gridiron. We're gonna crush them this time."

"We do every time." Hawk spoke with confidence and then turned his attention back to me. "See ya, Maya. I'll save you a seat tomorrow night."

"Good deal," I replied. "Go crush 'em," I added with a smile.

***

He wasn't kidding. There was, indeed, an empty chair next to Hawk awaiting my arrival that following night after the concert. And it seemed to be the only one. Everyone was already kicked back with fresh, casual clothes and partaking in some sort of beverage. It wasn't the whole entire crew—a more intimate one made up of mostly the band and those who immediately dealt with Finn. Their beach chairs were in a circle near Finn's bus so he and Lara could be close to the kids.

They didn't see me approach, which was just fine. It gave the writer in me a chance to observe silently and figure out the dynamics. What I witnessed was something I had noticed almost immediately since starting the tour—a true sense of ease and equality.

Coming from behind, I squeezed in between Hawk's chair and the empty one. "This seat taken?" I know my smile was as shy as my voice.

"It was taking on dust, waiting for you," Hawk replied in jest. "Sit, Maya."

As I did, a good part of the gang seemed to cheer out, "Maya!" as if I was Norm on that old television show *Cheers*.

I sat down. "Hi, everyone."

Whatever conversation had been happening prior to my arrival changed so everyone got to know me better. I had been introduced informally, or introduced myself over those past few days, but I got a better sense of individuals by sitting around and talking casually with them. And I'm sure they found out a lot about me, too.

At some point, Hawk had opened and handed me a bottle of beer. The whole transaction had happened so effortlessly, I hadn't even realized it. But there I was enjoying the refreshing lime flavor, and it was nearly half gone.

I held up my bottle in his direction. "Thanks."

"You got it," he said, and I couldn't help but think I liked when he was relaxed.

"Who won the game yesterday?" I looked at Carter because I felt like I was looking too much at Hawk. "Did you crush them?"

"Crushed." Carter nodded his head toward Hawk.

"Um, winning by one touchdown is not crushed." Finn spoke up, obviously having been on the opposing team. "And that's only because you cheated."

"What?" Carter's deafening bellow was in good jest.

Hawk was looking at my beer. "If it's not cold enough, you might need to go on an ice bucket run."

"Oh, geez!" I laughed. I liked his succinct, personalized wit.

"Maya…" Finn joined Hawk's and my conversation, giving up on the football trash-talking. "You said you weren't even going for ice that day in the hotel. What *were* you doing?"

Everyone's eyes on me, I spoke the truth. "I just needed space. I wanted some time alone to think."

"You sure didn't get that," was Hawk's commentary.

"No, guess not," I answered.

"You're not getting it now, either," Lara observed.

"This is completely different than my life at home," I acknowledged, momentarily bringing the bottle back to my lips. "I'm used to quiet solitude. I'm sorry it's taking me a little while to adjust."

"You're fine," Lara said.

"Maya, we're all used to this," Finn bounced off his wife. "Take as much time and space as you want. It's fine."

"Thanks." I smiled genuinely because I knew he meant it genuinely. "You know…" I said after a mini-beat. "I just might need a little of that quiet time right now." I took the final gulp of my beer and set the empty bottle down. "I'm just gonna go for a walk." As I started to stand, I couldn't help but see the eye shift Lara gave Finn who, in turn, did a head nod at Hawk.

Hawk looked at me as he shifted in his seat. "I know you're tough, but it's probably not a good idea to walk by yourself this late at night. It's dark, and there are still straggling drunks from the concert."

"Come with?" I didn't even try to disguise it. It was what I intended all along.

I did want some time alone…with him. I wanted to see if the little dance we'd started in March meant anything. I felt like it did, and I wished it did, and, by some of his comments, I hoped he felt the same. But that wasn't going to happen with a band full of brothers gathered around.

Hawk took the last drag of his longneck, silently stood up, and began walking alongside me through the grassy-to-gravely-to-grassy-again surfaces of the outdoor concert area. I was watching my feet more than anything because I was wearing simple sandals and didn't want to step on any of the miscellaneous garbage the ticketholders had left on the ground. But what made me look up and speak was the tremendous beacon from the sky. The nearly full moon was reflecting onto some type of water just in front of us.

"Is that a lake?" I asked, knowing Finn and his team had been to that venue many times in the past.

"Yeah. It's manmade…not big."

"Huh," I said. "I would have never guessed this was out here."

Standing at the edge, I could see it in its entirety a little better. The water was mucky and the entry into it looked rocky and steep. Regardless, it seemed like an ideal, quiet spot to sit for a moment.

"Yeah?" I asked, crouching to show I wanted to sit.

Hawk shrugged and joined me, both of us sitting with our legs outstretched toward, but not in, the water. "You cold?" he asked after a minute or two.

"Neh, it's refreshing."

And then after another beat, "So, honestly, what do you think of Camp Murphy so far?"

"I'm not sure what I expected." I was in a tranquil mood, just staring out into the water, while answering his question. "I guess it was so far out of my realm, I had no expectations. So it's hard to say."

"Well, that was a vague answer." He tossed a nearby rock into the lake...its splash was barely recognizable.

"Sorry. Yeah." I tried again. "What's not to like? I have a job that involves two of my favorite things. I love the music, and I love writing. And there's such a camaraderie."

"But sometimes too much?"

"No. I didn't mean that." I turned to face him. "I hope I didn't offend anyone." Geesh, really, truly.

"We all feel that way sometimes."

"Maybe it's the writer in me. I like moments like this. Moments to sit back and soak it in...to think."

Hawk turned to me then. After a second looking directly in my eyes, he used the exact words I had told him after our first kiss in the hotel. "Appreciate. Let it sink in."

"Exactly." I smiled just as his nose touched mine and our heads tilted in sync so I could feel the sight scratch of his beard before we kissed again...right there on the edge of the still lake.

I was internally sighing for a couple reasons. First and foremost, his lips felt magical. They were soft and feathery and gently sucking on mine. And second, I wanted that moment, and I knew it needed to be then. It was a rare chance for us to be alone in a calming, serene setting. The doubts needed to be erased. And if any more time would have gone by without my lips finding his again, I knew our chance would have passed, and we would have been stuck in that colleague-friendship zone. I didn't want that. Hawk had taken the first step at the hotel months before, and it was my turn to let him know I was ready. And I was. I had learned time and time again that every day counts. I didn't want to live with what-ifs. I didn't want to live in the past. I wanted to live.

When we stopped, my gaze bounced around his for a moment before saying, "You're not trying to influence me again, are you?"

"No, ma'am." He gave a legitimate laugh. "I'm sure glad I might have in March, though."

"Maybe." I smiled, repeating what he had said back then.

Knowing we should return, but not wanting him to think I was doing the quick running retreat like I had the first time at the hotel, I gave him a smile and then sat silently for a few minutes, looking out to the water. "Thanks for walking with me."

As he shot another rock into the lake, he said, "You shouldn't walk by yourself, Maya."

"I do like my alone time, but I wasn't exactly planning on it." I gave a sly smile, letting him in on my devious plan, and then reached out my hand as I started to stand.

He took the gentlemanly cue and stood while helping me do the same, all the while exhaling and slightly shaking his head at my comment. He got it. As we started walking back toward camp, I wondered if I had provided him with the best part of his day again. I know he had mine.

CHAPTER SIX

Concert days were a whole different beast than off or traveling days. Concert days involved a lot more attention from everyone on staff. Finn and crew had to scope out the venue, do sound checks, participate in meet-and-greets, and conduct interviews with radio people. Hawk was involved in almost all of that. Even though I still did not have a job description for him—but then, I didn't have one, either—he seemed to be Finn's right-hand man. And while I would sometimes be with them, I would mostly spend my time on those days talking on the phone with Reese and following through with social media posts. There were the standards—thanking fans for the concert the night before, counting down the minutes until the next concert, even the weather report was fair game.

And that was exactly what was causing havoc the day after my walk to the lake with Hawk. A big-time thunderstorm was threatening to cancel, or at least cut short, the outdoor South Carolina venue. Everyone was a little concerned. It had rained hard earlier in the day but quit rather quickly. It was the second round that had the potential for the most damage, though. No one wanted to cancel. That would mean rescheduling and refunds. But the safety of everyone—fans and crew alike—was the top priority.

When I popped in to a meeting of the minds to see if Finn needed me to post anything, he claimed they planned on going on as scheduled. I caught Hawk's glance and closed smile as he leaned over the table, making his already muscular arms even more defined. I smiled back and left them to their own.

Seeing Hawk made me flash back to our kiss the night before…not that it had been far from my mind in the first place. It was hard not to compare it to my time with Jeff. It wasn't that one was better than the other. It was that Jeff and I had been married for nearly seven years. While our love had not dulled, it had been a long time since we had been in the discovery phase—where everything was new, everything was an exploration, everything was an unfamiliar sensation. That was what each kiss had been with Hawk, and I knew there was so much more to find out and learn.

It wasn't going to be that night, though. I wouldn't even get close to him. Because even though the concert itself went on perfectly, there was a loud boom and the sky opened up during what had to be the last minute of the encore. Out from the clouds came a torrential downpour. I was in Finn and Lara's trailer watching the kids. Chance woke up with the loud clap of thunder and, especially in his freshly awakened state, was frightened. I brought him into my arms and rocked him the best I could. But even though I was good with the kids and could create terrific pillow and blanket forts, Chance wanted his parents.

Having motherly intuition, Lara rolled in moments later, looking like she had just been rescued from being thrown overboard. "Hey." She sounded winded.

"Mommy," Chance whined.

"It's all right, Little Man." Lara took Chance from me. "You're all right."

"Sorry," I said. "I tried."

"Thanks, Maya." Lara looked across her son to me.

"Finn and I can't even really do anything for him during storms." She looked back at Chance. "Bud, it's all right. I'm staying, okay?"

"I guess I'll go then," I said.

"No," Lara replied, still soothing Chance's back. "Just stay with us tonight. Everyone is taking cover. No one's moving anywhere once they're inside."

"It's that bad?" I peered out the window.

"Just a thunderstorm, but there's no reason to risk anybody. We're gonna pull out early and try to drive ahead of it." She finished her comment before picking up her ringing cell phone. "Finn?" She called her superstar husband by name. "Yeah, we're all good. Just getting Chance back to sleep." He was trying to close his eyes, but his mother's voice was actually making him flutter them open. "Yeah, I just told her." Lara looked my direction that time—me being the obvious "her" in the statement. "Okay. See you in a bit."

That settled, I was obviously in for the evening. There would be no after-show gathering. I wouldn't even sleep in my own bunk. Instead, I would listen to the sound of rain hitting the windows and roof and the rolling of wheels as we pulled out.

***

The next morning, we were greeted by the sun. And shortly after that, the sound of little pitter-pattering feet. Chance joined Lara, Finn, and me in the living area of the moving bus. Thank goodness he looked none the worse for wear after his nightmarish late-night wake up call. Glancing shyly at me, the little boy crawled into Lara's lap, while Finn went to get Arinn, who was calling out from her crib.

Right after finishing the ever-nutritious breakfast of pastries and coffee, Finn's phone rang. "Yeah?" He answered it immediately. "Yep. What's up?" He listened to the person on the other end. "Oh, yeah, right." There was another pause before he said, "No, I forgot. Hawk, can you take care of it?" he asked, revealing the caller. "Oh. All right. Hold on. Let me go into the other room. It's in there. And, plus, I'm being rude to these lovely ladies by talking on the phone in front of them." His voice faded as he started to walk off, obviously still answering Hawk's questions. "Arinn, Lara, and Maya."

Knowing Hawk was on the other line, damn it, made me think of him again. I tried to restrain myself, but I just couldn't help it. It was like I was a crushy, hormonal thirteen-year-old instead of a thirty-five-year-old.

Trying to act cool, I decided to see if I could get some information from Lara about the man who was still somewhat of a mystery. "So Hawk...he does a lot of stuff for Finn, huh?"

Lara scooted Chance back a little from the television set as she replied to my question. "He's a good guy."

I noted immediately how she answered. She could have gone into all of Hawk's duties, but she hadn't. She knew that wasn't what I was really asking. It was that woman-to-woman intuition thing, and, luckily, she was playing it cool with me.

"He's been such a great friend and more to Finn... and then to me and our kids, too."

"I can tell," I offered.

"He's one of those guys who will do anything for you once you get to know him," she continued.

"Yeah."

"I mean, you kinda know that, though, right, Maya?" Lara was keeping an eye on a rambling Arinn, who didn't have as much patience for the television show as her brother.

"Sorta. I mean, I'd like to." Oh, geez, did I just say that?

Lara's smile was so genuine I almost cried in embarrassment. "Let me tell you, Hawk puts everything into his job—too much, I think, sometimes—meaning there hasn't been a lot of time for relationships. I'm lucky. Finn has sacrificed a lot for me. And with the right person, Haw—"

Finn literally made me jump when he entered the room and interrupted our conversation. "And vice versa, Beauty. You've sacrificed a lot for me." He kissed her quickly on top of her head. "Are you talking about Hawk?"

Oh, dear God. I was absolutely mortified. Was I that transparent? Or had the country music singer been listening to our conversation?

"Oh, God." I looked at the phone in Finn's hand and trusted he had hung up. "Please don't tell him." I was resorting to my teenager stage again. "I know I have no right to ask you. You're like besties or something."

"Besties." Finn belly-laughed while sitting down with Lara and I again. "I have no omissions from my wife." When Lara smiled, he continued, "But if you ask me not to say something to Hawk and it's not going to hurt him, I'm good."

"Thanks," I said, hoping that was enough to just let it be.

But Finn had one more thing to add, and I was glad he did. "Let me just tell you something, and *you* promise not to tell Hawk." He paused, and the silence was my understood promise. "I have never heard the man of little words talk so much about someone." And then he poignantly tilted his head toward mine as if I didn't already know the person he was referencing was me…and I smiled internally.

***

Because we left the last venue ahead of schedule, we arrived early at the next. Having some free time before any of the preshow things needed to be done, Lara and Finn asked if I could take the kids for a little while. I was happy to because I really truly adored those kids, and I appreciated the honest, sort-of-advice the Murphys had given me the night before. It was also nice to see they seemed more at ease letting me do the kid part of my job.

As I played with Arinn on the blanket and watched Chance run around like a mad superhero saving the world, I saw Hawk approach our grassy spot near the bank of buses. "Hi," I said, thinking how the sun brought out the hues of red in his dark brown hair.

"Hi," he echoed, sitting down next to me. "How you doing?"

"Good." I gave the generic answer most humans did. "You?" I liked that he was once again sitting close to me and knowing, via Finn, that we both had been thinking of one another.

He didn't directly answer me but threw out another question. "You find it weird knowing you are basically watching them so mommy and daddy can get it on?"

If I'd had a beverage in my mouth, it would have been spit out. "They need time together," I tried instead. "It's hard out here. I'm sure especially for Finn."

"The crew's glad you're here. We love these little rugrats." Hawk tossed a soft ball toward Arinn, who giggled. "But rotating babysitting duty got old."

"That's what you were doing when—"

"Maya, watch!" Chance yelled while attempting to do a somersault.

I gave him two thumbs up and continued my thought. "That's what you were doing when everything happened at the hotel in the Keys?"

"Yeah," Hawk answered.

"Good job, Chance," I called out. "We're going to start calling you Captain Somersault."

"I good."

Hawk downright laughed because Chance was far from being good at tumbling. He turned his attention from the kids to me. "Maya, if I'm intruding, let me know. But why didn't you and your husband have kids?"

"We tried. I…I can't," I admitted and then made light of my personal situation. "It's actually kind of ironic. The name Maya means fertility goddess."

He nodded in silence, and I wondered if I'd just shot everything to hell before it had even started. Well, my inability to have children was the truth, and it was bound to come out. There was no denying it.

"We didn't know until a couple months or so before Jeff died. He was a rock. He helped me deal…" I stopped—not only because it was getting kind of personal, but it served no purpose other than to make me sad.

Hawk bailed me out. "I saw the pictures and articles about him Reese sent to Finn with your references and stuff. He seemed like a good guy."

"He was," I concurred but then decided to focus on the man in front of me. "What about you?" I turned the tables in hopes of revitalizing something. "You're good with kids. But, yet, it seems like maybe you don't want any of your own," I added because of the comments he had said at the hotel about being a grandparent figure and returning the kids.

"It was a bone of contention with my ex," he said plainly.

"Ex?" My mind swirled with potential information.

"Wife," was his one-word answer, and then he did his intense squint thing like he was trying to gauge how I was going to react. He let the fact he had been married sit with me a minute before providing the additional information I desired. "High school sweethearts. Married too young…right out of school. She wanted to be barefoot and pregnant, and I wanted to live. It got so bad I found myself counting her birth control. Our marriage was done by the time we were twenty-two." His reveal was more than I had ever heard him say before, and I think he realized it. "Sorry. You didn't need to know all that."

No, maybe not. But maybe, yes. After all, he knew so much about me already.

"Thanks for telling me. You keep in touch with her, then?"

"No," he said immediately. "Not at all. Just friends of

friends might mention something every once in a while. She remarried and has three kids…just like she planned," he tacked on at the end, in a bit of a spiteful way.

I decided it was the perfect opportunity to change the subject. "When did you start your job with Finn?"

"A little while after the divorce. I needed a change. I needed out. I moved to Nashville, where a buddy of mine owned a bar. So while I took some business classes, I bounced for my friend. Finn began playing there. It was the beginning of his career. We became friends, and he brought me on. I've done everything from selling merch, to bouncing, to driving, to bodyguarding, you name it." Hawk rattled off surely just some of his duties.

"He counts on you." I spoke with confidence.

"He can." He paused for a second and then said, "I'm driving one of the cars tomorrow. You wanta ride with? Won't—"

"Yes!" I interrupted, not needing him to say anything more. I would be more than happy not to be in the compact girl bus for a change and ride in one of the few cars that made up our road train.

"Well, that didn't take much convincing." He blew air out of his nose more than laughed.

"Can I put the windows down?" I asked one of the first things that had come to my mind when he proposed the idea.

That time, Hawk gave me a more legit, yet puzzled, laugh. "Sure."

"Great. That'll be great," I punctuated my acceptance.

"Well, I better get back to what I should be doing." He shifted onto his knees.

"I'll see you tomorrow, then."

"Not doing the concert tonight?"

"Nah. I'm gonna have to be writing and getting some of tomorrow's work done that will be too hard to do in the car," I explained.

"Good deal. If I'm driving in the morning, I'm not

staying up after the show." And he leaned in for a quick kiss. "Tomorrow."

Ah hell, I could really start getting used to that. The touch of his face on mine combined with the thoughtful consideration of getting some sleep, which he didn't even know meant so much to me, made me want that tomorrow even more. The open road, the freedom, Hawk…I couldn't wait.

***

The breeze through the windows helped create an easy flow of air in the silver crossover vehicle. Both the comfortable car and Hawk's masterful driving skills helped put me at ease. And he must have felt the same, since he opened up a lot about his family, which included, thank goodness, no other ex-wives.

I found out his parents were never married, yet had three sons together. Hawk's father had been in the armed forces and had been deployed for long times on end. When he would return home, he would, almost inevitably, knock up Hawk's mom. Hawk was the middle child. His older brother was married with a boy of his own. And his younger brother was married with a son and a daughter.

A couple years after Hawk's younger brother was born, his dad seemed to go through some sort of mid-life crisis. He bought a fancy car, met another woman and, instead of going overseas, retired early from the armed forces. His father married the other woman and Hawk's half-sister was born six months later. Though, somehow, his parents still got along.

Because he was driving, it was hard to make any eye contact with Hawk while he was revealing so much of his past. I wished I could. I wished I could look into those hazel eyes and see how he felt about what he was saying because his tone was almost as if he was reading a book or telling a story about someone he knew—not of himself.

Even though I didn't know Hawk well, I decided to dive in further. After all, since the first time we met, we always had an ease in our conversations. "Do you resent your dad?" I questioned, trying to put myself in his place.

"For which part?"

"I don't know," I answered. "All of it—not marrying your mom all those years and then turning around and marrying someone else."

"He was a good dad." He didn't shy away from my query. "I was young when the whole other-woman thing happened. So I didn't really know any difference. He was always around for us boys. But as I got older, the thought that he never married my mom? I'm not sure I agree with it. But that was their business." His slight pause seemed to be instantly filled with angst. "As far as Avia?"

"Who?" I asked.

And he clarified. "His wife. I don't have the best relationship with her or my sister. Avia was pretty manipulative. She got what she wanted." There was a pause again, and I let my obvious question hang silently. "She had their baby. I learned she had pretty much conned him into marrying her or she threatened to take the baby away from him. Like I said, if anything, my dad was a good dad. She ended up with most of his money, too."

"They divorced?" I asked, thinking settlement money.

"No, but probably would have ended that way. He died." Hawk just continued on. "It was an accident. He was a volunteer firefighter, and he fell. It was right when I graduated from high school." And then Hawk got married…I silently connected some dots on his personal timeline.

"Oh," I partially breathed, partially said. I wasn't any different than all those others who didn't know how to say their condolences.

"Pretty heavy shit for a lovely car ride down the interstate," he joked.

"Yeah, right?" I decided to assist in easing the intensity,

too. "Maybe we should start playing punch buggy."

"Two hits for the classic Beetle."

"You're on."

***

I think there were way more cows than Volkswagens on our drive before the meal break. So we ended up mooing more than punching. But either way, it was a fun release. I was glad we had a chance to talk and learn more about each other and, at the same time, have some fun, too.

Because we were in the car, we got to the designated meeting area a little sooner than the trailers and buses. Even though we would all split up and go to a few different restaurants, for a variety of reasons, Hawk and I still waited for the others to arrive. Just after we pulled into the parking spot and Hawk turned off the car, I noticed a blue VW Beetle across the lot.

"Punch bug blue," I called out, and tapped him on the shoulder.

"We're not moving. Doesn't count," he claimed.

"What?" I whined. "I thought until we said stop and ruled a victor, all is fair."

"I'll make you a deal." His eyes squinted at me. "Parking lot Bugs count for a kiss."

"Punch buggy blue," I repeated and, approving the amendment to the rules, I met my lips with his.

"Punch buggy blue," he said, once we parted, and then he kissed me again.

"Where?" I asked.

"Look in the rear-view mirror."

I did. "It's the same one!" I exclaimed with a light laugh.

"Are you arguing?" His eyebrows lifted.

"Uh, no, not exactly."

"Punch buggy blue," he claimed again and kissed me just a little bit longer. Before I could question, he said, "Side mirror. And look out, I believe you have a side mirror, too."

"Punch buggy blue," I called out before he had a chance to, but that one wasn't the best of kisses because I was laughing too hard.

CHAPTER SEVEN

I was super psyched. Over a week later, our caravan rolled into Baltimore for that city's stop on the summer tour. It had been nearly three weeks since I'd been in my hometown area. And while time had flown by quickly, arriving back made me instantly a little homesick.

I was watching the kids for most of the Baltimore concert, but Lara made sure to come back early so I could be with Sophia and Juanita at the tail end. Finn had finagled third-row seats for my friends and got them backstage after the final note was played. Of course, there were hugs and "how are yous" all the way around, even though we spoke or texted one another on a regular basis.

Then there were similar statements when Finn approached us. It was funny watching my two best friends be so star-struck. I had long since gotten over any of those feelings when seeing Finn or any of his famous friends. But those two were still giddy thirty-somethings.

"Have a nice break, Maya," Finn concluded his conversation with us.

"Thanks." I smiled, and then teased him. "And thanks for planning your schedule this way. It's perfect for me."

The complete tour outfit had a week off after the

Baltimore concert. Everyone was free to go home or wherever, just so they returned for the Pittsburgh concert the following week. I was basically already home. My house was less than an hour away. I was going to be in my bed, check in on things, and catch up with friends. And the trip to Pittsburgh was only a short bus ride away.

"That's really why I hired you. Your hometown fit into the break schedule."

"Ha, ha!" I laughed as my two friends watched. "If something comes up, let me know. And give those two little ones a hug from me."

"I will," Finn answered back as Hawk joined the scene. Bro-patting Hawk on the shoulder, he said, "Good show," which I noticed and liked about Finn. He always complimented everyone about the concert. He genuinely thought it was a team effort, although I was sure the fans wouldn't agree. "Catcha in a few." And the superstar took off.

"Hi, ladies," Hawk said to my friends.

"Hi." Juanita's eyes got even wider, if that were possible.

"You remember Hawk, right?" I asked Sophia and Juanita.

"Sure. Nice to see you," Sophia said with a slightly clipped tone. She remembered. She remembered all too well.

I looked up at Hawk, who I was pretty sure caught my sister-in-law's inflection. "I guess I'm ready to head out."

"Yeah," he agreed, and I don't think I was mistaken about the little crease of sadness across his face. "Everybody's high-tailing it out tonight. They want to get a start on break." Hawk wasn't, though. He was going with Finn, Lara, the kids, and a few others directly to Pittsburgh for the week. "You want me to walk you gals to your car? Need me to carry anything?"

I smiled at his genuine desire to protect and help. He would do it for anybody. But I also knew there was something special starting to happen between the two of us.

It was in the way we'd spoken with one another since the car ride. It was in the way the seat next to him at the couple of after-shows I went to was assumed to be mine. It was in the way that if we saw each other, which varied depending on schedules, he would kiss me or touch my hand.

It was my hand he was going for as we stood there backstage. Juanita noticed the motion and kindly took a step or two backward. But Sophia either didn't get the hint or purposefully didn't want to.

Not wanting any hurt feelings on the very first night of my homecoming, I took Hawk's hand and squeezed it quickly while not letting my eyes leave his. But just as fast, I let it drop for Sophia's sake. "We'll be all right," I claimed, while looking at the brawny hunk in front of me. "Thanks for asking. I'll see you next week."

***

We had an old-fashioned girls sleepover at my home that night. Sophia had gone to the house earlier in the day and opened some windows to air the place out. She also brought Allante back home. The spark in his elder step wasn't what it used to be, but that dog sure did find the burst of energy to run to me the second I walked through the door. He lapped me with kisses, and I hugged him extra tight. I'm not sure who was more excited to see whom. Pretty remarkable for a girl who was a cat fan growing up.

While there was a guest room and my master bedroom, Juanita, Sophia, and I decided to really play it old-school by camping out in the living room with blankets and pillows. It was very late at night, or really early in the morning, but we knew we weren't going to get much sleep. There was so much to catch up on. And besides, both ladies had taken off work the following day.

"No offense, Maya, but this is a little less luxurious than our last get-together." Juanita laughed, referencing the Keys.

"No doubt." I raised my head up from the floor pillow,

thinking of how much it reminded me of that time, though—my friends, a Finn Murphy concert, and being surrounded with blankets and pillows on the floor.

As if reading my dreamy mind, Sophia finally asked the question I knew she had been wanting to for a couple of hours. "Have you been seeing that guy?"

"Hawk." I said his name because I knew Sophia, by choice, had not. When she didn't acknowledge my clarification, I said, "Yeah."

Again, the silence lingered. And I felt bad. Somehow, my budding relationship with Hawk was harder on Sophia than on the widower in me trying to move on. Maybe it was because I was living it day in and day out, and I knew we were progressing at a natural pace. In contrast, Sophia had not been aware of anything since the night outside of our hotel door. I had purposefully not mentioned Hawk to either of the girls but especially not to Sophia. She was Jeff's sister. It was as if she was feeling a little like I had when I'd moved my wedding ring to the opposite hand. Seeing me have feelings for someone else was like tearing an adhesive bandage off a not-healed wound.

Feeling empathetic, I tried to downplay my answer but kept it honest. "Of course, I see him. I mean there's tons of people traveling with us, but Hawk and I are kind of in the inner circle."

"Geez," Juanita interjected, propped up on her elbow. "How did little Miss Maya get in the inner circle of Finn Murphy?"

"I know, right! I'm still trying to figure that out." I laughed.

"What's he like?"

Hoping Juanita was still talking about Finn, but even if she wasn't, I answered with him in mind. "You guys met him. What you see is what you get—absolutely genuine. He's hard on himself and serious about his music."

"Let's get back to the original 'him' question." Sophia sat up, pretzel-style. And just like that, we were back to Hawk.

"Did you two pick up where you left off, Maya?"

I sat up to meet Sophia and thought about the fact I still called her my sister-in-law. Should I? Was it still true? Or was it another "ring" I had to move? Oh, my mind was flurrying all over the place.

To further demonstrate that fact, I stumbled on my response. "No...yes." Juanita sat up to join us as I tried to explain. "The first week, I was just trying to get my bearings. Everybody was really busy, and I had to figure out exactly what my role was. There wasn't a lot of time to talk, and, you know, there are people everywhere."

"So the yes part?" Sophia wouldn't let it go. It was like she was trying to torture herself.

"Yes. We've kissed...a few times. We've talked. We know each other's pasts. We...yeah." That was it. That was the truth.

"You gonna sleep with him? Or have you already?" Leave it to Juanita.

I tried a *really?* stare at my friend who I knew, even in the darkness, understood but didn't care. So I sighed and answered. "We haven't. First of all, we're just getting to know one another." I looked from Juanita to Sophia. "Second, you guys don't understand, there's no down or at least alone time."

"Look at her smile," Juanita teased.

I couldn't help it. What she said was true. I knew I felt a little different every time I thought of Hawk. And saying his name only amplified my reaction. But I still felt guilty feeling that way in front of Jeff's sister and in the house I had shared with my late husband.

"You should be happy," Sophia offered, and I realized her voice was a little bit sad but also a lot honest and hopeful.

"Sophia..." I said her name, not knowing what else to do. When she nodded her head affirming her statement, I smiled again. "Yeah...thanks."

***

On Sunday, I joined Jeff's family for dinner. I loved spending time with the whole family but especially my nephews, ages ten and eight. Sophia and her husband, Walt, did a magnificent job raising them. Between Sophia's job as a dental assistant and Walt's job running a chain of family-owned restaurants, they were able to put the boys in a private school, which helped keep them grounded in the right way. Their oldest, Artie, idolized Jeff. He wanted to be a cop just like his uncle, and his passion hadn't changed since Jeff's death. If anything, it intensified, which worried Sophia. I tried to remain neutral, but pride and fear were strange bedfellows.

Being with them made me emotional to start out with. But then, in a role reversal, I actually started feeling a little wistful for the constant, rapid beat of the traveling summer band. It confused me a little. So I decided to blog that next day. I wasn't expected to. Finn wasn't looking for any work from me over the break. But I needed to.

After composing my thoughts on my laptop, I sat in a semi-meditative state, wondering whether to send my writing piece to Reese and Finn or not. It was sappy. It wasn't quite like the others I had written. It had more of the feel of what I had written after the Keys—my pseudo-letter to Jeff.

An incoming text physically shook me back to reality. I reached down for my phone and discovered Hawk's name on it. I wasn't much for signs, but the irony of him texting while I was getting sentimental about the roadie life seemed kind of cosmic.

I pressed to retrieve the whole message, wondering what was going on at their end. Was he meeting with Finn? Had something come up?

What time does your bus come into Pitt. on TH? I'll pick U up.

Figuring he must have been, or still was, in a meeting with Finn and my transportation concern arose, I wanted to let both men off the hook. The last thing I needed was a stressed-out Hawk picking me up. I did not want to revisit my Nashville arrival. So my text back was honest and pure Maya. *Tell Finn no. This was my decision to stay. I'll find my own way back to camp.*

I swear he must have been texting the second I pressed send… his response was that immediate. *Finn's not the 1 asking.*

Good thing we weren't live video chatting. My instant blush would have revealed too much. I smiled at his sweet sentiment and considered how to respond.

But he beat me to it. *What time, Maya?*

I could totally picture him with just those three texted words. He was confident I would give him the time yet exasperated I had initially wanted to handle the situation myself. When did I get to know him so well?

11:30 a.m. I texted back and then quickly followed up with, *R U sure? If Finn has U doing a lot of things, I'll get a cab.*

He can wait. I'll B there.

I loved his authoritative voice mixed with the repeated reassurance that he wanted to come and get me. Knowing it was what I wanted, too, along with not having the hassle of finding a cab, I typed back, *Thx. I'd like that.*

U got it.

I knew that was the natural close to our texting episode. But I didn't want it to be. I had already been feeling emotional when he had first texted. And I still was. But I was also feeling a little light-hearted. So I decided to take a leap… even though we were probably still considered to be in the shallow end of the relationship pool.

Punch buggy parked I typed with suddenly clammy, shaky, nervous hands.

But I didn't press "send." I read it and reread it again making sure there weren't any typos. It was as if it was a Pulitzer Prize submission.

He would get my meaning, right? He would appreciate it, right? It was just a cute close, right? It shouldn't be so hard, damn it. Oh, God, there…I did it. I pressed send.

Waiting for his response was possibly even more painful. But there it came. *That's cruel, Maya.* And then, just in case I needed clarification, which the insecure part of me most certainly did, he followed up with another text and a smiley. *Looking fwd. to that 'punch' at the bus terminal.*

I answered with a favorite Hawk term, *U got it.* and added a smile emoji of my own.

***

And after three days of shopping, meeting up with friends, and showering attention on Allante and my nephews, there I suddenly was, stepping off the Greyhound bus and following the line of passengers into the downtown Pittsburgh terminal. It was busy but certainly not a major hub. So I easily spotted my next handsome driver. Hawk stood tall just outside the row of chairs that made up the waiting area. Being away from him for a week seemed like a long time. And noticing the way he stood, watching me as I approached, without blinking once, told me the feeling was mutual. As a new relationship, we were taking baby steps but definitely stepping. First it had been on our long car ride a couple weeks before, when we got to know each other better, and then, ironically, being apart.

Just a step away, I lowered my eyelids in a rare display of shyness. But it didn't last. I could feel his warmth, and I knew if I looked up, he would be staring at me with the squinting eyes I knew were classic Hawk. I smiled at my accurate assessment after once again meeting his gaze and taking the final step to him. Placing my carry-on down on the floor, I tipped up onto my toes and lingered my lips on his.

"Much better than a punch." His smile was legitimate and so nice to see as he then leaned down to grab my bag in one hand and my hand in the other.

I liked that feel. That was something new, too. He had

brushed my hand before, just like our lips had brushed. But a complete, hand-holding, not letting go, walk together was something beautifully new.

"The bus ride go all right?" His voice zoned me back in.

"Yeah," I said, realizing the terminal truly wasn't that big, and we were already moments from the main outside door. "You should have heard some of the stories I overheard from fellow seatmates. I should give the ideas to my author friends."

"Really? Can't be any crazier than the Finnatics." Hawk referred to the ultimate Finn Murphy fans as he temporarily let go of my hand to open the main outside door.

"Who people have slept with, who has herpes, what daughter is marrying the wrong guy, who to vote for, why smoking is bad…. The list goes on and on."

"Come on, really?"

I nodded my head to affirm as he took my hand again and started leading us down the street. "Yeah, a little different than the luxury musical home on wheels I have been used to."

"You're spoiled." He shook his head in a teasing way.

"No doubt," I admitted.

"We're gonna make a stop and pick up some lunch for the crew."

"Okay. Anything good? I'm starved." That morning's solo protein bar had long since worn off.

"How do you feel about fries on your sandwich?"

"On?" Did I hear him right?

"Just go with it. You'll like it. It's what the people around here call a 'burg thing." I was finding out Hawk was, because of his years traveling with Finn, a scholar in the cultures of American cities.

"Yeah, well, I'm a Baltimore/DC gal, and we tend not to like anything Pittsburgh-related."

"That's sports." He let out a legit chuckle. "Besides, you and Lara get along." He noted that Lara Murphy's hometown was just outside of Pittsburgh.

"True," I admitted. "How did their visit go?" I knew Lara, Finn, and the kids were all bunking at her mom's house.

"Finn will be ready to rock hard tonight." Hawk said, and I realized we were at the car parked along the side of the street. "He'll need to get some of his be-nice-to-mommy-in-law business out." When I laughed, he opened the trunk and put my carry-on inside. "We went to a few breweries a couple of nights."

"Geesh." I was thankful my in-laws were tolerable. But then again, I never had to spend that long with them.

"How was *your* visit?" Hawk asked, as if reading my mind.

"It was good," I said, and waited for him to close the trunk so I could look him in the eyes when I said the next part. "It's good being back, though, too."

He lightly, carefully, pushed me against the car door and then leaned his whiskery face onto mine. He kissed me with a little more intensity than ever before. It was still soft, and it was still nice, but it had the hunger of a missing-someone kiss. "It's good having you back."

***

When we got to camp, it was back to business almost immediately. Hawk was definitely wrapped up in all of the preshow hoopla, and I had to get my bearings again by contacting Reese. Pittsburgh was, actually, a two-night event. The venue wasn't in the city itself but just outside of it and, because of its more intimate size, Finn sold out two nights in a row.

Then, the following week was a grueling one. There was one concert directly after the next, and picking up and traveling right as each show ended. As tired as I felt, it wasn't anything compared to those who actually worked the events themselves.

Finally, things settled down for a night after the concert

in Kansas City. We weren't leaving town until the next afternoon, so it was a post-concert party night. I was feeling more and more comfortable sitting around with everyone and just chilling with some cold beverages. As much as Jeff's family had become my own, the collective group of band and crew were beginning to be, also.

When everyone started dispersing for the night, Hawk walked me to my trailer. It was the first time in days we had actually gotten to spend any more than a passing moment together. And I was so glad to have the chance.

Regardless, I didn't let on. "You know, I think I'm pretty capable of finding the trailer," I teased.

"Really?" He went along with my humorous side. "You sure had trouble finding that ice." He referred to our very first meeting.

"Ha, ha! You're lucky I was there to save the day."

"You're right. I was definitely the lucky one."

Ah, hell, I walked him right into that one without meaning to. But it sure was sweet...as was the kiss that followed. While we didn't make a spectacle of it, we didn't care if people knew something was happening between the two of us. That was why I didn't completely stop the kiss but shortened it as Xristina, one of my bus mates, approached, smiled, and entered.

"Thanks for walking me to my door."

"It's kind of a thing with us, huh?" When I smiled in remembrance, he continued. "What are you doing tomorrow before we take off again?" Hawk asked.

"I don't know. Why?"

"It occurred to me that we've never been on a date."

His response threw me for a moment. What he said was true. I just hadn't expected it. We certainly were acting like we had been dating. And the implied, upcoming question made me both happy and strangely nervous. I suppose because, in a way, it was formalizing our relationship.

Knowing neither of us wanted me to hesitate, I replied with a cutesy answer. "What's all this kissing business been, then?"

"Very nice is what it's been." His smile was wide and genuine. I appreciated his serious side, but his smile—dang, when he let that out—it was amazing.

"I concur."

"You free then…tomorrow?" he asked, making sure we got back to the question at hand.

"Yeah. Finn and Lara are taking the kids to the petting zoo."

"I know." He knew Finn's schedule probably better than I did. "I have one of the cars. Anywhere you want to go?"

"I don't know. What's nearby?" I knew with the time constraints we wouldn't have time for a real meal or movie. Plus, I didn't know what he constituted as a date.

"There's a little shopping area or a mini-golf place—"

"Yeah," I replied.

"Which one?" He laughed through his nose.

"I know you don't want to shop." I understood that was just part of the male make-up. When he didn't deny, I continued. "I'm not good at the golf thing, but it could be fun, right?" I missed the things that couples or people with kids did—mini-golf was definitely one of those activities you didn't do by yourself or with a group of girlfriends.

"I'm sure it will be," he said, and I swear he did the one sweep of my body with his eyes.

***

That next day, Hawk helped me putt the damn little orange golf ball up mini hills, around curves, and through traps. But he didn't let me win. He did that pretty easily. It made me realize another thing about him. He was good at most sports and, while competitive, a humble winner.

We made it back just in time to board the buses and start out for the next city. Well, everyone that was, except for Hawk and Finn. They were heading to the airport so Finn could do a quick St. Jude's event the following day and then meet up with us at the next stop the day after that.

Before he left, Hawk butterflied a few kisses on my lips. "See ya, Maya. We'll look for another mini-golf course when I get back."

"I'm going to be practicing," I teased. "You better watch out."

"You do that." He smiled, brushed my hand, and left me sighing contently.

CHAPTER EIGHT

Geez, I flipping missed him. He had been gone less than two days, and I missed him. Meanwhile, there were longer times when we wouldn't see one another and I didn't miss him like I did when he was at the St. Jude's event. Maybe it was because he was actually miles and miles away—when normally, even if I didn't physically lay eyes on him, I knew he was near. But if I admitted it, it was because our bond was getting deeper. Every time I saw Hawk, my feelings for him changed...advanced ever so slightly. There was that still-unsure-where-we-were feeling, mixed with the take-my-breath-away feeling, and finally the calm, knowing-he-was-there feeling.

And I think I felt all of those rolled into one when he came to see me upon his and Finn's return. After a lengthy, sweet kiss, he took my hand and started to lead me toward the stage area. Before I could question, I heard the telltale signs before I even saw the visual. It was not only by the announcer's calls, but it was through the profanity that some of the crew were bellowing. And then it was confirmed by a glance at the large screen on the stage.

"We're watching hockey?" I spurted out and froze in place.

Because his hand was in mine, Hawk had to come to a halt, too. "Yeah. It's the Stanley Cup. The Preds are playing," he said, in an "obviously" kind of tone.

"You're a hockey fan?"

"Can't watch regularly, but yeah." He tugged at my hand, wanting to get closer to the group of our colleagues, but I didn't budge. "C'mon. We're already down two to zip and it's winner takes all."

"Hawk, I can't."

"What do you mean you can't?" Again, incredulous. "It's just for a little bit, and then we have to start getting ready for tonight."

"Go watch. Maybe I'll see you after the concert." I let go of his grip and started in the opposite direction…away from the "oohs" and "ahhs" that the fast game provoked in its viewers.

"Maya…" He stopped me with a brush of his hand, and I turned once again to face him.

It wasn't a secret. In fact, it was far from one. I just didn't like to think about it.

Regardless. "My dad played hockey."

"He did?" When I nodded, Hawk, realizing and empathizing with the loss of a father, asked another question. "Any good?"

"Yeah. Pretty good," I admitted and pursed my lips with a breath.

"What position?" His voice was soft—it helped.

"Defenseman." And then, because not saying it would almost be like lying, I added, "He played for the Caps."

"The Caps? As in the Washington Capitals?" Hawk's voice heightened a little at the shocking revelation.

"Yeah." Once again in my line of vision, the screen seemed larger.

"Who—"

"Noah Collins." I hadn't said his name out loud like that in a long time.

"Holy…" Hawk's eyes blinked wider, and his mouth

hung open momentarily. "Your dad was Noah Collins?"

"Yeah."

"He was one of hockey's greatest. One of the leading defense scorers in history." He recited a fact I had known and heard repeated many times in my life.

"Yeah."

"They still talk about him and that goal during the Stanley Cup, right before he—" Hawk cut himself off. "Oh, Maya, I'm sorry."

I moved my closed lips slightly at the sympathy. I was used to it—and it hadn't just been with Jeff or with my mother. My first taste with sympathy had been with my father. And just like Jeff, he had been a hero but in a whole other sense. He was a legend…the sports kind.

"It was right after the Stanley Cup parade. My dad wanted to celebrate with his family in Canada. They had done so much for him and his career—the lessons, the money, the time. My mom didn't go because she had been so busy attending the games, watching me, hosting the post-party at our house, and then the hot heat of the parade. She was tired and just needed a break. If she would have gone, I probably would have been an orphan that much sooner."

"Maya…" He touched the side of my face.

"I remember I loved being in that parade. I was right beside my dad. He was in his jersey and me in a mini-version. We were in the back of a huge, dark pickup, and I was waving to the crowd and throwing out complimentary T-shirts. Everyone was so happy—the crowd, my parents, me. And then it was all gone. I hate hockey. I associate hockey with driving to Canada. I associate hockey with the end." I couldn't help it. I turned a little so I couldn't see the screen. I had to.

"I'm sorry."

"I keep trying to remember how much my dad loved it, and I should, too, you know, to honor him. But I just can't."

"Why didn't you ever tell me what your dad did?"

"You never asked."

"No," he admitted. "I guess not. I guess I just figured it was a sensitive subject for you."

"But the thing is, he wasn't a famous hockey great to me. He was just my dad—a great one." I smiled. "And he chose to play hockey…and be good at it."

His eyes narrowed slightly. "Kind of like Finn."

"Yeah, yeah, I guess." The words came out slowly as thoughts materialized in my mind. "Go. Watch the game."

"Maya… You sure? I don't have to."

"Yeah. You want to, and I think I just might have some writing to do."

I pecked him on the lips. He didn't realize how much he had helped just by listening. And it had given me an idea.

***

Hours after the Preds lost the game but mere moments after the concert concluded, Hawk found me in a quiet, open, grassy area behind the parked buses. The blog I was writing was a little different than most of the others I had previously written. And because of that, I was having a bit of the infamous writer's block.

"Hey." He lowered himself to the ground where I sat pretzel-style, laptop in lap.

"I just can't seem to get this right." I breathed out a slightly frustrated burst of air. "It needs to have that *ahhh* ending."

"You'll get it." He moved to adjust his body directly behind mine. His legs were stretched out flanking either side of my slightly crossed ones, his head went to the side of mine, and his right hand softly stroked my thigh, which was only partially covered by my jean shorts.

It was exactly what I needed. I needed a pause…a break. I needed comfort. I needed him. And again, his closeness was new and appreciated and welcomed.

"Thanks," I said and hoped he knew it was for the encouragement, as well as the way he held me.

"All your other blogs have been great." His face pressed up against mine.

"You're reading them?" I turned as much as I could.

"Maybe." The inflection in his voice told me he had purposefully chosen that word because it echoed his statement back in the hotel in the Keys when he had first kissed me. "Maybe," I had come to recognize, was his equivalent to "for sure."

I placed the laptop on the ground to the side of us and carefully turned around so I was sitting on his legs with mine wrapped behind his back. "Sometimes it helps to take a break from what I'm writing and come back to it with a fresh pair of eyes."

"Okay," he replied slowly—his hazel eyes not leaving mine.

Our mouths were on each other's then, moving in the rhythmic sync we had come to know. His hands scooted my bottom so I was more snug against him, as I opened my mouth and let our tongues meet. I was losing all sense of place and time with the sensations electrifying my body.

When his hands searched under my loose, white sleeveless top and found first my stomach and then my bra-covered breasts, I moaned. I couldn't help it. It felt so good. It felt so right. It felt like it had been so long since I had felt.

My moan vibrated into his mouth and he broke our lip lock momentarily to say my name followed by, "God, girl, what you do t—"

"Wheels roll in ten!" It was Toot—the head of transportation on the road. He was calling out a general announcement, walking past all the trailers. The buses were pulling out earlier that night so we could get to a legitimate rest area the following day for a real break...even if it was just for a couple hours.

Hawk let out a different type of moan and his hands slowly moved away from my torso. Our clothed bodies were still pretty well interlocked and our faces were just inches apart. I searched his face—from his eyes to his mouth. It was there. It was definitely there—the sparks. I knew we had connected in so many ways, but this was the magnetism. There was no denying it. I wanted him. When a bout of shyness swept over me, I looked down, as if my actions just seconds before hadn't revealed all I felt.

He tilted my head back up and kissed me one more time. "Well, that will give me something to think about all night."

"Yeah," I agreed softly and then secured the laptop in my hands.

"C'mon." He gently lifted his body and mine until we were both standing. "Good night, Maya," he said, when we had walked the few steps to my trailer door.

"See you tomorrow." I kissed him quickly and entered the bus.

I tried to talk with the other girls in our bus, but my mind was elsewhere…singularly, solidly, sweetly elsewhere. I don't know if they noticed. I don't really know if I cared.

Once the bus started to roll, I retreated to my bunk. I didn't even take my clothes off to change into my regular pajama attire. I wanted to remain in the clothes he had touched me so passionately in. I lay there in my bunk and stared once again at the computer screen—a concluding sentence suddenly, magically materialized. I typed with satisfaction, reread the entire thing, and then shut down my computer. It was then that my phone, sitting innocently next to my laptop, lit up and vibrated. I smiled and nearly teared up when I saw the text. It was a stock photograph of a parked, red Volkswagen Bug.

XXOO, I texted back without hesitation or internal debate. It was what I felt. It was what I meant. And I believed he did, too.

***

For the next day's stop, Finn had bought out a campground well in advance. We would spend part of the day there. We could legitimately stretch out, shower, eat, relax. It provided camaraderie to those who needed the social aspect or the space to find solitude for those who just needed a break from everyone else. A few weeks before, I would have definitely fit into the latter category. But between being able to find alone time throughout the tour and simply enjoying being with everybody, I found myself eagerly joining in as a member of the sand volleyball game. Of course, it didn't hurt that I was on Hawk's team…and he was wearing just gray board shorts, which accentuated his athletic frame beautifully.

Our team had just scored off my great, but by chance, placement of the ball across the net. Extending a high five, Hawk slid me up slightly into his secure arms and kissed me. It was open and exhilarating and definitely brought flashbacks of the night before.

But it was interrupted by the master of the parade. "Maya?" Finn called out. He was less than fifty feet away from the volleyball court, standing on a slightly raised hill.

"Yeah?" I swiped at a piece of hair, which had fallen from my loose ponytail.

"Can I see you a sec?" Finn was definitely speaking to me, but the collective volleyball bunch all halted.

"Sure," I answered and started to naturally step away from Hawk.

"Today's not good," Hawk gruffly whispered as he squeezed my hand and handed me my red, white, and blue cover-up.

"What?" I questioned, but didn't wait for an answer.

I was in too good of a mood. The sun was bright. Everyone was relaxed. The tour was going well. My job was fantastic. And I felt so comfortable and happy with that man behind me who I knew was watching me climb the small hill.

Shaking the flowing top over my shoulders to partially cover my tie-dyed crop tank and gray shorts, I approached Finn. "What's up?"

"The blog." His first two words came out short and

plain, but the connecting question was much terser. It mimicked his hands, which were grasping tightly at both sides of his loose, white shirt. "What were you thinking?"

"Wha—" I started, a little thrown by his demeanor.

Not only was his tone the exact opposite of the game I had just left, but it was uncharacteristic of Finn. Sure, we all had our moments of crankiness, especially right before a show and when we had been working on limited sleep. And Finn had been noticeably stressed those first few days of the tour but with due reason…and Hawk had warned me then. Was that what he had just done a couple minutes before…cautioned me about Finn's disposition?

Before I could ponder any further or even complete my question, Finn amputated my sentence. "I thought we talked about not mentioning the kids. I know"—he emphasized that word—"we did."

"I didn't—" I started to explain but was immediately cut off again.

"And this thing about my pop?" His voice, while not yelling, actually escalated another notch. "You didn't know him. He has nothing to do with being out here—the road experience."

"I thought I was using kids in a generic sense of the term." I managed to get a complete thought in that time. I didn't feel like I was necessarily defending my choices regarding the blog, but I did want to explain, especially because it was the one I had been working and agonizing over. And, while he was my boss, I was confident of my own skills and capabilities and had always known Finn to respect that. "And the public knows you have kids, Finn. They—"

"But I told you not—"

"Okay." It was actually *me* who stopped *him* that time.

Realizing he had the final say and I needed things to stay genial with him, I apologized for what he interpreted as a misdemeanor. It was easy on my part. Finn Murphy was not a second-hand paperback writer I needed to fight with regarding correctly promoting his book. He was a superstar with an unparalleled career and, honestly, one of the nicest people I knew. And I would be more than happy to do what needed to be done.

"The part with your dad?" I continued. "I'm sorry. I thought the whole thing would be a change of pace—just something to honor you and your dad and all the fathers out there today." I spoke of Father's Day. "I didn't post it. You know I wouldn't until it got your approval."

"I should hope not."

"Okay, man, ease up." It was Hawk.

I hadn't heard or seen him approach. Finn and I had been in too intense of a conversation. But there he was beside us, sporting the form-fitting, white tank top he had previously discarded mid-volleyball game.

"She said she was sorr—" my defender continued.

"Hawk…" Finn's voice was as firm as his stare at his friend. "You better know how to separate business and pleasure."

I shut my eyes, hoping for calm or maybe a rewind. It was one of the last things I wanted Finn to say. In the back of my mind, I had been a little concerned if my blossoming relationship with Hawk would be an issue, since we sort of worked together. It hadn't seemed to be, though. Everyone knew and even embraced it. But then, there it was—Finn's comment.

And even worse was Hawk's reaction. "What? What!"

"Hawk!" I tried to halt the confrontation, which seemed to be looming. I purposefully widened my eyes at the bearded man whose ego was flexing as much as his biceps had been during the game. "I've got this."

I knew Hawk was frustrated. He had a practical death stare going on at Finn. But when he looked at me, and I pleaded with my eyes, as well as used the word "please," he stalked more than walked off. I didn't mean for him to leave. I just wanted him to calm down. I wanted everyone to calm down. The blog wasn't worth it. It was an easy fix. I just wasn't sure keeping my job or my relationship was going to be.

I started with the one in front of me. "Sorry about that."

"Don't apologize for someone else." Finn used, ironically, a fatherly tone. "He and I will be okay. That was nothing."

Oh. Well, that was news to me. "Me then," I said, needing to recover.

Finn was calmer when he spoke but just as adamant. "I get where you were trying to go with the blog, and I know it is personal for you—your father having been not only your dad but a well-known figure."

"Hawk told you."

"Yeah. Should he not have?"

"No. It's fine. It's not a secret."

"Maya, I get it. I just don't want it."

"All right." Simple enough.

Finn went on to explain. "It's just my dad didn't die that long ago."

"I get it. It's all right. Can I write something else?"

"Yeah, definitely," he answered, putting me a little more at ease. Finn tilted his chin in the direction of where Hawk had retreated—yards away, standing solitary and staring in the opposite direction of us. "Maybe write about how frustrating it is that there's no privacy on these tours." Returning his gaze to me, he let the silence indicate he understood how it felt to be in a relationship on the road. "And if it's okay, I want to keep the blog. It was beautifully written. Maybe someday you can help me make it into lyrics—a tribute to both our dads."

Truly touched, I told him so. "I would be honored. I'll get a new blog to you soon."

"Okay." He tried a smile and walked toward where I knew his trailer was located.

I took a deep breath. I needed to calm myself after my first real professional debate with a boss I admired and was glad to be employed by. And I also had to prepare myself for dealing with the other important male in my life.

"Hawk?" I asked tentatively, as I approached him from behind.

He didn't answer. He didn't even turn to face me. When I started to say his name again, he asked in a controlled, stoic manner, "Everything settled?"

"Yeah. It's fine."

"Great," he said with a sarcastic undertone and finally swiveled around. "You don't need me, then." He blinked his eyes and started his stride past me.

Having lived with a man, a cop at that, for many years, I recognized and understood the male macho pride—how incredibly solid and, at the same time, fragile it was. I knew I had a fine line to tread with Hawk. "Hey," I tried in a soft voice, while reaching out for his moving arm. "That's not…you just didn't need to defend me."

He stopped and faced me. His response was matter-of-fact…the fury obviously still bubbling underneath. "He shouldn't have spoken to you that way."

"You warned me." I just hadn't listened or investigated further.

"Nevertheless."

"What Finn said was right," I tried. "This is my job. What I wrote was my choice. It was my mistake. I, alone, have to live up to it." When Hawk didn't say anything—good, bad, or ugly—I knew I had to provide more. "I know it's kinda in your nature. It's what makes you so much you…your need to protect. Just, when it comes to my job, you can't, Hawk," I said with a little bit of pleading, while tagging on the most honest part. "It worries me what Finn said to you."

"He has some room to talk, bringing his wife and kids with him."

"Don't."

That was apples and oranges. That was spite. That was not true. And if Hawk was calm, he would agree. But even worse, if Finn heard what Hawk said, it would ruin everything for everybody. Again, just because of macho chest-bumping.

My one word must have come out as fearful as my internal thoughts because Hawk softened his tone and said, "Maya, he's on board with us."

"I thought so, too. Let's just not give him a reason not to be."

I let my eyes wander all over the dark scruff of his handsome face. I searched his deep eyes, his mouth, the crinkle between his eyebrows, trying to read what he was feeling. But he didn't give me anything.

With a semi-sigh, I touched his hand. "I gotta go find somewhere quiet and write a new blog." On Hawk's more audible moan, I said, "I need to make things better with him. You're not gonna go and…" I let my sentence trail off, looking the direction of where Finn and I had been standing.

Hawk understood and was at least calmer. "I'll stay out of his way. I knew it was going to be a rough one with his dad."

"I'll see you," I said, and then tacked on, "Sometime."

"Yeah," was his one-word response.

We had ended things better than mere moments before when Hawk had stomped off from Finn and me. Yet there was something lingering. Something had changed or maybe even needed to change.

CHAPTER NINE

It was a little harder to find solitude to write the blog. Part of it was because everyone seemed to be everywhere, mixing and mingling and, in general, having a boisterously joyous time. And I was not. Even when I found a spot way out past the trailers near the exit of the grounds, the noise in my head was loud. There was too much going on internally to properly concentrate—the words Finn had said to me, the words he said to Hawk, and my feelings on both.

I loved my job. It was everything I could have asked for in a career. It was a subject I was interested in. It gave me freedom, for the most part, to be creative. I was treated as a professional with valued ideas. I got to travel. And I got to meet so many genuine, nice, loving people.

And then there was Hawk. I was falling fast. And for the first time, sitting there near tears, I was realizing it. Rationally, I knew it was early. We hadn't known each other long, and we hadn't even slept together. But thinking about him and the implications of Finn's words made me realize how much I cared…how much I didn't want to be apart from him.

I needed to balance. I needed to find a way to have both. I needed it to work.

"Maya, hey, I was looking for you. I even tried your phone." Lara's voice slightly startled me because I had been so entranced by the cursor blinking on a still blank screen.

"Turned it off to concentrate," I said, while attempting to brush at my eyes.

The movement wasn't as discreet as I'd hoped, though, as she immediately said, "Sheez, what's wrong?" Wearing a white floral jumper, she sat down next to me on the long bench.

"Nothing. Nothing. Just a rough moment." I tried for a cheerful expression. "What's up?"

It was an epic fail, though, because she continued to probe. "Is it Hawk?"

Funny how that was her first thought. It just proved how much my relationship with Hawk was acknowledged and accepted. And maybe it further suggested that I needed to establish a balance.

"No." But I knew that wasn't the whole truth.

"Is it Finn? He's been great with the kids today, but it's been hard with his dad. But that's no excuse." She immediately forged on. "Did he do or say something? I'll kill him."

"No. No. No. He didn't do anything." Geez, that was the last thing I needed—Finn thinking I tattled to his wife. "No," I repeated. "It's just writer's block and PMS or homesickness. Not a good combination." I tried to dissuade the astute Mrs. Murphy with humor.

"I hear ya, sista." Lara seemed to accept what I knew was a very flimsy excuse. "If you're swamped, let me know…"

"What?" I asked, eager both for a change in subject and wanting to help the Murphys in whichever way I could.

"Do you think you could watch the kids for a little while tomorrow? There's some radio people coming to interview Finn, and I'm going to pick my friend, Vanessa, up at the airport."

"Carter's Vanessa?" I asked, recalling the drummer speaking a couple times about his fiancée.

Lara seemed amused by my response. "Yeah. She was my friend before she became Carter's."

"Oh." That was a fun tidbit. I got back to the question at hand. "I'd be thrilled to watch the kids." It would help me focus on something else.

"I'm excited for you to meet her," she spoke of my new, temporary bus mate, since the only coed trailer was the superstar's himself. "While Vanessa's on tour with us, I'm sure she'll help out with the kids, too. She's almost like a second aunt to them. It will give you more time for, you know, other things."

By the way she said it, I knew she meant Hawk. But I purposefully ignored the innuendo. "Yeah, I have some new ideas for Reese and Finn, but your kids come first. They are so great, Lara."

"We think the same of you." She returned the compliment but didn't really let the other subject drop. "You sure everything's okay?"

"Yep."

"I know you need your alone time," she recalled after the slightest of pauses. "So I'll let you be. FYI, though, we're ready to pull out in about a half hour."

God, it was that time already? Geez! How long had I been sitting there entangled in my own internal drama?

"I got it. Thanks. Whenever you need me tomorrow, come get me. I'll put my phone back on before then."

And then we were back on the buses again for the rest of the day and all through the night. I didn't receive any punch bug photos or other texts. But then again, I didn't send a smoke signal out either…and I had been the one who walked away.

***

I turned in a more Finn-suitable blog early that next morning. And taking Finn's suggestion, it centered around the lack of privacy on tours because, no matter how hard I tried, I couldn't get the subject out of my mind. I certainly didn't mention Hawk or anyone having a personal relationship on the road. I made it extremely general, citing cell phone use, bathroom time, and sleeping habits. But even before I started my opening sentence, I knew what my concluding one was going to be about—how special the friendships and bonds formed on the road were and how the private moments, although few, were so treasured and appreciated. And if you could manage the right mixture of both, you couldn't imagine a better life.

After it was posted, Finn was talking to press, Lara was picking up Vanessa, and I was sitting with the kids in the beachy area right outside our latest concert stop. It was then when I felt my shoulders being rubbed from behind. I didn't need to turn. I already knew those hands. I closed my eyes for a serene second and then put my one hand on Hawk's.

"Hi," I said as he joined me on the white, fluffy blanket. However, when he echoed my statement and started to lean his lips toward mine, I shook my head negatively and leaned back a bit.

Puzzlement seemed to streak across his face, but he did respect my intentions. "Maya…"

"Hawk, no. This is my job." I tried to explain the kiss denial. "In fact, this, those kids"—I nodded to the two happy Murphy offspring bouncing around in the sand—"are the most important part."

"I know tha—"

"Hawk, flip me!" Chance broke in to our conversation by running up to his dad's right-hand man.

Hawk squinted those mesmerizing eyes at me before getting up and obliging the energized four-year-old. Chance's giggly laugh was infectious, as his body was turned masterfully upside down and back again. I watched as Arinn pointed and laughed at her older brother and as Hawk lit up being the source of delight. It was nice seeing him like that. While he was easy to get along with, he was also serious when it came to his job, which was why I knew he should understand my dilemma and request.

Flipping Chance one last time, he landed both of them in a seated position next to me. "You having fun with Maya?" Hawk asked, poking the little boy playfully in his belly.

"Yeah." Chance's smile was like Finn's when he performed—large and genuine. "Where Daddy?" He obviously associated Hawk with being with Finn when on the road.

"He's finishing with the radio people," the elder explained, and then purposefully turned to make the point to me. "He won't be around for a little while."

I know he wanted his statement to resolve the boundary I had put up between the two of us. But it didn't. I wished it did. It wasn't that I didn't want to kiss him. God knows I did. And the proximity of his body and the resistance I knew I had to create was making that desire so much stronger.

Maybe I should have said all that, but I didn't. "Hawk…" There was a definite plea in my voice. "Just…please, just not right now, okay?"

"Maya, it's all right." He spoke plainly and clearly, practically punctuating each word.

I was going to call "uncle," but it came out instead as, "Arinn!" The one-and-a-half-year-old was threatening to toddle away. "Come here." When I started to stand, I said to her brother, "Chance, we're gonna go see if we can find some popsicles or something to cool down." Literally…in more ways than one.

Hawk, grumbling, stood up, bringing Chance with him. "Here," he said and started to help me fold up the blanket we had been sitting on.

"I got it," I proclaimed.

"Oh, for God's sake, Maya. I can help you." His agitation was clear and legit.

I didn't need to push him away with everything I did. Short of actually saying thanks, I managed a half smile and let him finish folding the blanket. When I hoisted my bag onto one shoulder and lifted Arinn into my arms, Chance automatically went to claim Hawk's hand.

Hawk looked a little deflated when he turned to the young Murphy. "You better go with Maya, Chance."

"Okay," the little boy said, and transferred to my hand.

"Hawk? You understand, right?"

There was another huge, angst-filled exhale. But it was followed with some hope. "Post-show, then?" he offered. "There will be friends and bonding and…"

I knew he had read it. I'd written it for public consumption, but it was as much for him. I wanted him to understand. I wanted him to know my feelings certainly hadn't changed.

"It's just the right mix," I said, smiling. "Yeah."

His soft smile back was reassuring. But when he started to conclude our visit how we normally did—a kiss—he stopped himself. "Damn it. We're gonna have t— Okay, see you tonight."

***

I didn't have to watch Chance and Arinn that night. Lara and Vanessa had them covered. But I didn't go to the concert, either. As much of a Finn Murphy fan as I was and as thrilled as I was having the job of a lifetime, I didn't need to see another show—at least I didn't need to watch night after night. I knew the songs, and I got how the behind-the-scenes system worked. That was enough. I don't know how they all did the same routine every time. But I guess, for someone like Hawk, who was managing more of the behind-the-scenes than hearing what was going on on stage, it was a new experience each time.

With the rare, private time to myself, I took a shower, followed up on personal correspondence, and rested my eyes for a moment before heading to the post-show gathering. I arrived just as the first few people were bringing out the chairs, so I helped. Lara and Vanessa, toting baby monitors, arrived next, and then slowly the band and some of the crew made their way to our intimate circle.

Hawk, whose all-black ensemble was a little sweaty from the hot summer night, flopped onto the empty chair next to me. Everyone knew by then to keep our seats together. It was both a little embarrassing and a little endearing. I hadn't seen him since the flip-me beach scene and was anxious to. I was eager for us to have a chance—since we were both "off work"—to just be together. He elongated his left arm so he could rest his hand on top of my right. There were a few soft rubs before he held it more definitively. It happened to be at the same time when Finn joined our group, sitting next to his wife and almost directly across from us in the circle.

When I redirected my attention to Hawk, he smiled. "How are you?"

"I'm good," I answered generically. "How was the show?"

As Hawk was nodding positively, Carter interrupted. "Hey, Maya?" And because he was seated next to Finn, the request of my name was loud enough to stop everyone's mini conversations. Knowing everyone was looking at me, my hand wiggled underneath Hawk's, but he wouldn't let me break our connection. "Yeah?" I finally replied.

"I think it's about time you blog about the band— starting with the awesome drum work." The drummer stated his case.

I chuckled along with a few others...everyone was much more relaxed since the concert and all that it entailed was over. "Because that's really what draws the crowds, right?" I countered in good humor.

Finn brought his bottle back down from his mouth and looked at me. "Maya, remember who signs your paycheck."

Hawk instantly, and almost through gritted teeth, said to the crooner, "Tell her you're kidding, man."

"I know he's kidding!" I exclaimed. "He knows I am, too."

I tried to ease Hawk's obvious tension with an underneath-hand-rub of my own, but his grip on my hand was at its firmest yet. He was still defending me, and he didn't need to. Finn and I were joking around. We got each other's sense of humor and Hawk did, too, if he would just loosen up.

Oblivious to the undercurrent, Finn bounced right back. "Yeah, I'm kidding. Although if you want the 'likes' instead of 'tears' or whatever emoji is in right now, go with the guitar section."

Two of the guitar players yelled out "Woo! Hoo!" and played a few chords, much to Carter's chagrin.

"Where's the love?" he joshed back with Finn.

"Don't look at me." Finn took another swipe of beer. "I hope it's that girl right next to you."

"Yeah, Carter." Vanessa, who had long, beachy brunette waves, countered with a playful punch on her fiancé's arm. "Where is the love?"

"It's on your finger, for one." He played with Vanessa's beautiful sparkling engagement ring. "And right here," he said, before giving her a show-stopping smooch.

When the "woo-hooing" died down, I asked the happy couple, "When's the wedding?" As the newbie in the group, I was still trying to figure out the dynamics, plus I was glad to get off the subject of the blog.

"Thanksgiving weekend," Vanessa answered. "After all this…and before the bad weather."

"Holiday nuptials…sounds nice," I commented.

I didn't, however, let it be known Jeff and I had done the same thing, except we had been married over an Easter weekend. It was irrelevant, and Hawk's hand was finally starting to loosen in mine. No need for a roadblock.

"How did you two meet?" The inquisitive writer in me always liked hearing those stories.

"Like this, actually." Vanessa held Carter's hand then. "They were on the road, and Lara was driving down to surprise Finn, and she needed a wing-girl for the ride." She glanced across Carter to where Lara was sitting on Finn's lap.

I saw Lara smile at the obvious remembrance and snuggle in even closer to Finn. They were so in love—even years into a marriage and two kids later. It was an awesome and inspiring sight to see.

"That night was kinda just like this." I refocused on Vanessa's dialogue. "We were unwinding with a little bit of alcohol and good music. It was perfect. Well, *you* know." She looked from me to Hawk and then at our hands combined.

Admittedly, that was a little awkward. Sure, everyone knew we were seeing one another. But to be compared to a couple who were engaged and planning their wedding?

Luckily, the proverbial bell saved the day. My phone was chiming beside me. Even though it broke the awkwardness I'm sure only I felt, I was concerned about the late-night timing.

"Sorry," I apologized, and Hawk finally let go of my hand so I could swipe at the phone.

When I saw the caller ID said Sophia's name, I was even more concerned. My former sister-in-law was not normally a late-nighter. She was kind of infamous, in fact, for her kids staying up later than her.

"I'm sorry," I said again to the collective group. "I should take this." Hawk partially stood as I did but then sat back down as I walked off.

As I stepped into my trailer, ironically gaining some of the privacy I had written about earlier, I found out the sad and scary reason Sophia was making that call so late at night. Her father had been admitted to the hospital. He had a pulmonary embolism. It was serious, but he was in stable condition. She wanted me to know, since I would always be a part of their family—neither death nor miles apart would change that I had a loving home base with them. But I also knew she just needed to talk. Her husband had gone back home to be with the boys, and she had coaxed her mother into sleeping for a little bit at the hospital, where she still was. I lamented that I couldn't be there for him, her, or any of them in person as we were states and states away. But she knew and understood. Besides, the preliminary outlook was, barring any setbacks, he should pull through and just needed to get blood thinners regulated and eat a different diet. I prayed with her and promised to keep talking as long as she needed me.

Somewhere in the middle of my conversation with Sophia, a text came in from Hawk. *Everything OK?*

His message helped calm me. It gave me a second to halt my conversation with a despairing Sophia and regroup. And it also made me realize that Hawk was connected enough to me to be concerned.

Jeff's dad is in hospital -- pulmonary. I typed back. *Sophia needs to talk. It's gonna B late. Sorry.* Because I was. I wanted to feel his hand secure but relaxed on mine.

He ignored my apology with another concerned query. *He OK?*

Hopefully…not out of woods yet.
Sorry.
Thx. Could U apologize 4 me please?
He ended with his Hawkism. *U got it.*

***

After the late night, I was able to sleep in a little the next day. We only had a couple hours commute to our next location stop. So we arrived mid-morning. I was busy looking up the posts on social media from the night before and reacting to the blog. And I called and talked with Sophia briefly, too.

And then I wanted to talk with Hawk. Although I would not change counseling my friend the night before, I was sad my time with Hawk had been cut short. I wanted to make sure we were simpatico. I had been thinking we were on the right track when Sophia's call came through. But for sure, we needed a chance to talk.

Knowing he should have some free time before the late afternoon and evening hoopla of the latest concert, I texted him. *Where R U?*

The text response came nearly twenty minutes later, after I had found a solitary spot to just sit, stare at my phone, and wait it out. *Just got to a gym.*

When time and motivation allotted, some of the guys would find a local gym at the concert stop and work out. It was another one of those macho things. But I had seen the regular gym rats still lingering around camp. So I hadn't considered that option.

Oh. I texted back. *I didn't know today was 1 of those days.*

Last min....just w/ Finn, was his reply back.

Sorry to interrupt, I typed, wanting to let the two men do what they'd set out to do.

You're not.

But I was. It wasn't the time to have a conversation. Plus, I wanted to actually see him.

Have a good workout, I offered. *Talk later.*

It was a second or so longer wait than his other texts, but then his reply was, *For sure.*

CHAPTER TEN

I did not expect to hear from Hawk before that night's concert. The best I was hoping for was a redo around the post-show circle. But hear from him I did.

I had been walking with Lara, Vanessa, and the kids around the grounds. There were concert-goers tailgating and meandering, but we went unnoticed, partly because of hats and sunglasses, but a lot because of the privacy Finn insisted on with his family. Pictures of the kids were very scarce. So it gave Lara, Chance, and Arinn some anonymity. We were heading back to the trailers so Lara could get the kids something to eat and calmed down before putting them to bed. She and Vanessa were staying with the kids that night, leaving me some free time before the after-show. They had just asked me if I wanted to stay with them for a glass of wine when a text came through.

Meet me backstage? It was from Hawk.

I typed back *After the show?*

No…now was his response.

"Everything all right?" Lara asked. "Is it your friend Sophia?" We had talked a lot about Jeff and Sophia's father during our tromp around the area.

"No. No. Everything's good." I looked back at my

phone.

"Is it Hawk?" Vanessa, I was learning, was bold, outgoing, and a little feisty—a style that seemed to both compliment and contrast her best friend's.

Before I could answer, a follow-up text came in from Hawk. *It will just B a couple mins.*

He probably thought I was hesitating…which a little bit of me was. I didn't want to interfere while he was doing his job, just as I asked of him the day before. But I also realized, considering the unique situation we were in—working for the same employer and being in the work environment essentially twenty-four-seven— the lines were going to be blurred. He asked me to see him, and God knew I wanted to. I was the one who'd initiated the contact earlier, anyway.

"Yeah," I replied to Vanessa first. "I'm just gonna meet up with him for a sec. Have some wine for me."

And then I texted back to Hawk. *OK. B there soon.*

"If you see my man, tell him not to use up all his energy." She smirked a sultry look.

Lara and I had a similar head shake as I said, "*If* I see him."

I put on my backstage pass lanyard and made my way through the mass of people who were all busy doing their own part to make the superstar's show spectacular. I had a pretty good idea where Hawk would be…or at least in the vicinity. And I was right.

Without being detected, I stood back, watched, and waited. He was helping move some type of equipment with a couple of the guys. He had such strength. But it wasn't just in those muscular arms. It was in the way he directed people—in an authoritarian way but not with one ounce of superiority. He knew what he was doing and people respected him for it.

When the other men moved on to the next project, Hawk turned. That was when he noticed me. "Hi." He wiped his hand on the thigh of his army-green cargo shorts.

"Hey." I took the couple remaining steps toward him.

But before we could get more than the single introductory words in, somebody from catering interrupted, asking about a delivery. Of course, Hawk knew. He seemed to have his hands in a little bit of everything.

Problem solved, he turned his attention back to me. "How's your...Sophia's..." He seemed to stumble on what to call my father-in-law.

But then again, so did I. We weren't truly in-laws any more. And I was only really realizing that, as my relationship with the man in front of me evolved.

"Stable," I answered.

"Good, right?"

"Yeah." Thank goodness. "They're probably gonna keep him for about a week, though. I'll tell you more about it later. I know you're busy."

Even though we had managed to have a minute conversation without being interrupted, it certainly wasn't intimate. There were people buzzing around everywhere. And I knew some of them were going to need Hawk's attention.

"Yeah." He couldn't deny it. "How about tomorrow?"

Admittedly, my heart sank a tad. "Yeah, I guess. But I thought I'd see you after the show."

He tilted his head slightly when looking at me. "Not going. I'm driving again tomorrow. You in?"

My enthusiastic, instant "Yes!" got an equally quick closed-mouth smile from Hawk. "Oh..." I amended, briefly remembering then what should have been my first concern. "Should I check with Fi—"

He cut me off. "Stop worrying about him. You can go!"

"Okay."

I regretted asking, not only because of Hawk's agitated state but because I already knew the answer. I hadn't asked the previous time if I could ride with Hawk. And it shouldn't have been any different. It didn't matter which of the onslaught of vehicles got me there as long as I was in one of them...and I got my work done.

That fact made me say my next thought, though. "I guess I should maybe go write the blog since I won't be able to do it in the car tomorrow."

"That's why I wanted to catch you now." He had brought his level back down to normal.

"Hawk, did Finn sign those posters?" Someone else was asking him another completely random question.

"Yeah, yeah," he answered. "I got him to take care of it."

"Good deal." And off they went in another direction.

"Sorry," Hawk apologized to me and said, "It's crazy."

"Yeah." Like I didn't already know. "You could have just texted me. You know my answer would have been the same." I brought my cheeks up in a subtle smile, hoping he realized how much I truly wanted to be in the car with him that next morning.

"But then, Maya, I wouldn't have gotten a goodnight kiss. You are going to let me kiss you, aren't you?"

If his magnetic, piercing eyes didn't totally do me in, it was the way he asked—the sweet yet needy desire in his voice. Our lips hadn't touched one another's since the interrupted volleyball game and, hell yeah, I wanted them to. I didn't think, and I didn't verbally respond. I just took the remaining step closer, locked on to his eyes, and let my lips do the rest. The constant hum of all the commotion around us seemed to disappear during the soft, therapeutic kiss. When I dipped my head onto his sturdy, strong chest for a second afterward, I felt it sag in a calming way.

"Hawk? Finn's ready."

On Shelly's voice, I pulled away. Time to go. Definitely not time to be in his arms.

But Hawk grasped my hand. "Tomorrow," he said.

***

Headlights beamed onto the vast field full of vehicles ready to set off once again to our next destination. Those and the barely beginning to rise sun were the only things that illuminated my way to Hawk, who was standing propped up against the vehicle awaiting my arrival. We were both casually dressed for a long day of car travel. He was in a navy-blue hoodie and light cargo shorts, and I wore a white tee and jean capris.

"Good morning." His quiet voice came out a little gargled, most likely from not having used it yet that day.

"Hmmm…" I managed. "Getting there."

He opened my passenger door and waited for me to sit before closing it. Someone had taught him really nice manners. Internally attributing it to his practically single mom of three boys, I watched him enter the car via the driver's side.

After starting the ignition, he took note of my belongings. "I thought you said you were going to get your stuff done last night." It was an obvious reference to my laptop.

"I did," I answered. "Even stayed up a little late, working ahead. This is just in case something comes up." And I carefully stretched to put it and my phone in the back. After latching my seatbelt, my next move was to push down the window a tad.

"You warm?" Hawk's voice was definitely perplexed. "It's so early."

I barely got "Just like the fresh air" out when a yawn escaped. "Sorry."

"If you didn't have that coffee," he noted the travel mug I had immediately snuggled into one of the cup holders between our seats. "I would tell you to go back to sleep."

"It's for you. Wanta make sure *you* are awake."

"I am."

"For sure?" I know I sounded like a nag, and I tried so hard not to be, but it really, truly couldn't be helped. "It's just such an early start, and I know—"

"I'm fine, Maya." He put his hand on the mug. "But I appreciate the gesture, and I'll take the coffee. Thanks." At least he sounded legitimately grateful.

After watching him take his first hearty sip, I asked, "Is it all right?"

"Yeah."

"You shouldn't be all that surprised," I said, upon the inflection of his one-word answer. "I pay attention, remember. Just a bit of cream, right?"

I did pay attention—a people watcher. Not only did I pretty much have Hawk's coffee order down to a science, I also noted he was mainly a beer and occasional wine drinker. But no matter how much he drank—and it seemed to be significant enough—he never appeared to get drunk or lose control. I was a little less aware of his food habits, though. But from what I could gather, he ate simple, wholesome kinds of food...not a lot of sweets. It showed in his build— his solid chest and those well-defined, muscular arms.

"Might need a little sugar," he teased, and leaned his coffee-flavored mouth onto my freshly toothpaste-minted one. "Perfect," he concluded after the kiss. "Go ahead. Go to sleep."

"You sure because I could—" God, Maya, I cursed myself for nagging.

"Yeah, Mai. I got the coffee *and* your window open." He shook his head, still in disbelief of my act. "And if you snore, it will keep me even more awake."

"I do not snore!" I exclaimed. I knew that for a fact— Jeff had told me I was such a silent sleeper, he had sometimes wondered if I was alive.

"I guess I'll find out." Hawk tipped the coffee mug back up to his lips and started the car down the road.

***

I really hadn't expected to fall asleep in the car, no matter how little slumber I had achieved the night before. I never thought I would feel comfortable enough—either physically with a window as my pillow, mentally being in a moving vehicle, or emotionally with someone I had not slept next to before. But exhaustion must have won…and won quickly. I didn't recall too many road signs or buildings before my eyes must have shut and put me to sleep.

When I did wake, the first thing I observed was the sun was definitely up. The next thing I noticed was Hawk's hand lying casually and protectively on my leg. "Hi," I said, turning just enough to straighten up but not dislodge the placement of his fingers.

"Hi," he echoed.

"Where we at?"

"We're officially in Nevada."

"Hmmm," I murmured, still trying to adjust to my awake status. My sleep hadn't been long, but it had been legit. "I missed the big border crossing."

"It was terribly exciting," he mocked. "A snore."

"I did not," I protested, knowing exactly what he was implying.

There was the tiniest bit of a belly laugh. "No. You did not." He rubbed my leg and then went to put his hand back on the steering wheel.

Missing his touch instantly, I took his hand back. He managed a side glance at me as I placed his hand on my leg. "It felt nice. And I do like when you protect me, Hawk."

His eyes were more direct as he said, "We need to talk about all of that." But he let his hand remain.

"It sounds like I'm going to be scolded." I tried to make light of the situation even though I knew when I said it and how I said it, it alluded to the source of tension that had been between us since Father's Day.

"Maya…" My name came out like a disappointment. "No." He self-corrected, took an anticipatory breath, and said, "I talked with Finn. That's what the whole gym thing was about."

"What?"

At my tense query, he once again removed his hand. He had talked with Finn, and by our conversation starter, there was no doubt it was about what went down between the two of them and me. God, who initiated that conversation? And what did it mean?

"I know you didn't want me to, but I did," he continued. "I had to because you backing away or whatever is going on is not gonna work. I can't…I need…" He swung his index finger back and forth between the two of us. "I need this to be okay."

The awkward way the last part of his statement came out, plus the fact he was the one who brought the subject up with Finn, made me realize how much he cared about me…about us. It made me proud and appreciative of the man just inches away from me. But then, it made me nervous. What was the end result of their conversation?

"What did you say?" My voice was quieter in anticipation of a verdict. "What did he say?"

There was a small exhale before he replied. "Like I told you, he didn't give that comment the other day a second thought. You and I don't have to pretend we're not together—at any time," he emphasized. "He was going to talk with you and make sure you knew that. He actually felt bad. But I offered to drive today so I could…so we could talk."

"Okay." I felt like some of the weight had been lifted off my shoulders.

"Okay?" Hawk dipped his head a little toward mine. "Okay I talked with him? Or…"

"Okay with, yeah, all of it," I clarified, while still processing the information and knowing it would make things so much easier and relaxed between the two of us. "I didn't like it either, you know. I was just worried. I was worried about your job, about—" I started to explain.

"I know. I'm telling you, you don't have to be. If you want me to have Finn talk with you…"

"No," I replied immediately.

It was embarrassing enough. I certainly didn't want to rehash it with Finn himself. I would much rather deny and forget those past few days or so even happened.

"I'm good," I reiterated. "It's…it's good."

Besides, I didn't need the country singer to tell me. Lara had, in a roundabout way, already done that the day before. When the subject of Hawk and me came up—thanks to Vanessa, of course—Lara had said how happy both she and Finn were that Hawk was happy. I didn't tell Hawk that, though. He was way too macho for such girly talk.

"Good." We drove in silence for a minute or so before Hawk, looking straight ahead to the windshield, said, "What are you going to do during the Louisville break?"

"Uh…" I scrambled my brain to the apparent change of subject. "I don't know. I probably should go back home. I haven't given it much thought, and I know I should. It's coming up so soon."

"A week. Well, six days." He was more specific.

"I know. I guess you're staying in Louisville. You're like 'I stay with the president, sir' on these deals, right?" I joked since Finn and family were staying with his mom in that town where he grew up.

"Ha!" He seemed to appreciate my comparison of his job to a Secret Service agent. "I never thought of it that way, but, yeah, I guess, pretty much. Mostly everybody is going into Nashville since it's only a couple hours away and home. I could, but…" He paused and finally did a side glance at me. "Finn offered to put the two of us up at the Galt House. It's a nice hotel by the river." His eyes were on mine as I quickly processed the offer and what it suggested. His voice was a little slower with the actual question. "Whatcha think? Would you want to stay with me? We'll have some free time. I could show you around town. We—"

"Yeah." I didn't need to hear any more. "Yes," I clarified, a little louder and enthusiastically.

Yes, it sounded like a fantastically marvelous idea. It was a chance for us to really be alone together. Besides the golf outing and a few car rides, we really had never been. And I knew what a hotel for a few days or so implied. And I was ready. I was so ready. I wanted to let him know that those past couple of days had nothing to do with the intensity of my feelings for him. And I knew by not only the hotel offer but the talk with Finn, his hadn't either. The fact that it was Finn-endorsed was the icing on top of the cake.

"Sounds perfect." I summarized my internal thoughts verbally and succinctly.

His voice and composure seemed to ease. "I was hoping you'd say that."

"Then why is your hand still on the steering wheel?" When I smiled, he smiled back and placed his right hand back on my left thigh. And I knew not only was everything back to normal, it was even better.

***

"Hey, I just wanted to let you know we'll catch up with y'all. I'm detouring through Vegas. Maya's never been, and I thought I'd show her." Hawk was on his phone, speaking with Toot.

As he listened, I watched out the windows. It had pretty much been deserted highway roads since we left California. I could not possibly imagine how the glamor and lights of Vegas were going to pop out of it. I had never had any desire to visit the notorious gambling city. But since we were right on top of it, I was anxious to at least witness what I had only seen on television and in the movies.

The whole summer had been like that, day after day. I had never ventured much in the United States before then. When I was little, we took trips to Hawaii, Disney World, and California, but I only had photo memories…not real ones. Other than that, I had pretty much stayed in the Maryland/DC area, besides when Jeff and I went on our honeymoon to Germany. Oh, and the Shriver family reunion in Connecticut.

I refocused on Hawk's voice. "No, not hitting the tables or slots," he said into the phone and then seemed to tag on,

"No, not the buffets, either." He laughed and listened to the head driver again. "Elvis…?" He looked over at me. "Whatever, Toot. I'm hanging up now. We're just driving through. We'll be right behind you. In fact, we might be ahead, how some of you drive."

And before I knew it, I was the stereotypical tourist. I had the window all the way down and was taking videos and pic after pic of all the ostentatious buildings on the Strip. It was just around eight in the morning. So there were enough cars on the road, but Hawk still managed to drive slow for my benefit. Mandalay Bay, Luxor, Excalibur, Tropicana, MGM Grand, Bellagio… I managed to take it all in with audible awe and wonder in my voice.

"I can't even imagine the insides of some of these places." My head was cranked up, looking at the towering buildings above.

There was an edge of amusement coming from the driver's side. "It's like Disney for adults. It's fun. But when we're here, we rarely get a chance to see a show or tour anything, though."

"ACMs?" I knew the award show was broadcast in Vegas annually.

"Yeah." He paused before continuing. "Yeah, you should come. You would like it."

"I'm sure I would." I was thinking the show was nearly a year away, and God knew where I would be then. Deciding to get myself out of my hasty funk, I decided to stay in the beautiful, amazing present. "Thanks, Hawk."

"For?"

"For riding me into Sin City." As soon as the words came out of my mouth, I realized the non-intended sexual innuendo. When he squinted his eyes at me in an obvious debate on how to react, I admitted my word blunder. "Go ahead, laugh. It was funny."

He nodded his head. "Any time, Maya." And on the repeat, he said it slower. "Any time."

I was thankful there was enough traffic to keep the

driver's eyes more on the road than on mine at the moment. The pull between us was undeniable, and I knew it was going to cultivate into something magical…soon. Without saying it, we both knew the invite of Louisville promised to be *that* time…when all of those feelings that had been building could find their proper home.

I wanted to take in the sights, sounds, and heat of Vegas while they were still fresh in my mind and write them down. So I reached into the back and pulled my laptop up front with me. It wasn't anything formal—just some notes. But once I got started, I found my fingers dancing on the keyboard.

As Hawk made our way out of the Strip and into a little less busy commercial area, it was like any other suburban town. There were grocery stores and big-box chains. I didn't bother to look up. I just continued to type.

But when Hawk not only stopped the car but put it in park, it forced me to take note of our location. It had only been about fifteen minutes from the Strip. Why were we stopping? We couldn't have needed gasoline yet.

I laughed loud and quick once I did a double take of the multitude of cars parked around us. The rows immediately in our line of vision were all…Volkswagen Bugs. We were in the parking lot of a VW dealer.

"Parked bug." Hawk chuckled, seemingly causing his eyes to light up and his eyebrows to rise.

"Quite a few," I noted with good humor.

"Mmmm-hmmm. Better get started."

I laughed through our first smooch then sank into the rhythm of his mouth. I liked the feel of his hands on my ribs. I liked how natural everything seemed between us. I liked—

"Maya…"

"Mmmm," I mumbled, thinking he was just calling out my name.

But he wasn't. "There's somebody coming." When my eyes flew open and our lips completely parted, Hawk questioned, in an obvious reference to the salesman walking toward us, "Do you want to car shop?"

"Uh…no." I laughed in a mortified way.

"You better think of something quick then." Hawk rolled down his window completely.

"Hi, there, folks. Can I interest you in something? Look at one of our Beetles? Maybe take a test drive?" Oh, Mr. VW Vegas definitely went to Classic Car Salesman School 101.

Ready for Hawk's challenge, I spoke from across the gear shift. "Sorry. No. Definitely don't need a car. We're from out of town and just looking for a place to get some ice." I almost laughed when Hawk swung his head toward me, obviously amused by my excuse.

The dejected salesperson answered nonetheless. "In just another block north"—he pointed that direction—"there's a convenience store and gas station. They sell it. There are big freezers right outside the doors."

"Ah, I knew we were close," I flat-out lied. "Thanks. This one just needs to trust the GPS." I mockingly rolled my eyes and shook my head at Hawk, giving the salesperson my old-married-couple routine.

"Sure you don't want to look at a new one? Built-in GPS in the—"

Oh! I had to give the guy some credit. He did want a sale.

"No. No thanks," I started, but was interrupted by the loudspeaker system requesting a salesperson to the main showroom.

After the salesman's quick retreat, Hawk rolled up the window and burst out laughing. "Ice?"

"I thought you might appreciate that."

"Didn't realize it was your go-to line."

"Only around you." I smiled.

"Good." Using his index finger, he touched my bottom lip and gently pulled it down. He then replaced his finger with his mouth, dropping his tongue inside and letting it sit there for a second before our tongues started playing with one another's again.

CHAPTER ELEVEN

The concert the next day was a biggie. It was at the famous Red Rocks location in Colorado. So it involved a little more with press, set-up…everything. We had arrived at the grounds past sunset and all basically went right to sleep. I knew Hawk had to be exhausted. Besides a few rest and food stops, he had basically driven the whole day and then had to be up first thing in the morning to go with Finn to do radio appearances.

I had a little more of a casual day at Red Rocks, working on updating all of Finn's social media accounts and bouncing ideas off Reese about online giveaways. And later, I would watch the kids because Lara wanted to be at the show. I knew there would probably only be a slim window of opportunity to see Hawk before the post-show, and I wanted to take advantage of it. I felt an even stronger bond since our car ride, and the pull to be near him and see him was great.

Before going to the Murphy trailer to babysit, I made my way over to where I knew Hawk would most likely be—in the midst of all the preshow hoopla. Sure enough, I found him bent over a table writing something down. He did not see me approach. I knew not only because his back was turned but by the way he reacted when I tapped him on the shoulder.

"Why can't you just leave me alone for a damn second?"

Startled by his abruptness, I quickly agreed. "Okay. I'll just—"

He swirled around just as quickly. "Oh, shit, Maya, I didn't know it was you."

"Mmmm."

"What? What's up?" His voice was still tense, but his eyes looked softer. He was busy. He was stressed. He didn't need a visit from me.

"Nothing." I stated the truth. "I'll see you later."

"Maya…" His voice stretched out just like his hand did toward my arm.

"No. It's okay." I meant it and went to squeeze his hand quick, but his phone went off. "I have to be with the kids, anyway. Later," I reiterated, and I think I heard him swear as I walked off.

***

I put our interaction behind me and spent a nice evening with Chance and Arinn. After the show and Lara's return, I went back to my trailer. I knew I had a few minutes before everyone gathered for post-show, and I wanted to freshen up.

Hair and teeth brushed, I was a few steps out of the trailer when Hawk appeared. "Wanted to make sure you were coming tonight," he said.

"Hey." I smiled at him. "Yeah. I was just heading over." I started walking, assuming he would join me.

But instead, he halted my action and took both of my hands in his. "You know earlier wasn't about you, right?" His question was in obvious reference to his previous gruff disposition.

"Yeah, I know." I did, but it was nice that he was concerned and felt a need to explain.

"There was just so much shit going on. I sometimes get—"

"Oh, I know." I opened my eyelids a bit in exaggeration.

"Oh, you do?" He seemed almost amused, as if I truly had never seen him stressed before.

"Yeah." I thought for a second and then went for it. "Like when you came to pick me up at the airport."

"Hmmm, yeah." He paused himself. "But that *was* a little about you."

"What?" I dropped my hands when he didn't answer. "Wait? Are you being serious?"

"Yeah," he admitted.

"What did *I* do?"

"You were there." He didn't say it like it was a bad thing. It was more like a remembrance.

"More, please," I prompted as my curiosity grew.

"I didn't know what to expect. It was a little weird seeing you again. *And* things were crazy." He tacked on the last part as if to justify his feelings about being reunited with me in the beginning of May.

"Weird, yep, just what I wanted to hear. You contact Hallmark yet?"

"Maya!" Exasperated, but with lightheartedness, he lightly pushed me.

"I got it." I let him off the hook, relishing the fact that we had been on the same page since the tour had started.

"What did you want earlier?" He got back on subject.

"Nothing. Really," I answered. "I was just thinking of you and had a minute and thought I would say thanks for offering to drive yesterday. It was so nice. I'm so glad we had that."

"Oh, geez, now I feel doubly bad."

"You should!" I teased.

"Can I make it up to you?" His tired-looking eyes perked a little at the suggestive question.

"I bet you could." I played right along.

It wasn't even a second before he had his hands wrapped

around my head and was kissing me like a thankful dog let in from the rain. Our lip-lock was, in fact, so amorous, it caused me to take a step back so we were braced against the trailer's side. With the intensity only growing, Hawk took my hands in his and brought them together above my head. It made his firm, strong body lean even more into mine. Oh…uh…sheesh, we may as well have been doing it right there.

"Hawk…." I finally managed to get out.

"Yeah…" His slightly labored breath mimicked mine. And then he repeated, a little more subdued, "Yeah."

He brought our arms down but kept them entwined as he took a mini-step back. Pursing his lips to breathe out, his intense eyes did not blink as they fixated on mine. He then kissed me a couple more times but quickly, as if he knew if he would linger, he wouldn't be able to stop.

Feeling so relaxed and desired, I smiled the softest of serene smiles and squeezed his hands. Internally, I kept thinking Louisville…Louisville. Instead, I said out loud, "I think I need a drink."

"Mine is going to be a double for sure," he agreed, and together we made our way toward the rest of the crew.

***

After a few more of those nights of almost-painful goodnight kisses, we were in Louisville. I was finally, truly going to be alone with Hawk. And while we had definitely been leading up to it, and I had been eager to arrive, when we first walked in to the massive hotel room that early evening, a few butterflies invaded my previously calm nerves.

I followed Hawk into the living area of the suite, complete with wall-length armoire, fridge, coffee table, and sofa. Next, we entered the dressing area with adjoining bathroom. And then, finally, was the bedroom. With the exception of Finn and Lara's suite in the Keys, it was bigger than any hotel room I ever remembered being in.

As Hawk set our bags down in the corner of the bedroom, I exclaimed, "Geez, is this a penthouse? I mean, besides the size, how many floors up are we?"

"Good thing for elevators." On my dismissive 'hmmm,' he continued. "Finn doesn't know how to do things halfway…at least when it comes to friends and family." There was a bit of awkward silence between us then as we stood next to those two queen beds. "Look, Maya, no pressure. There are two beds or even the whole living room. I don't want you to feel—"

I was going to reassure him that none of that was necessary, when his phone announced a text. "What?" I asked after he quickly looked at the electronic device.

"Damn it."

"What?" I asked again.

"Something with the trucks. I'll be right back. Sorry." He fit the phone back in his pocket. "It'll take me longer to get back and forth through the hotel and out to where the trucks are than to actually solve it."

"It's fine," I reassured him. "Go do what you need to."

"All right." He looked at me a sec, knowing our serious conversation had just taken a reprieve. But instead of saying anything more, he quickly pecked me on the lips, swiped one of the room keys from the top of his bag, and left.

I was actually a little glad for whatever was wrong with the trucks and that Hawk was the multi-task man to fix it. Because now that I was in the hotel room in Louisville, I needed to, like other wonderful things, soak it in and breathe. I was determined to get the little jitters out of my mind and focus on how much I wanted the night, week, and more.

I distracted myself by putting my clothes in one of the drawers and checking my phone. And then I went for the shower. God, it was just what I needed. It was so much more spacious than those cubbies on the road, and the hotel's honey-scented shampoo was luxuriously heavenly.

The grime of traveling truly felt removed.

Afterward, I put on the fresh undergarments I had brought into the bathroom. It was my nicest black lace bra and panty set. I had planned on sliding into the jeans, tank, and wrap I had also brought in, but now, much more relaxed, I felt sexy. I knew in that moment, I didn't want to wait until later that evening to determine sleeping arrangements. In fact, I wanted to be in a bed and not sleep. I wanted him. And I wanted him to know I wanted him.

I applied a sparkly pink lip stain and fresh mascara and decided on nothing more, makeup-wise. After all, Hawk had seen me for months with minimal makeup on. Who was I trying to fool? Scrunching my fingers through my hair to bring out the natural waves, I started the hairdryer to finish my look.

When I turned the blower off, I could hear the television in the bedroom. Knowing I hadn't turned it on, I realized Hawk had to be back. Just a quick, small flutter hit my body, but I decided it was more out of anticipation. I left the jeans and tank folded on the towel rack and tied the black wrap around my torso. It was the best I could do without just walking out in my underwear. And I think it pretty much did the trick. It hung down to mid-thigh and exposed just enough of my bra to tease. I knew he wouldn't be expecting it, but I was pretty sure he wouldn't be disappointed.

Then, before I opened the door, I saw it. And I had a decision to make. The skinny gold band, engraved with a J, heart symbol, and M, glistened on the shelf where I had put it pre-shower. It was automatic that I would put it on. While it no longer resided on my left hand, it had a permanent space on the opposite ring finger. But it didn't feel right. It didn't feel right putting the ring on, knowing what I was planning—hoping—I would be doing very shortly. I looked at the mirror. I looked at the ring. I closed my eyes. I thought of Jeff. I thought of Hawk. And I put the ring securely in my makeup bag and opened the bathroom door.

I saw him immediately via the lengthy mirror in the

dressing area. His back was toward me as he was half sitting, half lying on the first bed, watching some sort of news program. When I entered the room and got into his peripheral vision, he popped off the bed and fumbled for the remote, eventually getting the television off.

I stood still, waiting for him to approach me, which he did. There was a slight exhale from his mouth as he scanned my attire. "You look…God…amazing."

My top teeth, which had been digging deep into my bottom lip since exiting the bathroom, released their grip as I smiled. Any doubts I may have had were erased by his words…and the adoring way he looked at me. He took the final step and kissed me sweetly and then with a little more hunger.

Stopping and holding me just at arm's length, he asked, "Now? Yeah?" When I let my eyes blink positively on his, he asked, "Do I need to get anything?"

I shook my head without breaking my gaze. "Not because of me. I'm fine." I realized how much of the dating crap I had forgotten about, having been married for so many years.

"I'm good," he confirmed.

"And you know the thing with…I can't get pregnant." I always hated the words infertile, infertility—they seemed so diseased and incompetent.

He brought me back to him and, while running his hands through my hair, I could feel his tongue explore deeper and greedier into my mouth. I know I moaned in pleasure as I let my mouth dance with his. He broke for a second and then swept the covers and sheet down on the bed he had just been sitting on. And then he scooped me up into those damn, strong arms and gently laid me right in the center of the mattress. I watched as he stood and discarded his red T-shirt. Of course, I had seen him shirtless before. But this was intoxicating. His broad chest led down to where he was removing his buckle from his jeans, showing off his defined V. It was like my private strip show, and I was just taking pleasure in watching. He silently removed his jeans, letting them puddle on the floor, before sitting directly next to my outstretched legs and untying my wrap. When I helped him shrug it off my shoulders, he let out another audible, appreciative breath.

And then we got lost in one another. His mouth was all over my torso. My hands wove in the short strands of his hair and then roamed down his back. My head tilted back. My eyes closed. And when he entered me, he settled for a moment, allowing both of us to feel that new, spectacular connection we both knew had been building since almost the first time we met. And with the strength and silence I knew as Hawk, he made love with me in the most clenching, squirming, feeling-every-wonderful-molecule kind of way.

***

Afterward, I lay in his encompassing arms. We were both silent, allowing our breaths to regulate. I ran my index finger in a slow, small pattern through the little bit of light hair on his chest and then rested my lips there for an extended moment.

"That was some meet-and-greet." He touched the side of my face.

I laughed lightly at his comparison of a concert event with how I met him upon returning from the trucks. "And we still have another bed," I teased, feeling lighter than I had in such a while.

"Oh, my God, woman." His chest bounced my head in laughter. We lay like that for another moment before Hawk took his hand to tilt my chin and, consequently, my eyes toward him. "Mai?" By just the way he said my name, I knew he was turning a little more serious. "I have wanted you...us...for so long."

I propped myself onto my elbow. "It was better than I even imagined."

"You were imagining it?" He seemed intrigued.

"Oh, yeah," I admitted, glad to still have such an easygoing give-and-take with him. "And I am a writer. I have quite an imagination."

He did a light chuckle. "Welcome to Louisville." He pecked me on my lips.

"My new favorite town."

He kissed me again, and I turned to snuggle my back against his front. We lay there for a bit...me feeling his breathing in my hair and his one finger ever so slightly moving back and forth on my hip. Was it right that it felt so right?

"Look at that gorgeous view." I spoke of the spectacular, peachy sunset above the still water.

"I am." His simple words made me turn. His eyes were only on me.

CHAPTER TWELVE

"Oh, look who decided to show up." Sitting at the hotel bar, Yogi, one of the few crew guys staying in Louisville, nodded in Hawk's and my direction.

Hawk had agreed to meet up with him and fellow crew member Dominic, prior to his reentering our hotel room and seeing me in just my undies. He offered to cancel, but I didn't want to. I was happy and energized and wanting to see the town, and Hawk was more than thrilled to be my personal tour guide.

Dominic, on the stool next to Yogi, chimed in with, "Did you two get tied up? Or...were you just on a missionary?" He smacked Yogi on the arm at his own sexual reference.

Hawk pulled out the tall bar chair for me. "You sat here this whole time and that was the best you could come up with?" He shook his head mockingly, as I sat down next to our two fellow roadies.

Probably fresh out of college, the dark-haired bartender placed two napkins in front of us as Hawk sat next to me. It made me look closer at the bar itself. Live fish were swimming inside it.

"Maya, what do you want?" Hawk asked.

Having been momentarily distracted by the fish, I refocused by first turning to the two smartass crew members and then to the bartender before saying, "A screaming orgasm on the rocks."

As Dominic and Yogi practically spit out their drafts and Hawk's eyes appeared to widen, the bartender smiled. "Really? Because I know how to make them."

"Uh-huh." I didn't exactly know what I was ordering, but it sure did shut the two hecklers up. "I know someone else who might, too," I whispered and scrunched my nose at Hawk.

Looking quite amused by my sass and relaxed state, Hawk shook his head and ordered a Kentucky Bourbon Barrel Ale. "Put it on the room." He slid the key toward the bartender.

"I'll get it." I furrowed my brows at Hawk as the bartender walked off.

"Tip the guy. The rest is taken care of."

Before I could argue, Yogi piped up. "So how do you like Louisville so far, Maya?"

"I haven't seen much. And before you start with all the other innuendos, I was married to a cop, boys. There's nothing like the city's finest doing some beer talking. I could keep it up all night."

"That's what *he* said," Hawk tipped his head with a smile.

"Don't you get in on it, too!" I warned, but laughed just the same.

He placed his hand on top of mine as Dominic offered, "Sorry, Maya. We're just joshing you…really more Hawk, here. We luv ya."

Hawk rested his foot on the bottom of my chair just as the bartender placed our drinks in front of us. I twirled the little black straw around in the glass and then took a sip. Hawk watched from the top of the bottle raised to his mouth. But I couldn't hide it.

"Pretty strong?" he asked.

"Yeah," I admitted.

He tilted his head toward the drink in my hand, and I slid it toward him, knowing he wanted a taste himself. "It's good," he offered after a decent gulp and brought our mutually tasting mouths together in a kiss.

The four of us talked a little shop, discussed our plans for break, and then ventured out to, within walking distance, Fourth Street Live. There wasn't a concert or special event going on that night, but you wouldn't have been able to tell. The area was abuzz with people meandering in the middle of the closed-off street. I felt energized just being there. Having had a late lunch, none of us felt like eating at one of the restaurants. However, Dominic and Yogi wanted to go into the bar with the dueling pianos and drink, sing, and be merry. I felt like that was what we did every night on the road and decided to pass. I reassured Hawk he could go, but I knew it wasn't really his scene, either. So the two of us parted ways with the single roadies and started making our way back toward the hotel.

We had one stop on the way, however. And what a delicious one it was. The Fudgery had every scrumptious, sinful kind of sweet you could imagine, from caramel apples to chocolate-covered pretzels. I just wanted its namesake, though. Hawk and I bought three different fudges to split— rocky road, chocolate nut, and creamy vanilla. We were nibbling on them as we reentered the Galt House and Hawk's phone started to ring.

Glancing at the ID, he said, "Sorry. It's Finn. I should take it."

Just about to enter the hotel's conservatory, I replied, "Go ahead. I need to check my stuff, too."

"What's up?" Hawk answered the phone and then, after a pause, said, "Thanks." He listened to Finn as I pulled out my phone. "Great." There was another pause on Hawk's end before, "Yeah." And then another pause and another, "Yeah." Such guy talk. "No. It's okay. I wouldn't have answered it, chief, if it wasn't." Hawk looked at me as we both came to a natural stop in the conservatory. When I pointed toward the little gathering of empty seats, indicating I was going to rest there, he nodded back. He didn't join me but instead walked back and forth in the area as if he were my private guard. The protective streak was so naturally embedded in him.

I crawled onto the ledge area that was not exactly a seat but gave me a fantastic view of the town since the conservatory was also a glass skywalk. I could hear Hawk talking with Finn, but I drowned out their conversation and instead got on to social media to post my latest location— Louisville. I did not, however, post the hotel's name, in fear that somehow Finn's fans would figure out my personal page and, God knows, do what.

What I did type in however was, *Fudgery = the way to a woman's heart.*

Placing his phone back in his pocket, Hawk leaned over and looked at my screen. "I thought the screaming orgasm was."

"I can add that." I smirked.

"I would say 'dare ya,' but you just might." He sat down next to me.

"What did Finn want? Everything is okay with you two, right?"

"I told you it is. Do you think he would have put us up here, if it wasn't?"

"No. I know." I did know. There was just that slightest bit of second-guessing. It was the part of me waiting for the rug to be pulled out from underneath me…again.

"Maya, Father's Day just wasn't a good day for him. And me? I was frustrated on so…" He paused and looked at me in a knowing way. "So many levels. Not so much anymore." When he touched my nose, I blushed at his sexual innuendo. "So, to answer your question, the phone call was about…Clooney's in town producing or directing a movie with Jennifer Lawrence. And because Clooney, Jennifer, and Finn are Kentuckians—is that the word?—they want to do the whole dinner thing. You know…be seen around town, promote themselves, the state, good freewill, all the shit. And also talk about getting Finn to do some songs for the soundtrack. It came up very suddenly."

"Hmmm. Cool."

It was way cool. While not usually star-struck, that news gave me some major food for thought. I didn't let it show, though.

"So I need to set up some things on our end—make sure there's proper security, service, you name it."

"When are they meeting?"

"Friday. Got a couple days." He put his phone solidly back in his pocket. "You ready to head up?"

"Yeah. Sure." I placed my phone back in my purse and stood.

Hawk immediately took my hand in his. I loved that. Jeff had held my hand but only when he felt like there was a reason to—either romantically or in a situation where he felt there should be cautionary measures. Hawk did it automatically...all the time.

"Start thinking of places you want to see tomorrow," he said as we made our way to the elevator, whose doors opened just as we approached.

It was on the very next floor when a huge crowd of people swarmed into the rising glass box with us. There was a convention taking place in the hotel and, by the noise and badges plastered on every shirt, it was obvious some sort of ceremony or dinner connected with it had just let out. Because we were the first ones on the lift, Hawk and I found ourselves being pushed to the very back of the elevator. I looked to the closing doors as more and more people actually wanted to enter.

"What's the capacity on this?" I questioned, knowing we were way too far back to read the sign near the doors, and it was way too loud for probably even Hawk, standing next to me, to hear. "No. No. That's enough. It's not like there isn't another elevator. Geez, wait an f-ing minute for the next one."

I knew he heard me that time because he looked at me the best he could, considering we were smashed like sardines next to one another, and said, "Although there's something to be said about togetherness."

The sound that came from my mouth was nowhere near a complete word. It was a mix of a mumble and a cry. And it only partially reflected the terror I was experiencing.

"Mai? What's wrong?" He noticed right away.

"I...I..." Every word included a big breath until I managed to spill out five all at one time. "I'm a little bit claustrophobic."

It was something I didn't advertise and certainly didn't anticipate letting Hawk know about, especially on our first night together. But, God, right then, my symptoms were extreme. I was getting in major panic mode. I needed help. As much as I didn't want to admit it, I needed him to help me.

"I'd say more than a little," he acknowledged, and I could see the concern hit his eyes. "Maya? What do you want to do? Do you want me to get them to stop the elevator, and we get off for a while?" Of course, our room was nearly at the top of the twenty-five stories, and we had started at single digits. "Maya?" he asked again when I didn't immediately answer.

"It...will...take...just as...long...to do that," I managed.

"Here." He turned me so I could see out the back of the all glass elevator. He managed to squeeze behind me, surely shifting people around with his towering frame, but neither of us cared. Wrapping his arms around me from behind, he asked, "Does that help?"

"Yeah. Yeah," I repeated. I wasn't sure what was exactly helping—being able to see out or feeling the security of his arms—but it did a little. "Keep me distracted somehow."

His mouth against my ear, he whispered, "If we weren't in a glass elevator or with all these people, I would definitely know how I could do that." His hand danced a little right below my breasts, managing to get a little belly laugh out of me. "I don't want to see any of the Abe Lincoln stuff tomorrow. You good with not doing that?" He continued talking, which was really the distraction. And he was smart asking me a question because it forced me to concentrate on what he was saying, not on…on—

"Sure." I spit out.

"Churchill Downs? Historic district? We could go into Indiana."

"Uh-huh." I could feel his head swing around as the car stopped and only a couple people, of course, got off.

While I was trying to think what Indiana had to do with anything, Hawk spoke as the elevator started to lift again. "Maya, geez. How come you're like this? You're all right on the buses, right?"

Um…uh…well… Again, it wasn't something I liked to draw attention to.

"The buses, Mai?" he prompted again when I didn't verbalize. "They're not exactly roomy."

"Yeah," I said. "Yeah. Don't really enjoy them so much," I admitted.

With the "bing" of the elevator, Hawk firmly took my hand and started getting us through the group smashed in the glass coffin with us. We were finally on our floor. Two people got off with us but headed in the other direction. I took a couple deep breaths as I saw the elevator doors close and resume their tower of terror upward.

Feeling like I was gaining some of my composure back, I tried to continue the line of conversation more rationally. "I tore the drape thing off my bunk right away." I spoke of the bus's individual sleeping compartments. "And"—I touched his hand as we started walking down the hall toward our room—"I love when you're driving one of the cars."

"Ouch." He turned to me mid-stride. "Well, that left a mark! I thought you just wanted to be with me."

"I do." I tried a smile, but I was still really trying to

concentrate on regulating my breathing again. It felt better that we weren't in the elevator, but even the long, narrow hallway was a little stifling. "It's definitely a win-win." I spoke of Hawk's driving, while looping my arm around his back.

"Want to stop a sec?" he asked, most likely feeling the vigor of how I clung to his side.

"No. I'm good." I nearly got the complete thought out before he literally swept me off my feet. I was suddenly tossed and cradled into his arms as he continued to walk down the hall. "Geez, put me down. I'm okay."

"I don't mind." His eyes were so close to mine as he continued. "You're usually so self-assured and strong. Besides, you told me you like me protecting you. And I like doing it…apparently, especially in hotels."

With a soft smile, I managed to laugh at myself. "Silly how a packed, enclosed box will do me in every time."

"Do you know why?"

"Put me down, and I'll tell you." After a couple steps, he granted my request, and I repaid him with the answer to his question. "The car accident my dad was killed in?"

"Yeah?"

"I was the only other passenger. It was later at night. And from what they pieced together, he fell asleep driving. We went off the road and down a deserted embankment area. Because it was at night, no one saw the accident. When they found us at daybreak, my dad was dead. The front was totally smashed in. They said he died instantly. And I was trapped. The front passenger seat was pretty close to me. I was asleep, but it was obvious I had been crying."

When he looked at me, I could see the mix of sympathy and concern. "I read a little about it online after, well, after you told me who your dad was."

"Yeah. I figured you might. Anyway,"—I continued as we neared the room and he got the key out of his pocket— "that's what my grandma always blamed my claustrophobia on."

"Well, yeah, it definitely makes sense. It also explains how conscientious you are about making sure I'm awake enough to drive."

"Yeah," I lamented as he inserted the key. "Sorry. I can be a little pesty about that."

His eyes squinted at the same time his nose scrunched. "You look like him…your dad."

"Yeah?" I relaxed into a bit of a grin.

"Definitely your smile." He touched the upper, right corner of my lip. "The way it goes up just a little bit there."

"Yeah. But my eyes are closer to my mom's, and I definitely have her widow's peak." When he tilted his head in question, I lifted my bangs to reveal the slight V shape dip of my hairline in the middle of my forehead. I had always hated it and the name and, therefore, always wore bangs. After I explained it and the irony for both me and my mother, I quickly changed the subject. "Thanks for talking me off the ledge."

"You sure you're okay? This room might be a little small," he jested at the ginormous size of the suite, while double-checking to make sure the door was shut behind us. "Or do you still need me to distract you?" There was a little of that seductive tone back in his voice.

"Yeah, I might need a little help yet," I bounced back, reaching for his belt.

"You know, the very first words you said to me were 'Take off your belt.'"

Ha! That probably was true. I laughed and then tried to think of his words to me. Not knowing exactly, I countered with, "The first thing *you* did was throw me into your hotel room."

"It was meant to be." And he gave me a full-fledged grin.

Hawk made love to me slowly and gently, as if he truly was calming me from my panicked state. And his kisses on my body and in my hair afterward were as soothing as a warm bubble bath on a yearlong vacation. In fact, so much so, they put me right to sleep.

***

When I woke, it was the middle of the night, and Hawk was not in bed with me. Adjusting my eyes, I realized he was not even in the bedroom. A little concerned, I tossed on the shirt I had previously been wearing and wandered out to the lamp-lit living room area.

Stretched out on his side, Hawk was sound asleep on the sofa. His laptop, on the nearby coffee table, stood propped open, as if waiting for his fingers to drum on the keyboard. He looked comfortable enough. But even in sleep, he seemed serious.

I wondered if I should wake him. Would he want me to? Or was it the opposite? After all, why had he gone out to the sofa in the first place? Did he not want to sleep next to me? Or was it something else? I touched his laptop, but it had gone to sleep and was no use in solving the late-night sofa mystery.

Shaking my head at trying to figure out another one of the newly dating roadmaps, I settled on getting the extra blanket from the bed and resting it on top of him. It was the non-mom mom part of me. When he shifted a little into the blanket and became more relaxed, I turned off the light and ventured back into the bedroom. It had been an exhausting, emotional day, and my mind, completely wide awake, was thinking of it all.

CHAPTER THIRTEEN

His text of, *Yes please. C U in a few.* didn't give me a lot to go on while waiting for him in the conservatory that next morning. Leaving him sleep, I had placed a note next to his laptop telling him where I would be and to let me know if he wanted some coffee. Now with two hot beverages and a granola bar on the mini-table beside me, I had no idea what that day—the morning after—would bring.

For some weird, backward reason, I pretended not to see him until he was sitting down in the matching chair on the other side of the table. But I had. I had seen, and maybe even felt, his presence from the moment he first entered the area. I wanted to see him, but, yet, was anxious.

"Needed some of that alone time?" he questioned, looking across the table at me.

Meeting his eyes, I managed a closed smile, while pushing his coffee in his direction. "No. No ice bucket runs."

Realizing I was doing it, I purposefully tried to stop my thumb from playing with the non-existent piece of jewelry on my right ring finger. Not only was I concerned about Hawk's choice of sleeping venues, but thoughts of Jeff had invaded my mind that morning. It wasn't exactly guilt. It wasn't exactly remembrance. But there were definitely parts of those mixed in with the knowledge that I had let myself feel again, in every way.

"I thought maybe *you* might have."

"What?" Hawk brought the cup back down from his lips. "You talking about last night?" When I didn't respond, he gave a quick narrowing of his hazel eyes and continued. "I went in the other room to work on some stuff for Friday so we didn't have to deal with it today. You were sleeping so peacefully, I didn't want to disturb you." On his explanation and slight pause, I started to relax. "Mai, I didn't know I fell asleep. If I had woken up, I would have come back to bed."

"Oh. Okay." Even though I hadn't outwardly admitted to my insecurities, I'm pretty sure he had guessed. "I'm glad you slept," I offered instead.

His soft smile told me he not only knew we were on better footing but he understood the meaning behind my last comment. "I did. Thanks for the blanket," he said, and then questioned the more serious of my phobias. "How was the elevator this morning?"

"Empty, thank goodness." I breathed in a coordinating, cleansing breath.

"Good." He was finally able to take a second sip of coffee before leaning across the small table and peering at my tablet. "What are you doing?" he inquired.

"Same as you." I tilted the screen a little more so he could see the information I had collected on the film. "Looking for stuff I can send to Finn to help on Friday."

"Great. Don't overwhelm him, though. Just bullet some stuff."

"Already done, hotshot." I sent the info to Finn and looked at the casually dressed, gorgeous man next to me. "Don't act so surprised," I teased. "I know what I'm doing. I forwarded it to you, too, so you can schmooze when you're dealing with them." On my last word, I heard his phone make a sound, announcing that my electronic message had come through.

"Schmooze,"—he emphasized after resting his cup back on the table—"is not in my word bank. Unless it's because a certain pretty claustrophobe is upset with me for sleeping on the sofa."

"If she starts flirting with her tour guide today, I bet she's probably not too upset." Placing the tablet on the table, I leaned over to said tour guide and pecked his lips.

Hawk took my hand in his and brought it up to his lips. I was pretty sure he'd noticed the absence of my ring the night before but had not brought it up. But now, the next day, I was positive he knew.

"Maya…"

"Can we not talk about it?" My request came out in a choppy almost-whisper, as I shifted in my chair.

He hesitated but then concluded with his go-to line. "You got it."

Our phones made us break our eye lock with one another and instead look at our screens. We both had a text coming in at the same time. No wonder—it was a joint message from our host and boss.

We both read Finn's text. *Thx for the info. I'll look it over. Hope U enjoyed your special day yesterday.*

"Oh, geez." I rolled my eyes. "What a fraternity I walked into." Before Hawk could say anything, I started typing back my reply to my employer. *No prob. My pleasure.*

I forgot it was a group text until I heard Hawk's phone acknowledge my reply seconds after I sent it. He looked at his screen, smirked, and started typing. When I tried to look, he purposefully sheltered it from my view. After a few more finger hits, he looked up and smiled…and then I heard the new message sound on my phone.

Oh, it was mine, too ☺ was Hawk's text to both Finn and me.

"Oh, my God!" I screeched at his obvious sexual reference.

"Well, it was." His eyebrows lifted in a jovial way.

"Wasn't what I meant, and you know it."

"Wasn't what Finn meant either…about the special day."

"What are you talking about?" I countered. "I already dealt with Tweedledum and Dumber at the bar last night." I glanced at the nearby conservatory bar. "Everybody knows. It's kind of—"

"Only Finn knows it was my birthday," Hawk interrupted.

"What?" I beseeched. I heard him, but I had to connect the dots. "Yesterday?"

"Yeah," he answered as casual as ever.

"Hawk!" I side-swiped him with my arm. "Why didn't you tell me?"

"I don't tell anybody. Finn knows because of the personnel records. I'm not a big celebration guy."

"Oh…my…God." I shook my head.

"What?" He nonchalantly took another sip of coffee. "What difference does it make?"

"I don't know. I could have done something. We could have—"

"We did, Maya." He reached over and laid his hand on top of mine, just like he had so many times at the post-concert gatherings. "That was the best birthday I've ever had." And even though I knew there was an obvious, silent reference to the first time we made love, I knew he was being very honest, too. "Are you ready to go?" He took another swig from the cup and stood up.

"Hawk!" I wasn't over the birthday reveal yet. I legitimately wanted to recognize it somehow.

"Come on." He held out his hand for me. "There's some cafes just down the road. Let's go get breakfast. I seemed to have worked up an appetite yesterday." His eyebrows shifted again as I honored his request by standing. When I handed him the second half of the granola bar I hadn't eaten, he took a bite and said, "Thanks."

"Thirty-eight, right?" I sought confirmation of his new age.

"Yep."

"I can't believe you didn't tell me." I gathered my things in my purse.

"I just did."

"Yeah, but—"

He interrupted. "When's your birthday?"

"I'm hungry, too," was my non-answer.

Grabbing my arm, he gently stopped me from walking off. "Maya?" he questioned with a look on his face that said he knew my birth date was going to be as equally as intriguing as his. "Tell me." With the way his eyes narrowed at mine and the way his sexy voice demanded a response, I knew I had to tell him.

"Cinco de Mayo." I shook my head, having been used to hearing the funny comments throughout my life. "I know— May, Mayo, Maya. My parents were way too cutesy."

"The fifth of May." He accurately converted from Spanish to English. But he wasn't making fun of my birthday in connection with my name. He was putting together when it actually was. "That…" he started. "That was…it was our first stop." He spoke of the summer's first concert date. "You were with us."

"Uh-huh. My official first day of work. Like I was going to say something then." So true. Not giving him a chance to agree or argue, I leaned in to his side and said in humor, "Hey, I just realized I got to see you in your birthday suit on your birthday."

I felt his body bounce from his chuckle before he said, "You know, I believe it's my birthday week…"

I rubbed his hip where my hand had been resting and then stopped mid-stride as another text came in, apparently just to my phone. "Sorry. Let me see."

I pulled the phone out to read Finn's text. *Hope U R joining us on Fri.* When I showed it to Hawk, he shrugged as if he agreed, but it was up to me.

I can, I texted back. *Prob. B important to get on social media. U want me to blog, too?*

If U R willing. But I was asking U as our T.M.I. boy's plus 1. Good either way.

Embarrassed all over again by the T.M.I. comment, I started playfully hitting Hawk, who had read the message from behind my shoulder. On his laugh, I typed back, *Thx. I'll B there. Let me know if U need anything else. Tell Chance & Arinn I said Hi.*

"I told you he is okay with us." Hawk bumped his hip with mine before leading us to the adventure of the new day.

***

It was weird being with him practically twenty-four hours a day. Weird…but definitely not in a bad way. I had initially worried it would be. But we were pretty simpatico. We got to know each other outside of having the country music world as an immediate backdrop. We weren't pseudo co-workers but simply a carefree couple learning the minute, silly things about each other. After all, we had gotten the heavy stuff out early in our relationship.

Those two sides of us merged on the night we met Finn, Lara, and an exclusive few from the film. I wasn't as nervous as I thought I would be, and I think a good part of that was those few, carefree days prior with Hawk. Although we came as a couple, we were introduced in our career roles and maintained professionalism throughout. But that didn't mean my heart didn't pitter-patter, sitting so close to Hawk in his all-black shirt, blazer, and slacks ensemble—such a striking, sexy contrast to his usual summer attire. And I'm pretty sure he felt the same way about my selection of clothing, since he would casually touch the spaghetti strap of my black dress when we stood near one another and got even more adventurous under the table where the lacy part of the dress ended at my knee. It was only the third of July, but the fireworks started shortly afterward in the hotel suite.

I stayed out of Hawk's, and really everyone's, way for the concert at the end of the week. It was time to get back to business, and I knew Hawk took his job very seriously. And with everyone returning and it being Finn's hometown, there was a different buzz occurring that day and into the night. I didn't go to the show, though. The kids were staying at Finn's mom's place, so I didn't need to watch them. I just wanted to stay in comfy sweats and follow up on some of the social media aspects of Finn's career and check in with my father-in-law, who had been released from the hospital.

I left the living room lamp on as a nightlight for when Hawk would eventually make his way back to the hotel suite after the concert. It wouldn't take him long because the venue—the Yum Center—was actually connected to our hotel. It was just a skybridge and parking lot away. But, regardless, I knew I would be asleep.

I wasn't necessarily a sound sleeper, though. It was years of worrying about Jeff's late nights on the force. So even though I'm sure he was trying to be quiet, I did hear Hawk enter the room later that night.

"Maya?" he whispered as I felt the weight of his body sit on the bed.

"Hmmm?" I answered.

"I didn't want to wake you but, sweetie, I smell like a brewery. So I wanted to let you know I'll just sleep on the oth—"

"Oh, no. You'll sleep right here," I corrected, and rolled onto my back to see him.

"Are you sure?" he asked, but he elongated his body to mimic mine.

"I've smelled be—that's…" I changed my words, knowing it wasn't beer.

"Champagne. Wearing it more than drinking it. Finn signed on for the film. There was just a little thing backstage."

"Huh," I said, but it came out simultaneously with a yawn. "Good for him."

"Sorry. Go back to sleep."

My eyes were focused completely on him. "Yep, as long as you are, too."

We had been in the same bed that whole week, and I was already used to and loved it. He carefully planked his body above mine and began a light lapping of kisses on my mouth before letting me turn again and lay my head on his chest.

"Maya…" He sighed out my name peacefully before we both drifted off to sleep.

***

I caught on pretty quickly to the reason behind the sudden increase of Hawk driving one of the cars during those first few weeks back on tour. Well, the reason was really two-fold. I accepted the first—Hawk wanting us to have our alone time together. But the second, I could not. I know he wanted to spare me any unnecessary time in the cramped up, not-well-ventilated trailer. Although thoughtful and kindhearted, I did not want him driving so much. It would have been different if that was all of his responsibilities, but that was far, far, far from the truth.

"I'm fine." I tried to reassure him, even going as far as saying if he wanted to drive, so be it, but I wasn't traveling with him. I think he knew it was a bluff but, regardless, he obliged my request and didn't drive as often.

It was hard, though—the coming back to reality. Back on the road meant back to not seeing one another all the time…sometimes not even once a day. And if the week or so leading up to Louisville had been mentally and physically hard wanting to be with him, *after* Louisville was equally as painful. We were used to being together, and now there was the constant traveling circus around us. There were nights when I had to just rely on a sexy goodnight banter via text. And there were other nights when sitting around the post-concert circle holding hands had to suffice. But there were also times when we found a way to go on a joint "ice bucket" run—a rare empty bus, a back-wooded area, or even a hotel room when he was driving and we had a spare day between concerts.

***

It was at the end of August when just an intimate few of us traveled to Nashville for a quick overnighter. Finn and Lara were attending a party his label was hosting where one of the highlights was his touring success. Hawk went just because he always did, and Reese was flying in to have the publicity side covered. But it wasn't a kid-friendly party. So I was also making the trip. I was staying at Finn and Lara's Nashville ranch with Chance and Arinn. Even though it would have been cool to be at the party, I was just fine chillin' in comfy clothes inside an expansive home with every modern amenity. I did not mind at all being the glorified babysitter that night.

Hawk returned before Finn and Lara. He said he wasn't really needed and he missed me. He definitely got brownie points for including the latter. After hearing about his evening and knowing the kids had long since been securely asleep, Hawk and I moved to the guest room. We could have waited for Finn and Lara to come home and then gone to Hawk's townhome, but it was late, and we all had a predawn flight out the next morning. So it made more sense for us just to stay there overnight.

In the instant he kissed me on the bed, my cell phone chimed. I knew it wasn't a call or a text. It was the sound I set for my reminders. I saw Hawk glance at the bedside clock. It was exactly midnight.

"Cinderella, do you need to go home?" he jested. But when he saw what I was sure was a horrified look on my face, he rapidly changed his tone. "What?"

"I…I forgot," I managed. "How could I forget?"

"Maya? What?"

"It's…it was Jeff's birthday." Only then did I look at

Hawk.

"Oh."

When he softly touched my cheek, I said, "I'm sorry."

"For what?" His hand went down to mine. "You can talk about him." We had always been open when discussing our pasts, but still...

"Thanks," I acknowledged. "I just...I...I feel bad that I forgot." It was one of my remember, forget, remember, forget things. "I feel a little guilty about it."

We both sat there for a moment, unsure of how to proceed. Was that the end of the topic? Was that the end of the night? I gave him a small smile, and he did one back. He feathered a few kisses on my mouth and then laid both of us down, drawing my head onto his button-down-covered chest.

"We can, you know...if you want to..." Still snuggled in to his side, I made the offer of sex.

He sat me partially up so we could look eye to eye. "Maya, please tell me you don't think that's what I'm—what we're—all about."

"No. No," I reiterated a second time, because I didn't. But hearing him actually say those words, I felt like I was fighting off some tears. It was nice to verbalize, in a backward sort of way, that we were emotionally on the same level. I didn't want any awkwardness to creep in to the silence that followed, though. So I inserted some humor. "This is like some kind of bad soap opera."

"Huh?"

"My husband busting in just as we got into bed."

By the shake of his head and the couple small sounds of laughter, I knew he appreciated my effort. Though, in a more genuine tone, he followed up with, "You good? You need some time?"

"I'm all right."

"I'm glad you're here with me," he said with a slight smile.

"Oh, God..." I thought about how I would have felt

being miles away in a stale bus. "So am I."

He kissed the top of my head and readjusted our bodies so we were both more prone again. We wouldn't make love. It felt a little weird after the reminder alarm. But lying there with him, knowing I had made peace with where my life was, meant so much more.

CHAPTER FOURTEEN

"Thanks. It's more than generous, but I…"

When I verbally stumbled, Finn continued with his pitch. "Then what's the problem? You'll like it. There are great eateries and shops and…people." He purposefully paused as both of us looked across our latest concert venue to where Hawk was speaking with some fellow road travelers.

"I don't know. There is no problem. It's just a…" *A leap, closure…real.* But while those thoughts silently circulated through my mind, I saw Hawk look directly over at us and give a quick wink. That encouraged me to finish my words to Finn. "It's an amazing offer and yes…yes, I am ready."

"Great, Maya. I thought I was going to have to bring in the big guns to convince you." Obviously noting my scrunched, perplexed face, he explained. "My two little darlings."

I smiled, thinking of Chance and Arinn. "They would have sealed the deal for sure."

Finn nodded in Hawk's direction. "Go over there and tell Brawny he has ten minutes and then it's time to roll. They'll be letting people in soon."

I laughed at the jestful, yet fitting, name Finn used for

Hawk. While the superstar walked off, phone already to ear, I strolled toward the tall, handsome, dark-copper-topped man. On my approach, our other tour mates walked away.

"Something I said?"

"No. More like something I said." Hawk smirked. "I told them if they knew what was good for them, they would let me have a few minutes with you."

"Hawk!"

He ignored me, obviously having an agenda of his own. "Everything all right?" He paused for the slightest of seconds. "You've been a little moody the past couple of days." When he saw me do the "stand up for women" thing with my glare, he retreated slightly. "All right—not moody. How about 'off'?"

"No. You're right. I've been, I guess, distracted."

I had been. I knew it. The tour was soon coming to a close, and all I could think about was how everything was going to end. It reminded me of how, before she left, Vanessa had said she felt at the beginning of every August. As a reading specialist for a school district, she knew turning the calendar to August signified the end of summer break. I knew I should soak up the time remaining on tour, but my mind was too clouded with finality.

"You wanta tell me what it's about? Did it have anything to do with what you and the chief were talking about?"

"Yeah. And I'm sure you already know."

"No, Maya. I wouldn't be asking if I did."

I couldn't help but be a little surprised, especially because I could tell his response was legit. "About the possibility of me moving to Nashville and staying on permanently as part of Finn's team. Not so much with the kids." I knew, and Finn had confirmed, that he and Lara did not believe in nannies and wanted to raise their children as normal and on their own as they could. "But I would be blogging and the social media accounts…dealing with some of the Nashville stuff if Reese can't make it there. You two didn't talk about it?"

"No," he replied, and I was a little shocked but, admittedly, a little proud that the offer was purely about my work. "He has said how great it is that you've been a part of this craziness. We talked, but I didn't know about a permanent job offer."

That was all Hawk said, though. He didn't give me any more of his insight on the subject. I had no idea what his thoughts or feelings were on the matter of my possible employment or residency.

Knowing his opinion mattered pretty much more than even my own at that point, I asked the direct question. "What do you think about it…if I took the job?"

But what I got was the question bounced back. "What do *you* think about it?"

Hoping his reply wasn't a stalling or deflection technique, I went for my honest answer. "I think I'd like it an awful lot."

The grin on his face was bigger than I had ever seen from him. "I think I'd like it an awful lot, too."

I wasn't going to lie. There was an actual flow of warmth throughout my body. Pure relief. I believed the thing between the two of us was more than just a summer fling. And his answer pretty much solidified it for me. Between Finn's offer and Hawk's response, the clouds had definitely lifted.

"I don't know, though." I felt light and carefree again—enough to joke around. "Maybe I might need a little influencing?"

The way his eyes lit up acknowledged that he remembered the first time he hadn't been trying to influence me into taking a job. I flashed back to the kiss outside my hotel room in the Keys. It was what had started it all. And the kiss then on the field of one of the most popular baseball stadiums in the country, even exceeded that first one.

"That may have worked in the beginning," I joked. "But you have to step up your game, mister."

Before I could get the last word out of my mouth, he

had me in his arms and glided us both onto the turf. One of those rare but captivating Hawk smiles spread across his face as he planked above me. His kisses, mimicking mine, were sweet and soft and full of happiness.

***

Telling Hawk my plans was a lot easier than telling Sophia. While she had championed every blog and success I had that summer, I think it was under the guise of knowing it was a fifteen-minutes-of-fame kind of deal, and that I would return to Maryland when the leaves began to change. After all, it was what I had thought, too.

I had gradually made a new life with new possibilities all around me, though. But Sophia hadn't been a direct eyewitness to it. And in the midst of still worrying about her father, who was almost back to normal, it hit her hard. It was like my move was not only going to be one of physical mileage away from their lives, it was as if Jeff was leaving all over again.

In the end, though, I knew I had hers and the entire Shriver clan's support and blessing. With Jeff's dad in the real estate business, he was going to take charge of the sale of my house, and I was most grateful. That was going to be the emotional part for me. After all, the light blue frame abode in suburban Maryland held so many memories of my life. It had first been the house where I would visit my grandma. Then it became my safe haven when my world fell apart and my grandmother became "mom." And finally, it had been my first and only home with my husband. Every wall, brick, and appliance had some kind of memory to me. I would need support for sure.

And that time was coming soon. The tour was reaching the finish line. Finn was going to celebrate his September eleventh birthday quietly at home in Nashville before his concert stop there. And then there was just one more gig two days after that.

Because there were a couple days of break before the Nashville concert, Hawk secured one of the cars and the two of us were making a pit stop at his mother's house in Oklahoma, since it was basically on the way. I was excited to experience a part of Hawk's life that I could only imagine through the limited stories he'd told me about his family and growing up. But I was also nervous. When he talked about his mom, it was always in adoration and pride about what she had accomplished on her own. I didn't know how I was going to stack up. Jeff's parents had been a hard sell in the beginning. It wasn't that they didn't necessarily like me, it was that I don't think they took Jeff and me seriously. Until me, he had a different girl at almost every holiday celebration. Hawk, I knew, because of distance alone, didn't see his family very often, much less bring someone home with him. So I wondered how my visit would play out.

"What should I call her?" My stomach seemed to knot just a little bit tighter as the GPS showed we were getting closer.

"Who?" Hawk had his left arm casually dangling out the window as he drove with his right.

"Your mom. Who else?" I knew I couldn't call her Mrs. anything because she had never married...to Hawk's dad or anyone else, for that matter.

"Della." He pronounced his mother's first name just as calmly as he had spoken before.

"Yeah?" Was that disrespectful? Too personal?

"Call her Della. It's her name. Why? What should I have her call you?"

I shook my head at his absurdity and then answered. "Right now? Tired bitch."

He did an airy laugh and switched steering wheel arms so he could rest his right hand on the back of my head. "Why don't you just stay at the house, and I'll go by myself to pick her up at the airport. You can rest."

"Really?"

It was someone else's house. Wouldn't I be intruding?

But, God, I knew I could really use a quick snooze to refresh. Between the constant movement of being on the road and the decision to upend my life permanently, I had felt more emotional and tired than usual.

"Sure," he replied. "What's the point of you having to deal with the crowds and traffic and luggage? We won't be too long. Plus, it will give me time to personally warn my mom about how weird you are."

"Hawk!"

"Maya…" His voice was calming. "I know you're tired. It's fine. And as far as weird, wait until you meet my brother."

I shook my head once more. The easy banter between the two of us relaxed me once again. I was anxious and excited to meet his family. It was not only going to be his mom—who was flying back from a trip—but also his younger brother, sister-in-law, and their two kids who lived in another part of the state. Hawk's older brother, following in their father's footsteps, lived on a military base overseas, so he would not be joining the rest of the Brannigan bunch.

By the time we were at Della's farmhouse, which was surrounded by the peace and serenity of just open fields, the fair weather had turned. It had started to drizzle. But even worse was the force of the wind. We scurried onto the extended front porch as Hawk found the front door key hidden under a flower pot. Was it really that simple and innocent in the small Oklahoma town? You would have never dared do that where I was from. Besides, Jeff would have had a fit. I was surprised Hawk didn't, too.

"I know." He shook his head, seemingly reading my mind. "It's not normally here. She insisted on leaving it for us. But, really, this place isn't too far removed from Mayberry."

I followed him into the home. It wasn't the house where Hawk and his brothers had grown up. It could have been, though. It was big enough. It was a house that Della moved into a few years before when a lonely, old woman, who had been Della's travel customer, died and willed it to her. She wanted Hawk's mom to start her own travel business instead of working at an agency. And Della had—right there out of her home.

Hawk first showed me his mother's home office—a room located off the foyer. Hanging on the walls were photographs and memorabilia of all the places around the world she had traveled to. There was also a large map and a globe. And, of course, there was an impressive desk, as well as a tall stained-glass lamp, computer, and chairs for customers.

Nearby was the expansive kitchen-dining area. It was obviously a part of the residence area of the house. But Hawk said his mom did as much business there as in the office. He bragged about her baking skills and how she would often butter the customers up around the large, old, homemade oak table that could fit at least ten.

The central living room was where I felt most comfortable, though. There were pictures of Della—petite with short blond hair—surrounded by her family. And there were plenty of photos of Hawk's brothers' children and a few of Hawk, Liam, and Jacob, with their matching noses and smiles, growing up. I kind of felt bad that Hawk didn't have any more recent photos but realized that was how it usually worked. I knew it. Jeff and I had seen it at his folks' house, too—it was always all about the kids.

"You and your brothers look a lot alike," I commented.

"Yep." He was almost a little bashful as I looked around.

"But your hair is a little darker," I noted.

"I got dad's hair, one hundred percent. They're a little more mom. And Jake's a little taller and Liam has a little wider of a face." When I touched Hawk's face, which was just perfect to me, he said, "Get some sleep. The front two bedrooms upstairs are open. Pick one. I'm gonna head out. People will be driving like they've never seen a raindrop before." He shook his head at the potential inept drivers on the roads.

"I don't know if I will be able to sleep. Maybe I'll watch a little TV and rest my eyes," I said. "The sofa is fine."

"Wherever, Maya. Make yourself at home. I'll see you soon." He first looked at me and then around the room before giving me a kiss.

"Drive safe." I just couldn't help it.

***

My phone. Yep, it was my phone. It was ringing. I must have fallen asleep on the antique, high-backed Victorian sofa. But for how long? It was dark outside. I sat up a little straighter and grabbed my phone from the coffee table.

After acknowledging the mid-afternoon time, I answered my cell. "Hawk? Hey."

"Mai—"

I cut him off, playing forecaster via the picture window. "Those clouds sure are heavy and dark. What's up with your mom's flight?"

"It was rerouted. Haven't you seen the news?"

"No. I was sleeping." I breathed out a gust of air. I had been out. I must have been more tired than I thought. I hadn't even put on the television.

"There's a tornado warning."

"Huh? Really?" I took another glance out the window—the wind had picked up since Hawk had left, but there wasn't any rain.

"You need to get in the storm shelter."

"What?"

"Right behind the house, next to the garage, there is a set of doors on the ground. They're red. There's no key, just a simple latch." God, he was serious.

"Like *The Wizard of Oz*?" That was the only association of tornados and storm shelters I remotely had.

"Wha—?" He wasn't up for my movie reference. "Yeah. Yeah."

"I'll be fine here," I insisted.

"You'll be fine because you are going to go into that cellar." His directive was punctuated with clipped force and, I knew, concern.

"I'll be fine," I soothed. "I'll put the TV on. I'll stay away from the windows." I knew what to do. "It's just a little wind. Besides, macho man, you forget how we met. I'm pretty capable of—"

"Maya, this isn't an active shooter!" he boomed, causing me to not only stop mid-sentence but flinch. "And it's not a thunderstorm we're going to out-drive. I've been through these before. You need to get in the cellar. You don't have a lot of time." I could hear the elevation of stress in his voice not only because of the storm but because of my obstinate stance.

That didn't help me because, despite my façade, the tornado, with its winds already battering against the house, scared me. But I couldn't go into a storm shelter…not in a dark, small, closed … "I…Hawk, no. I can't." That time, my voice came out in more of a plea.

"Maya!"

"There's no windows, right? It's underground…small?"

He either realized then or understood that yelling at me wasn't helping. "Sweetie, I know. You need to, though. You can do this. I'll talk with you as long as I can, but I'm afraid the cell service might not work down there." He had me for a second with his offer of continuing to talk, but the thought of not having any communication…forget it.

"No, I don't think I can."

"You can. Just stay down there until someone comes and gets you or you can tell it's absolutely still…for a while. They're not letting us leave. We're in the tunnel connecting the airport and the parking. When they do…when I get back on the road, I'll be there as soon as I can."

"You need to be safe!" I exclaimed, rising from the sofa in full stance.

"I am." I know he was speaking as calmly as his body was letting him. "Momma usually keeps a flashlight in the top drawer next to the stove. Go, Maya."

"Haw—"

"Maya, don't make me stand next to another grave." He said it gut-wrenchingly slow because of the impact it had on both of us. After a pause, he added his own plea. "Please."

I was in the kitchen on his final word. I knew what it was like to stand at a grave, especially in front of one whose life could have been spared if they hadn't thought they were invincible. "All right. I have the flashlight." I found it right where he had said.

"Good." His exhale was strong. "Mai? I—"

But I couldn't hear anything more. The phone was already breaking up, and I had just stepped outside. The kitchen's back door was a beast to even shut.

"Sheez." I gasped for air from the effort of the door shutting and just trying to stand upright. "It's really bad," I yelled over the wind and into the phone. "I'm outside. I'm going to the cellar doors. I'm…God, I'm a little scared," I admitted. I was far from "a little."

"I know. You got this. You got this, Maya. I know it." His voice was going in and out, but I could hear it and at least know it was him. "Keep breathing."

"You're breaking up." It was hard to talk and try to get the damn, old shelter doors undone. "I've got to put the phone down for a sec." When I didn't hear anything from his end, I let out a small wail and shoved the phone and flashlight into my pants. It was the only place I felt they wouldn't fly away.

Finally, I opened the red doors. The howling wind was not only deafening my voice, but it was blowing me around. I knew it was serious. I had to get in the shelter. I couldn't even look up. There were leaves and other debris whipping around. I kept my head hung and found my way, inching down the first few steps of the dark abyss.

I flipped on the flashlight. Thank God it worked. When I looked downward, there wasn't much to see. It was a simple, plain, yet solid, cold cellar. Suspended on the steps, with the doors wide open just inches above me, I put the flashlight back in my pants and pressed the speaker button on the phone.

"Hawk?" I tried again.

"Maya!"

"I'm in," I screamed, knowing it was going to be nearly impossible for him to hear me. "But I have to shut—Oh, God." Just the thought of shutting those doors made me want to vomit.

"Maya? I'll be there as soon as I can."

"All right…Okay." I reached up and yanked until they closed.

"Feel how mu—"

And, nothing. He was gone. We were disconnected. I kept shouting out his name. But it was no use. I climbed down the remainder of the steps and placed the flashlight on the ground so it was beaming straight up. I then placed my useless phone next to it. I'm sure it was searching and searching for a signal, just as I was. It wanted a connection to the real world just like I did—not inside a dark and dusty cave.

I laughed, almost in hysterics as I thought of Finn's similarly named song. I even tried to sing a few verses in hopes it would get my mind off my predicament, but it wasn't working. Even through the solid captivity of the cellar, the circling wind was making so much noise I couldn't even think or hear myself sing.

It was stifling hot despite the little rectangle that supposedly provided ventilation. I had only been in there a matter of minutes, and I was considering stripping out of my clothes. I knew I was panicking. I knew I was panicking instantly. I considered opening the doors back up and just going for the house. Maybe there would be a bathtub to lie in. Wasn't that what you were supposed to do? But when I inched back toward the first step, the winds were howling. It was like a piercing alarm was vibrating as loud as it could in an attempt to break my eardrums. And then there was a thunderous, metallic boom like something had exploded right above my head. That, intermixed with the recollection of Hawk's words encouraging me to breathe, gave me the courage to be entombed a little longer.

I closed my eyes. It didn't do much good to have them open, anyway…it was so dark. I tried meditation. I had seen Finn do it a couple times on tour, and it calmed him. But the storm that was raging inside my body was battling with the fierce one just feet above. I tried timelining every second from the moment Hawk and I first met. I imagined I had my laptop and was editing the scenes, as there were things I forgot and retraced back to and things I wanted to bold and highlight and exclamation point.

And then, finally, there was stillness. There was stillness above me. My pursing lips slowed, and I took a deeper breath. The storm seemed to be over, and I would be able to leave. I decided to wait just a couple more minutes to be sure. I had been able to hold out that long. A few more minutes, knowing freedom and genuine air were just on the other side, was doable.

The silence remained, so I exhaled a couple more times and started to climb— cell phone and flashlight intact—up the steps. I had no idea what to expect when I would eventually make my way out of the escape hatch. Would there be total destruction? Or broken windows and shingles? Or simply trash tossed around? All I had to do was spring open those red doors, and I would find out.

But they didn't open. They… Oh, my God, wouldn't move. Well, there was a little wiggle, but the doors were not going to budge. Oh, my God! Oh, my God! Oh, my God! Having just regained a slight semblance of regular breathing back, I began to downright hyperventilate. I pushed. I clawed. I screamed. I went back down the steps and sat and tried to calm. My thougsht process was not rational. I thought I was actually losing my mind. I could not think straight…at all. I climbed the steps once more and pushed and clawed and screamed again. Nothing was working. I went back down, cursed my useless phone, cursed Hawk, and cried…hard.

CHAPTER FIFTEEN

There was some kind of metallic, scratching noise that made me rub at my eyes and listen more closely. My breathing, still erratic, was getting in the way of my ability to hear. I needed to calm down and concentrate. There was definitely a voice mixed in with the other sound. And…I think it was calling my name.

"Yeah. I'm down here." I was so beyond all sense of normalcy that it took me a couple tries to use the right amount of force in my vocal cords to let the person above know I was in the hellhole below.

"Hey. I'm gonna get you out," called the voice. "You all right?"

"Yeah," I managed and, in essence, lied. I wouldn't be all right until I was out.

"Okay. I'm just gonna need a little help. He's on his way. Just be a few minutes. Hang tight," came the voice, which I determined belonged to an angel.

There was help. Help was there. I just needed to hang tight. Like, what else was I going to do? Besides go completely mentally mad, of course. I leaned against the wall and tried to breathe and listen. Then another voice joined the first, followed by a lot of noise and grunting before there was a sudden rush of natural light filling my tomb. I shielded my eyes momentarily to let them adjust before looking up. There was an older gentleman, with scraggly, blondish-white hair, looking down at me.

"C'mon, little miss." He reached out a hand as I began to climb the steps. "We got you. You're okay."

When I made it to the top, my knees practically gave way in the exhilaration of fresh air. I started to shake a little. Everything was a blur. The man who had helped me through the shelter doors asked if I wanted to sit down. I could tell he was a little concerned.

But I couldn't. I couldn't sit. I was too wound up and needing... "Where's Hawk?" I turned from the first man, who was obviously a firefighter—the suspenders and emergency four-wheel-drive vehicle were tell-tale signs—to the younger version by his side. I had expected it to be Hawk, but it wasn't.

"We got a call from Alex," the chiseled, light-brown-haired man said.

"Al—? Where's Hawk?" I asked again.

I needed Hawk. I needed him. Everything was too much. I could maybe handle it with him beside me, but—

"Maya? You're Maya, right?" the elder asked.

"I don't feel good," was my response.

"Let us look at your hands," brown-haired prompted.

"What?" I peered at the raw scrapes and scratches that had formed from trying to make my escape. Despite the blood, I hadn't felt them at all.

"What were you trying to—" was all fireman number one got out before my stomach retched, and I promptly threw up on the grass. "Geez, little lady, take it easy. You're okay."

I sat down that time—on a large, downed tree trunk. It was right next to the red doors of terror. Oh! The tree had fallen on the shelter. That was why I couldn't get out. I looked then to the house. It appeared all right. Thank God. It was still standing—doors, windows, roof, all looked intact.

The younger man cautiously handed me a mint from his bag. "You think you're done?" He spoke of my unexpected upheaval.

"Uh-huh." I gladly sucked on the red and white peppermint. "Thanks."

"When was your last tetanus? That shelter is pretty old."

"Uh…uh…" Trying to remember something like that was pointless when I was having trouble just concentrating on simple things like my name and where I was. "A while," I admitted.

When the walkie-talkie on his hip started beeping and sounding out a static noise, he flipped it into his hand and turned to the lighter-haired fellow. "You better take her to the clinic just as a precaution. I'll follow through with these."

I looked to the other man who said, "Good deal. Call Alex. Tell him what's going on. And I'll call this in and meet up with you after."

I picked up my phone. I needed to call someone, too. But I couldn't. The damn thing was dead. It wasn't that there wasn't any service. The battery had run out. Damn it!

As the younger man quickly packed up and took off in his blue sedan, the second firefighter's phone started ringing. He was immediately engaged in a conversation, while leading me into his truck. I followed, still kind of in a fog, but knowing I did need to get my wounds checked.

The ride to the medical facility wasn't too far from Della's home. It only occurred to me as we pulled up that I should have seen about locking her door and grabbing my purse with my insurance and credit cards. But I hadn't. I could have even called Hawk from the landline, since the fireman was on his phone non-stop. But I hadn't. I wasn't thinking clearly yet.

The clinic was fairly busy, as should have been expected after a weather system like that blew through. Luckily though, it seemed, by my car window observations and listening to the fireman's dialogue on his phone, the storm wasn't as bad as what had been predicted. And my wait in the clinic wasn't going to be, either. My fireman hero, who I learned was named Elijah, coaxed the receptionist into moving me up in line.

I had just turned my paperwork in and Elijah had gotten off his phone when Hawk streamlined through the doors. It didn't take him long to spot the two of us sitting in the row of connected chairs. It was an even shorter amount of time for him to get to me.

"Oh, shit!" He shook his head as I got up, and he gently brought my weathered hands into his.

I clung hard to his torso. And for the first time since those tears in the storm shelter, I cried. I had never done so in front of him, but I didn't care. I knew I could. I knew my real shelter from the storm was in my arms.

"Breathe, Mai," I heard him murmur from behind my back.

Knowing I was finally able to do that again, I pulled my body a little apart from his. "I didn't want to go down there."

"I know," he concurred, and tucked a piece of my hair, which probably looked like Medusa's, behind my ear.

"There are a lot of places I need to—" Elijah rose to his feet, too.

Hawk extended his hand out to the firefighter as I sucked back into my man's side. "I know. Thanks. Thanks, Eli. And thank Gavin, too, for coming and calling me. I owe you both."

"John's kid owes us nothing," he said, and then I realized the connection—Hawk's dad had been a firefighter. "And your mom…well, there's no one better."

Another Della admirer, I thought, as Hawk said to Eli, "You oughta do something about that." It was an obvious attempt at a set-up.

"I have." The older man shifted a little awkwardly on his feet.

"Really?" Hawk asked the question in a light but legitimately inquisitive way and then added, "A little conversation-starter for dinner tonight."

Elijah shook his head and turned to me. "It was nice to meet you. Get those hands looked at. And make sure to tell them you threw up. Whether it was dehydration or nerves, you should check it out."

"Yeah," I agreed. "Thanks." We watched Elijah exit before I said, "I'm sorry."

"For what?" His look was incredulous.

"For not listening when you asked me to go down there right away. For being such a baby." A few fresh tears emerged in my eyes.

"Maya…" He cupped my face with his large, comforting hands. "I know how hard it was for you. I would have never, ever asked you to go down there if I thought there was another way."

"I tried hard not to panic." I started to retell my scary tale as Hawk brought his hands down to my hips. "I did. But especially when the doors wouldn't open…"

"I'm sorry, sweetie. I got here as soon as I could. I—"

"I know."

"I couldn't understand why you weren't picking up your phone. I knew you would be out of there as soon as you possibly could. I knew there had to be something wrong."

"I'm okay now," I said, and that time it was almost the truth. "And just so you know, I wouldn't have gone down there for any other person."

He kissed the top of my head as a sign of his gratitude. "C'mon, let's sit down."

But as soon as we did, Hawk's phone rang. He looked at it and said, "It's my brother Liam. It's probably about my mom."

"Where is she?" I was trying to recall what Hawk had told me prior to all of the storm shelter mess.

"The plane ended up going to Will Rogers." When I furrowed my eyebrows, Hawk explained. "Airport. Let me get this."

Listening to Hawk speak with his brother, I gathered the other airport was closer to where Liam and his family lived. So they were picking Della up and then meeting us back at her home. Hawk then explained to his brother where he and I were, and they had a light banter about the Elijah-Della connection.

The doctor's assistant called my name while Hawk was still on the phone. I reassured him that he could keep talking, and I went in for the poking and prodding. First was the dreaded height and weight, followed by routine questions, and then the additional wait for the doctor in the exam room. After my wounds were cleaned, they didn't look so bad. All I needed was some gauze and ointment momentarily and, of course, the lovely shot. She encouraged me to drink plenty of water and ran blood tests just to double check everything. But because my stomach had immediately settled, the vomiting was most likely due to my panicked state and lack of air.

When I went to leave and sign any papers at the front desk, the receptionist said everything was already taken care of. She was able to look up my insurance by the information I had given them, and the co-pay had been paid. I turned to Hawk, who had come to my side. I knew I was going to have to ask him to foot the small bill, but it was obvious he already had.

As we walked out to the parking lot, I asked, "So when I pay you back for the copa—"

"Don't be ridiculous. You don't have to pay me back."

I had figured that—it really was minimal—but that wasn't where I had been going with the line of conversation. "Should I make the check out to 'Alex'?" When he squinted those mesmerizing eyes at me and shrugged, I concluded with, "Really? That's you, right?" My mind was clear again and was able to replay things that had happened since the first of the winds blew.

"Yeah."

"What? What's with Hawk?" We stopped in front of the SUV.

He related the story of how Alexander was, indeed, his formal name. But shortly after he and Finn met, Finn started jokingly calling him Hawk due to his precision to detail and looking out for everything…Hawk eyes. And it stuck. No one knew him by Alex at Team Murphy.

"Hmmm," I said, looking him up and down.

"I'm the same guy," he seemed to tsk more than say. "I don't even think about it until I come home."

"Uh-huh." I offered little again and then started to walk away.

"What are you doing? Where you going?" he immediately questioned.

"I'm not getting in a car with a guy I just met seconds ago," I teased.

He carefully took my wrapped hand and turned me toward him. "First of all"—a knowing grin spread across his face—"you went into a hotel room with me in even less time and didn't know my name." When I smiled with remembrance, he continued in a more serious tone. "And second, you know me. You know me better than almost anyone."

"Alex?" It wasn't flowing off my tongue the right way.

"Yeah."

"I think I'm gonna stick with Hawk. You're definitely more of a Hawk."

"Yeah, I kinda think so, too."

***

Thank goodness I had time to shower, reapply some makeup, and change into fresh clothes before meeting Hawk's family. Medusa, as a descriptor of my appearance, would have been too kind. I'm surprised Hawk hadn't run out in horror or had me committed when he saw the mess I was in at the clinic.

When I came down the stairs, everyone was gathered in the enormous kitchen. They were a boisterous group, having not seen one another in a while and replaying the excitement of the day. I was able to stand back and simply observe without being noticed for a moment or two.

"So, you know, Momma"—Hawk was leaning against the woodblock counter—"it was Eli who rescued Maya."

"So I heard." She was standing at the sink washing some vegetables.

"Oh, yeah?" There was no mistaking Liam. "From the source?"

"Yes, boys. He told me you would be harassing me about it."

"No harassing, Ma." Liam spoke again. "We like Eli."

"And we kinda think you're okay, too," Hawk teased.

"Well, how nice of you to say, middle one," she bounced right back.

"Should we invite him over for dinner?" Hawk continued.

"No." She shook her head at the teasing. "He said to have fun with y'all tonight and tomorrow he would come and take care of the tree."

"Momma, you know we—" Liam halted his own sentence when he spotted me. "You must be Maya."

"The bandaged hands kind of gave it away, huh?" I tried a non-standard reply as all eyes swirled to me.

"Oh, you poor thing." Hawk's mother wiped her hands on a dish towel. "I'm so sorry that happened to you."

"Yeah. I think I may need you to book me a trip to somewhere sunny and calm—no winds...lots of open space." I jokingly appealed to the travel agent in her.

Hawk took the few steps over to me. Kissing the side of my head, he said, "You look nice."

"Thanks." I smiled.

"Hi, Maya. I'm Liam." He stretched out his hand. "I'm the handsomest and smartest of the clan."

Hawk swatted his brother's hand away. "And also the

most modest." He then went on to introduce Liam's wife Keita and their two kids, eight-year-old Landon and six-year-old Neve, who were both very engrossed in their electronics at the table. "You hungry?" he asked me.

"Actually, famished." My stomach was eager to be replenished.

"Good," Della said. "There's plenty. I wanted to cook." She pouted. "But because of all this delay business, I just picked up one of those precooked turkeys. And there's tons of veggies, bread, and chips. I just finished the coleslaw. It's going to be make your own salad or sandwich, if that's all right. And then we can all catch up and get to know Maya better." With her open invitation and genuine smile, I could see why so many people adored Della.

***

Later that evening, Liam and Keita went out on a date night. Their anniversary was that weekend, so they took advantage of having three built-in babysitters. While Grandma Della was baking with the kids in the kitchen, Hawk and I found some alone time on the porch bench. We lay there with my head on his chest and our feet intertwined, watching, after some brief rain, the peacefully clear sky.

"Hawk?" I broke the serenity of the silence.

"Mmmm?" He appeared to be in the same mode.

But I hesitated. Suddenly, I didn't want to say what had calmly and naturally flowed into my mind. I was afraid it might not be the right time and actually ruin the perfect moment.

"What, Mai?" He kissed the top of my head.

"I—" I hesitated again, but that time it was because I noticed Landon and Neve, who had auburn hair and freckles like their mom, standing at the doorway.

"What's up, super spies?" Hawk jested to his niece and nephew while adjusting our bodies slightly.

"Gram says it's time for the game," announced Neve.

Her brother added, "And she needs you to open a jar."

Hawk *hmmffed*, patted my leg, and said, "All right."

As we both stood up, I turned to Hawk. "Y'know, I think I might just go to sleep."

"Yeah?"

"Well, the nap I wanted earlier was rudely interrupted," I said with a slight smile. "And with all that's happened, it's been a pretty tiring day."

"I know. It has been," he concurred.

"Spend some time with your mom. You never got that chance to tell her how weird I am. But I think she pretty much found out firsthand." I had been more nervous about meeting Hawk's mother than meeting Finn or any of the celebrities that summer. And, of course, the first time I did, I had just torn up her storm shelter and had cuts all over my hands.

"I'm pretty sure she thinks the exact opposite." He caressed my face. "I'll be up soon. It won't take long to beat these two, hands down."

"Nu-uh!" the kids said in unison.

I couldn't help but smile. The Brannigan home was Americana. And Hawk was definitely a good part of that.

"Good night." I let my lips touch his.

On their "Eewww," Hawk started shooing Landon and Neve into the house. But then he turned to me and said, "Mai? Me, too."

Me, too? Me too, what? I stood alone on the porch, wondering what he meant. I backtracked our conversation but couldn't decipher his meaning. Surely it wasn't what I had started to say and wasn't able to finish. Was it?

***

When I woke the next morning, his arms were securely wrapped around my body in a spooning position. That was different for us. When we had the rare opportunity to actually fall asleep in the same bed, we didn't usually end up that way. We were normally more spread out.

I started to play with the light hair on his arms, thinking how much more rested I finally was and how much the man saddled up with me had to do with it. I could tell his breathing was changing and he was beginning to wake up. So I replaced my fingers with my lips.

"That's a nice hold you got there," I noted.

"I figured it worked in the elevator."

"What?" I tried to turn, but his embrace kept me still.

"When I came to bed last night, you were crying out in your sleep about needing air."

"Oh," I more exhaled than said. I didn't remember dreaming, but it didn't take a genius to understand my distress.

"You calmed when I brought you close to me like this."

"I...yeah. Thanks."

"It wasn't exactly a hardship." I could hear his smile even though I couldn't see it. "How you feelin' now?"

Refreshed, ready, a little horny...I pulled his index finger into my mouth and began slowly sucking. My emotions were on overload from the harrowing experience, as well as his capacity to understand what I needed in the middle of the night.

"Maya..." He purred out my name.

I released his finger and brought our hands together. I guided them from just under the waist of my tank down to my panties. When I felt his manly reaction start behind me, I pressed into him a little. His breathing was starting to become labored, like mine had been in the storm cellar. So, I turned toward him. I knew my eyes were a blue blaze of heat. I could feel them.

"God...hell...this is gonna be...I—" He started pulling down his sweats as I yanked off my top and tossed it aside. "We gotta be quiet, okay? There's lots of ears around here."

I started kissing his chest as he wrangled me out of my panties. There was the slightest of pauses as our gazes connected before he let me connect our bodies from the top. His hands were on my bottom and I could feel our mutual need. Ah…God, the release…from so much.

The knock on the wall was an obvious reference to our inability to be quiet. Thankfully, we knew, by the force and location, it was Hawk's brother. Della's room was across the hall and the kids were downstairs in sleeping bags. Still, my eyes opened just a little more from being caught.

"I told you to be quiet." Hawk had the silliest of sly grins on his face.

"Me?"

He readjusted us so I was lying flat on the bed. With a soft kiss, he entered me again and rolled his hips for a more serene, uninterrupted finish. I laid lax in his arms, feeling more protected than ever before.

CHAPTER SIXTEEN

By the time we made it downstairs, the kids had already finished breakfast and were in the family room, watching something on TV. Della, Liam, and Keita were gathered around the country kitchen table with food on their plates and coffee in their mugs. Hawk kissed his mom on her cheek and encouraged her not to get up. He pulled out a chair for me and turned around to the stove area to fix our breakfast plates. Sitting down, I managed a slight smile at Della at the head of the table but had a hard time meeting the eyes of Liam and Keita across from me. Thin walls and all of that.

"Someone got up on the right side of the bed," Liam started right away.

My gaze bounced everywhere as a heated blush rose to my cheeks. "Sorry about th—"

"Coffee, Mai?" Hawk saved me.

"Uh…" I turned around to face him, and he threw in a quick wink. "Tea?" I suggested, thinking between the tornado terror and facing Hawk's family, I needed something calming, not jittery.

"I'll get it." Della rose as Hawk set our plates of bacon, cheesy eggs, vegetables, and bread on the table.

Sitting next to me, he spoke to his younger brother. "Someone was out late on date night. Checkin' out the shocks on the minivan?"

"Maybe…" Liam's inflection and use of the word sounded so much like Hawk's, I had to laugh silently.

Both Keita and I shook our heads as the brothers grinned, and Della set the tea bags in front of me. "Boys…."

"Sorry, Momma." They both chuckled.

"Maya, go ahead and eat. Don't let this Neanderthal get to you." Hawk looked from me to Liam.

I loved watching the brothers together. As an only child, it was something I'd totally missed out on. "I…you know, I'm suddenly not that hungry."

Della examined my plate while handing me the hot water cup. "You're not another one of those vegetarians, are you?" She reclaimed her seat at the head of the table. "Yesterday you ate—"

"What?" I queried and looked at Hawk.

"Oaklee." His ex-wife's name came out blandly from Hawk's mouth.

"No, ma'am," I denied. "No, not at all. I like meat."

"Don't even say it!" Keita smacked her husband's arm before we went another round of sexual innuendo.

"I'm just not that hungry," I explained. I was still having mini-waves of nauseous panic from being stuck underground…although I was trying to conceal it.

"Good." I refocused on Della's voice and the shake of her head. "That little cheerleader… Can't believe Max has put up with h—"

"Momma." The way Hawk used his mother's name was a clear indication he didn't want to talk about his ex any more. He turned to me, instead. "You want to try something different?"

"No." I placed my hand on top of his. "I'm sure I'll regret it halfway out of town, but I…no." I quit dunking the tea bag and took a sip.

"I'll pack you a doggie bag," Della offered.

"Great." I took a bite of the whole wheat toast just so Hawk wouldn't keep staring at me. "And I would love the coleslaw recipe from last night."

"Oh, sure." His mother seemed pleased I took interest in her cooking. "It's so easy."

Thankfully, we managed to get back to a normal conversation, which included everything from Landon and Neve's school, to exactly how close Della and Eli were—regular companions but nothing serious yet, to my life in Maryland. Nothing was too personal. It just gave us all a better glimpse into each other's worlds.

While Hawk went upstairs to get our bags and Keita and Liam were rounding up the kids and their belongings, I helped Della put some food together for our trip. "Thanks." I nodded at the to-go containers.

"No problem. I hope you feel better."

"I already am," I said. "I don't know…these past few days have been a whirlwind. Making the decision to move to Nashville and having to look for a place to live and then, of course, the fun time I had feeling like I was buried alive under your garden." I tried to bring humor to the image that shattered my brain just thinking of it. "I think I just need to relax and quiet the spinning."

"That would do it." She seemed to look me up and down before saying, "Maya? You seem like a genuine person." Before I could answer that I try to be, she continued. "I'm trusting you have Alex's best intentions at heart. He deserves that."

"Of course," I partially stuttered, not quite sure how to take her comment.

"It really has been so nice meeting you." She gazed at me and then gave me a hug, adding to the confusion about what she was thinking.

I wasn't going to get a definitive answer then, though, because Hawk reentered the kitchen, oblivious to any of our conversation. "Well, we need to take off." He gently strung his hand through my still-bandaged one.

"You!" His mom pointed her finger at her son. "You need to call and visit more often."

"Yes, Momma." He sighed in a good-boy, Southern way.

"I expect to see both of you sometime soon."

She reached up on her tiptoes to give her tall son a hug, and I pushed away the uneasy feeling I'd had just seconds before. She had included me in the future visit. Maybe the little warning was just a protective momma kind of thing. Maybe. Hopefully.

***

We stopped for gasoline not too far from Della's home. I wanted some gum and soda. So I told Hawk I would run into the accompanying convenience store and be right back.

Both of us outside of the car, he brought me into his arms. His eyes met mine and the slightest of smiles emerged. He kissed me then. "Besides the obvious, Mai, I had a really good time. I'm glad you came."

I know my eyes shone. I could feel them light up like the bright Oklahoma sky above. I kissed him back sweetly. "Besides the obvious," I smiled, "me, too. And punch bug, by the way."

He looked around and saw the white, classic Beetle parked in front of the store. "Two for a classic," he recited, and kissed me twice.

I strolled happier than ever into the convenience store. A woman around my age with dark, full brunette hair, that hung halfway down her back, was at the glass doors when I entered. I said excuse me and went on my way to quickly pick up peppermint gum, a soda, and unsweetened tea for Hawk. After I paid, I swung around to be face to face with the woman again. Well, not exactly face to face. Her curvy figure was, actually, a good bit shorter than mine.

"You're the one?" she queried. Her dark eyes matched her hair color.

"Huh?" I turned a little more definitively toward her.

"You're the one with Alex?" Before I could answer, she continued. "I heard you were at the clinic yesterday." With that comment, I noticed she was wearing a nursing smock. She was kind of intense and really had me at a loss, since I had no idea who she was. "Don't expect much," she predicted ominously. "He's not made for happily-ever-after."

"Uh…"

"Hey, Mai, what's—" Hawk cut off his own words, as I turned to see him entering the store. Then he said her name. "Oaklee."

"Alex!" She threw her arms around him.

And he just as quickly pushed them away. I looked at her in a whole new way then. Hawk's ex-wife. Hmmm…not at all the tall blonde I was expecting.

"How are you?" he asked his ex, while carefully taking my bandaged hand in his.

I took note of the way he spoke to Oaklee. It was in a very even-keeled demeanor. It wasn't done with anger or with criticism but definitely not with enthusiasm. It was as if he was speaking to a waitress at a restaurant or a casual business colleague.

"Good. So good." She seemed suddenly bubblier in his presence. "Max, the kids…we're all good."

"Good."

"I'm sure he'd like to see you." Her Southern drawl was much more pronounced than Hawk's.

"We're actually heading out of town right now." He gave my hand a gentle squeeze.

"It was nice meeting you, Oaklee."

"You, too." She said it in an even tone, but I was pretty sure she didn't mean it.

And with that, Hawk turned us, and we walked hand in hand back to the car. He waited until we were on the main road before broaching the obvious subject. "So what's going on in that head of yours?" He glanced quickly at me and then back at the road.

"Because I have such an imaginative one."

His chuckle was partial. "Yes. I know you must have questions."

"Just one," I admitted.

"Okay…." His breath out was huge.

"You were married to *her*?"

"A life time and a different person ago." He sighed again.

"I should hope so."

His belly did a one-huff laugh. "Wasn't what you were expecting?"

"I hadn't thought much about—"

"Maya…" He said my name in the "c'mon, get real" kind of way. "I know you had to."

"Okay. Yeah, maybe a little." White lie.

"You're nothing like her," he said in a reassuring way.

"If you're talking personality, I'll take that as a compliment."

"It's a compliment in every which way." His soft voice changed then as it was registering what I said. "Why? What? What were you two talking about before I came in?" In the time it took me to debate on how to answer, his scruffy face definitely turned my direction.

"Nothing. Really," I insisted. "She was just introducing herself. But she sure seemed to sing a different tune when you walked in."

"Good thing I'm tone deaf," he joked and made a definitive nod in my direction. "Everything worked out the way it was supposed to. Believe me, I have no regrets." He placed his hand on my thigh.

I could hear the sincerity of his voice. I could see it in the way he'd treated her as a casual acquaintance. I could feel it in the way his hand caressed me. The lingering mystery of Oaklee could be put to rest.

***

I thought I would have been more tired after traveling most of the day. But I wasn't too bad. Entertaining Chance and Arinn at the Murphy abode while Hawk, Finn, and Lara were at the Nashville concert kept me awake, for the most part.

But after I put the kids down—prayers and bedbugs routines intact—I knew then that *I* wasn't going to be too far behind. I found my way under the sheets of the Murphy guest room. It was going to be my new temporary home since Finn and Lara had offered to put me up there while I looked for a permanent place in Music City.

Feeling even closer to him since the visit to his hometown, I texted Hawk. *Tornados & storm shelters…U sure know how to show a girl a good ole southern time* ☺

His text came back a couple minutes later. *Knocks on bedroom walls…*

Not only did I smile with heat rushing to my cheeks, but I sent him a similar emoji. *Made it all worth it. Going to sleep. C U tomorrow, right?*

U @ my place…can't wait.

I was internally melting as I typed, *Punch buggy parked. Back at ya.*

***

My stomach was rumbling worse than when I had first gotten out of that death trap of a shelter. I was more dazed than when Finn had first offered me the initial job. I was in a state of disbelief, similar to when I was on my way to the hospital the last day of Jeff's life.

And, yet, it had to be true. I had even double checked. And there I was standing in front of Hawk's door. It was the first time I was ever at his place, and it was going to be with such shocking news.

"Hi, Mai." He greeted me with a hug.

I looked in his eyes, wondering if I could pre-read them…wondering if I could predict the future…if I could tell how everything was going to go…how he was going to react…if it was the last time I would look in those eyes…if that had been our last embrace. "Hi." I got the one word out.

"I'm glad you're here. What's up? What took so long?"

I had originally planned on coming hours before—us spending more of the day together. But a mid-morning phone call had changed all that. I had needed to regroup and take as much charge of the situation as I could before finally making my way to his Tennessee townhome.

"I…I had to take care of some things."

He had my hand and was leading me through the hardwood hallway into the similarly floored family room. "If it's about the move…"

"No."

"Come on, sit down." He started toward the neutral-colored sofa. "I want to talk to you about th—"

"Hawk…." I didn't sit.

So neither did he. "Maya? What is it? What's wrong?"

I dropped his hand and turned from him. I looked down at the brown and white Oriental rug, over to the inactive brick fireplace with expansive art piece of the Nashville skyline above, to the beige-carpeted stairs leading up to the rest of the home, and to the door leading to the back yard. Finally, I glanced at the three framed photos of his family. I looked anywhere but at him.

"Maya?"

"I'm pregnant."

Whoosh! Did that just come out? Did I just say that? It was the first time I had said it out loud, and it made me feel like I was upside down all over again.

"What?" It was one word, but it seemed to take forever coming out of his mouth.

"I'm sorry." That time, despite mine blurring, I managed to look into his eyes.

"What?" It was the same inflection and rhythm of his previous question and the same as I had been feeling all morning since I'd first heard. After a beat or two, there was another one-word question—the other one I had immediately had, too. "How?"

"I don't know. I swear. I swear, Hawk. I don't know. I wouldn't have known, but they called with the results of my blood work. They said it was normal, except I was—" I recalled the stunning phone call from the Oklahoma clinic earlier that morning.

"I thought you couldn't."

"I...I know. I don't know how it happened. I swear. I didn't do this on purpose. I wasn't trying to trap you." Once I had gone to the pharmacy, once I had confirmed it with an over-the-counter test, and once I had parked the car in an empty vacant field, that was all I could think about— what he would think...how he would react...how women in his past had dealt with pregnancies. "God, I would never do that."

"You're pregnant?" He needed to hear it again.

"Yeah," I confirmed. "I even took one of those home tests."

"Ah..." He breathed out. "Jesu—"

"I'm sor—" I tried again.

"All right...enough. I heard you." His tension was quite apparent.

I closed my eyes, wanting us both to take a moment. And then, I tried again. "Hawk?"

His exhale was extreme. "I...wow. I need some time. I need some time to...damn...think." He took a mini-breath. "Wow."

I wanted him to say more. But when he didn't, I guess *that* was my answer. And it was really what I had expected all along, anyway. My shoulders drooped as I said, "I'll leave."

Surprisingly, he said, "No. No. Stay. I'll go. Just give me a little bi..."

His voice dropped off as he looked at me for a solid few seconds, blew out some air, and exited through a side door.

It must have led to the garage because, in the matter of minutes, I heard the garage door opening, an engine starting, and the door reclosing. He had left.

***

I waited awhile. Eventually, I had settled my nerves enough to finally sit down on the sofa. I played with the throw pillows, but I did nothing much more than get lost in my own thoughts. I knew what Hawk was thinking and feeling because I was pretty much feeling the same. The pregnancy was beyond a surprise. It was impossible, as far as I had been told. But it was real. It was true. And I had to place my feelings of shock into a compartment and understand what I felt about the actual life that was suddenly, miraculously inside of me. It was something I had wanted for so long and then had learned to cope with not being able to ever have. It wasn't how it was supposed to happen. God, no…not at all. But, somehow, it did. And I…I wasn't not going to be happy about it…even if it meant losing the one person who had brought me the most happiness in so long.

It was well over an hour, and I hadn't moved. I didn't feel like I should have gone up the stairs to the main part of Hawk's home. It seemed like an invasion, since he hadn't personally brought me up there himself. Just as I was about to use the powder room, my cell phone rang. Springing it free from my purse, I was disappointed to see it wasn't Hawk. But it could have possibly been the next best thing. At least the caller could provide some answers.

The person on the other line was my doctor from Maryland—the one who had said Jeff and I couldn't have a baby. She was the one who had turned my hopeful world into a barren one. And I was hoping she could explain how it could possibly be that it was becoming reversed. I had called before going to Hawk's but had to leave a long-winded message on her voicemail. I hadn't expected a phone call back that late in the day—after hours. But I was glad she did. It explained so much.

When I got off the phone, things were at least clearer on the how. But I knew it probably didn't make much difference where Hawk was concerned. I had thrown a bucket of ice in his face with no warning. And he hadn't gone for a short little stroll to get more. He had been gone for a while. He didn't want to see me. And I didn't blame him.

I took out the notepad and pen I always kept in my purse for blog inspirations and wrote a short but heartfelt note. *I'm sorry. I can't tell you how much. But I understand. It's my fault. I don't blame you for hating me.*

Emotional, I waited a little bit until I knew I was calm enough to drive. The bandages on my hands were beginning to unravel as I entered Finn's Range Rover he insisted I use until I got back to Maryland to reclaim my own car. I peeled away at the gauze until it was completely off. The marks were still there, but the healing had already begun. I wondered how long it would take for my heart to do the same.

CHAPTER SEVENTEEN

When I arrived back to the Murphy abode, thanks to a great car navigational system, I made an effort to appear semi-normal by taking some deep breaths and pasting on a smile. With the kids surely in slumber-land, Lara, Finn, Carter, and Vanessa were gathered in the great room. I knew the engaged couple were going to be there. Right before my earthshattering phone call—one which no one knew anything about—Lara had told me Vanessa was going to be in town for a short visit.

"Maya," Finn said upon my entrance. "Didn't expect you back so soon."

I'm sure they didn't. I suspect they didn't think I would return at all that night, considering the limited time Hawk and I had together as a couple. A sleepover was probably more than expected.

"Yeah." I tried a simple answer with no explanation, but I saw all four of their faces wanting more, and knowing Vanessa, she would ask. "He had to leave." Well, that was the truth. Knowing I didn't want to or had the energy to get into it any more, I then said, "Sorry, I don't want to interrupt. I'll just go to the guest r—"

"No. No," Lara interjected. "Don't be silly."

"We're just doing wedding plans," Vanessa jumped in. "Join us. The boys aren't listening to reason, anyway." She nudged Carter who shook his dark, loose hair.

"Maya, drink?" Finn asked, starting to stand.

Oh, God, yeah. A gallon of your strongest. You know the bourbon you like? Yeah, that.

"No. No. Thanks." I listened to sensibility instead of desire.

"So we were actually just discussing you two." Vanessa was looking right at me.

What was she talking about? Who? What two?

"We are doing the invitations," she continued in her fast-paced Vanessa way. "We were going to write 'Hawk and guest.' But should we just put your name on instead? Yeah, right? Is that proper etiquette?"

Oh. "Us" two. I was pretty sure there wasn't a "two" any more.

"Who cares about etiquette?" Carter sounded very much a man and groom-to-be. "They're both going to be there. I'm not even sure why we are sending half of these people an invitation. They know when. They know where."

"We have to send invitations!" Vanessa practically shrieked. "Maya, what do you think?"

I could hear some sort of buzzer, and I wondered if it was real or if it was just in my brain. Maybe it was the signal that my time was up. My time was up for the fantasy world I had been living in since the Keys.

"I don't need my name written on anything."

"Well, I…" Vanessa started.

But I was focusing on Finn, who was standing at the monitor. It had been a real buzzer—the one that said the main gates were opening to allow someone up the long drive to the house. I saw the driver's face in the gunmetal colored truck just before it roared up the hill. Of course, it was Hawk.

"I'm going to the guest room." When Finn's eyebrows burrowed and he jerked his head slightly at me, I clarified so there was no doubt. "I don't want to see him." And I walked away.

I didn't want to see him. I had enough for the day. Well, I had enough for a week. It was too much. I couldn't deal with disappointing him. I couldn't deal with having him being angry with me. I just needed to be alone.

I shut and locked the door and then went into the adjoining bathroom. Sheez, I hadn't done as good of a job as I thought I had. The mirror proved that. Although there wasn't any running makeup, my face was blotchy and my eyes were weary red. I was positive then that the four in the great room had noticed and had initial questions but had been too polite to ask. But now, for sure, they were rapidly putting the pieces together.

Since the guest room was only feet away from the great room, I could hear Hawk entering. "Is she here? She's here, isn't she?"

"Yeah." I recognized Finn's voice.

"I figured she wouldn't answer her phone. So I just drove over here." Hawk sounded hurried, rushed…anxious.

"What's going on?" Finn was getting closer.

"She didn't tell you?" So was Hawk.

"No."

There was a hearty knock on my guest room door. "Maya?" When I didn't answer, Hawk called out again, "Maya?" I sat on the bed and listened as he tried the locked doorknob. "Come on, open the door." That time, I swear it sounded like he had been drinking, which was strange because even when he drank, he didn't sound like or appear as if he had. "Maya, open the door." After another unsuccessful attempt at the door, he yelled, "Damn it."

I thought of the irony then. Jeff had quite a few nights of getting drunk after we found out we *couldn't* have a child. And, now, there was Hawk drinking and swearing over the fact that he *was* going to be a father.

I felt bad. I knew it was my fault. But still, I didn't want to see him…especially in the state of mind he was in. It would tear me apart. If there was even a semblance of hope that we could at least talk about it, it couldn't be then.

My thought was confirmed with, "I'll kick it in if I have to."

"No." Finn's response was immediate and firm. "No, you won't."

I could hear a little bit of a ruffle and then Hawk's voice softening just a tad. "Finn, man, this is my thing."

"This is *my* house." After a few seconds pause, the crooner said, "Come on." There was another slight hesitation before, "Give it a night. Whatever it is. Give it the night."

"I—" Hawk started.

"I'll call you a cab," Finn offered, and I buried my head in my semi-sore hands.

"I'm not that drunk."

"Even if you're not"—Lara obviously had joined the men— "you shouldn't be driving."

"Lara's right," her husband agreed.

"We'll take him home." It was Carter's turn. "We were leaving, anyway. Nessa, grab my keys. I'll get his."

"Great," I heard Finn say. "Come on. Go home. We'll talk tomorrow."

"Maya…" Hawk's voice trailed away.

There was a long bout of silence only interrupted by a few monitor beeps indicating exterior doors opening and closing. And then there was another knock on my door. I knew it wasn't him. The knock was too soft…too diminutive.

"Maya? It's Lara," she said before confirming, "It's just me. Can you let me in?"

Of course, I did. Not only was it her house, but I wanted someone to talk to…to confide in. And I knew Sophia couldn't be it, for obvious reasons. Juanita would listen. But there was nothing like talking with someone person to person.

We looked at each other in silence before both sitting on

the made bed. Finally, she asked, "What's going on? I don't think I have ever seen Hawk like that. He likes to be in control."

"Is he?" It hurt *me* that I hurt *him*.

"Finn is talking with him, and Carter will make sure he gets home all right. I'm not sure how drunk he is, but it's obvious he's upset."

"Yeah. I threw something pretty big at him."

Lara waited. She didn't flinch. She didn't question. She just waited, knowing that if I wanted to, I would tell her more. I suppose it was a mom tactic. One that maybe I needed to pay attention to.

"I'm pregnant." It was weird, but it came off more naturally that time.

"Oh." There was the look—not as bad as Hawk's or as surprised as mine, but there was definite shock. "I thought..." She paused. "I mean...I thought you couldn't."

"Oh, believe me, me, too. Jeff and I...we tried for years. We finally did all the fertility testing. And they told me we couldn't. I was devastated. We had wanted kids—maybe four—one for each of our hands, we used to joke. First a boy, then a girl...." I shook my head, realizing I was rambling. "When I found out we couldn't, I bolted out of the doctor's office. Jeff eventually found me down some random corridor. I took to my bed for a couple days. I wouldn't even talk about it. And, of course, he was upset, too. And then he died. He died a few months later. Oh, Lara, how can I...?"

"And you're sure you're pregnant? Not too long ago I was convinced—"

"The blood results came in from Oklahoma, and I even picked up one of those kits, totally not believing. But it's true."

"Congratulations." She smiled. "You have a miracle."

"Not quite. There was a mix up...well...Yeah, it's close to a miracle. I just wish I could be completely happy about it."

"Tell me what happened with Hawk...."

***

I felt nauseous that next morning. And it wasn't because of the pregnancy. I was playing with Chance and Arinn in the Murphy back yard when I heard Hawk's truck approaching. It had to be him. It had the sound of a big, extended RAM 1500 like I had seen him in, via the monitor, the night before. And I knew he was due to pick up Finn right around that time.

The two men were heading to the final concert stop that night, which was only a couple hours away. Then they would be back home in the wee hours of the morning. Lara wasn't going, though. She and the kids were supposed to go house-hunting with me. But considering the pregnancy revelation, I wasn't sure that was an option anymore.

I had ignored Hawk's "we need to talk" text from the night before—those were never good words—and had then turned off my phone altogether. But now I knew he was in the house and was once again just a door and a few feet away from me. I couldn't be that big of a wuss. I needed to face him sometime. So I started the kids and myself back into the house. At least I would have the buffer of two adorable children and two other rational adults, who both now knew everything.

"Have you told her that?" I heard Lara say as I approached the open screen door.

"You saw." It was Hawk's voice. "She won't even talk to me. She ignored my text. She just thinks she knows how this is all going to play out." There was no doubt they were talking about me.

"You walked out on her." The way Finn said that made me know I had an ally on my side. It was as if he was putting himself in my shoes. He got it. "You don't do that."

"Finn..." Lara's pronunciation of her husband's name was a partial sigh.

"I know." I could hear the empathy in Hawk's voice. "I was just thrown. I came back."

There was no harnessing the two Murphy children. They bustled through the door directly ahead of me. Chance raced toward Hawk, and Arinn kind of wobbled behind. It continuously amazed me how good Hawk was with kids—those two, his brother's kids…

I locked eyes with the tall, broad, brooding man, as Chance bounded into his legs saying, "Arinn stinky."

"Yeah," I agreed. "Someone needs their diaper changed. I'll do it." I started to pick up Arinn.

"Maya…." There was a plea and want in Hawk's voice.

"Not now." I had such mixed feelings right then. Seeing him with those kids made me vulnerable, but knowing what he'd said about how things were going to play out made me leery. I couldn't have my fear confirmed, at least not there in front of everybody. "There's too much going on. And there's not time, and I…" I took a deep breath and looked to Finn for help.

He did. "We *do* need to be going."

"Shi—" With a glance at Chance, Hawk stopped himself from downright swearing. "Man, you are always late. We can be—"

"We'll be back early tomorrow. Maya, you'll be here, right?" he said in a way where I knew he was giving me a reprieve but also hoped for some kind of resolution the following day. Having two of his closest employees in the situation Hawk and I were in was far from desirable for Finn…and it made me shudder, recalling my hesitancy earlier in the summer regarding personal versus professional.

"Yeah," I agreed immediately, while looking at Hawk, who shook his head.

"Let me give Princess Stinky here"—Finn gathered Arinn into his arms—"a kiss before you get her changed."

After he did, I took refuge in climbing the stairs and escaping into Arinn's nursery. I didn't need to wish either

Finn or Hawk good luck. I didn't need to see Lara kiss her husband goodbye, while Hawk stood nearby. And I certainly didn't need to see him leave again.

***

I had Arinn in my lap, reading her a rhyming book. She kept pointing to the cat. And then she would try to turn the book upside down.

"Stop that." I tickled her and turned it back the right way.

"Stop dat," she mimicked, with the same inflection as mine.

I put down the book and asked her, "Arinn, where is your foot?" When she grinned and pointed to the appropriate body part, I asked another. "Where are your ears?" With another right answer, I said with glee, "Oh, my goodness! You are so smart!"

"Oh, my goodness!" she repeated, and I laughed.

"That's nice to see." Walking into the room with Chance, Lara joined us by sitting on the floor.

"Yeah." I knew I was going to be a good mom. I felt it already.

"Chance, take Arinn and go play with one of the puzzles over there," Lara directed.

"Mommy..." Chance semi-whined at the baby puzzles.

"Thank you, bud." That was all she had to say for Chance to give in—I needed to start taking notes. "How you doing?" Lara directed the question to me with the kids not really out of earshot but at least not directly listening.

"I...I feel so high school. Getting pregnant and not thinking I could. Oh, you wouldn't know."

"I know more about that than you can possibly imagine." She seemed to shake imaginary cobwebs from her brain and then continued. "Hawk would make a great dad."

"I know." My face had a legitimate smile, but it was also a sad one. "I actually kinda told him that the first time we

212

met. He probably thinks it was my opening—bait, hook…"

"He doesn't think that, Maya."

"I'm so sorry. You and Finn don't need this drama. This wasn't why you brought me on. And, now, God knows, I probably shouldn't even look for a place to live. I can't work for Finn. I'll have to leave, or Finn should just let me go."

"What? No!" she said immediately. "No. And I say that for me and Finn. No. We're looking for a place for you. Maybe we should add a few houses instead of just townhomes since you might like more of back yard with a little one." She looked down at my not-for-long flat stomach. "And I won't say another word, but you *do* need to talk with Hawk."

Yeah. I know. But I dreaded it.

***

"Why is he calling me? Shouldn't he be on stage?" Lara reacted to her phone belting out the song "Roxanne," which I had come to know as her personalized ringtone for Finn.

Sitting near Lara in the great room, I glanced at the clock on my laptop. But I didn't need to. Arguing or not, I was pretty much as attuned to what and where Hawk should be as Lara was to her husband. Yes, I had been imagining what he was doing most of the day—having more bro-talk with Finn, meeting location representatives, organizing equipment placement, and at that moment in the evening, patrolling backstage as the crowd sang along to a Finn Murphy hit. I looked at Lara with the same amount of inquisition as she had on her own face.

"Finn? What? What's going on?" she answered and then gave him a chance to actually respond. "What! What? Are you okay?" She shot up from her seated position on the sofa.

Her disposition instantly got my attention. I put my laptop down and repeated her query. "What?"

"Yeah," she said into the phone and took a big breath

before repeating again, "Yeah. You're sure?" She pressed the phone tighter to her cheek and, after listening again, talked in a way that I knew she was having trouble hearing. "Hawk?" She looked at me, now standing, too, and then listened some more. "Uh-huh. She's right here." Her eyes appeared a little bigger that time before she said, "Okay. Hold on."

When she pulled the phone away from her face, I asked again, knowing there was definitely a cause for concern, "What?"

"There was an incident," she said slowly. "Hawk got Finn out of the way, but in the process, Hawk was hurt."

Oh. My. God. It was happening all over again. Jeff…Hawk…

"Is he dead?" I hardly heard my own words. They came out in a horrified whisper. "Was he shot?"

Did some fan go crazy and Hawk interceded? Oh, God. No.

"Oh, Maya. No. No. Finn wants to talk to you. He'll explain." I tried to concentrate on Lara's words. I think they were saying something positive…something not completely heartbreaking.

Still, I took the phone from her hand and spoke into it slowly, "Hello?"

"Maya?" Finn's voice came from across the line. "Listen…on the opening number…" There was a lot of background noise—more than usual, even with him presumably being backstage. "A piece of equipment broke loose from above. Hawk saw it happening. He pushed me out of the way, but he slid and fell pretty hard off the side."

"Oh, God. How bad?"

"His one side is banged up. Thank God there's always medics on site, right? They took him to the hospital but assured me he'll be all right. Need to run some scans, whatnot. He'll be home tomorrow at the latest." A smidge of the background noise faded, and I heard Shelly say everything was almost set before Finn continued. "Just living up to his name again—eyes on everything. Probably saved my life."

"So he's okay?"

"Yeah. He'll be sore. But he knows how to shield."

Finn didn't need to tell me that. I knew that. Hawk, after all, had done the same thing with me the first time we met in the hotel in the Keys.

"Should I call him?" I asked.

"You know what he told me when I said I was going to call you and Lara?" When I didn't answer, he spoke, anyway. "He said, maybe she'll actually talk with me now."

"Yeah." Admittedly, I felt regret.

"Can you put my wife back on the phone? I want to make sure I tell her how much I love her before I get back on stage. They're just about ready again."

"Yeah. I sure can." I smiled softly at his sentiment and returned the phone to Lara.

"Hi, Cowboy." She was more relaxed, knowing her man was safe. "Yeah." She listened again to the phone as I walked to the patio doors to look out into the darkness and try to reclaim my breath. "Yeah." After another pause, she said, "I love you, too. Forever."

Between Lara's concluding words to her husband and what Finn told me Hawk had said, I didn't hesitate to pick up my own phone and call the protector himself. Unfortunately, though, I got his voicemail. "It's me. I'm sorry. I'm sorry about…well, you know what. And, Hawk, I'm sorry you're hurt. I want to talk. It just wasn't right this morning. Tomorrow. All right? I'll come by your place. But will you please just call me back, and let me know you are okay?" Not knowing what else to say, I ended the call and wiped my eyes. They were still dry, but they were envisioning the horror that had taken place on the concert stage not long before. And it wasn't hard for me to imagine, since I had months of firsthand experience being in nearly identical settings.

"How did you find out about your husband?" Lara,

approaching my side, asked in a gentle way.

"His chief on the force called. By the time I got to the hospital, it was too late. We didn't even have a chance to say goodbye or say anything at all."

She looked at me in a knowing way. "When Finn was in an accident a few years ago, all I kept thinking was… what was the last thing I said to him?"

"Yeah." I sighed, trying not to recall my sadness.

"You'll have that chance with Hawk."

"Yeah." It should have made me feel better, but it didn't. "If he calls me back."

CHAPTER EIGHTEEN

Lara and I tried to get back to what we had been doing before Finn's phone call, but I think both our minds were preoccupied. It wasn't until my phone rang sometime later that I felt a little more at ease. Lara looked over, and I did a half-smile. Understanding my facial gesture, she exited the room to give me some privacy to speak with Hawk.

"Hello?" I answered generically, despite knowing the caller.

"Hi." His reply was so non-descript.

"Hawk?"

"Yeah."

"You all right?"

"Yeah. Broke my clavicle."

"What? What is that?" I felt a little like I had when I was in the damn storm cellar. I wasn't thinking straight, out of pure worry.

"Collar bone."

"Oh. Oh, God. Is it serious?" A broken anything didn't sound "all right."

"No. It's fine." There he was, once again, in a way, protecting me. "A sling and some good meds. A specialist is gonna look at it tomorrow just to make sure I don't need surgery. It's late, so they're keeping me the night." When I didn't, or couldn't, say anything, Hawk asked, "Maya, you still there?"

"Just breathing," I admitted. I could. I had needed to hear his voice in order to truly believe he was all right. "I'm glad you're okay."

"Yeah."

"Can I see you tomorrow, then?"

"Yeah. I'll be home."

"Good."

It was weird. We had basically been dating for months and yet never really talked on the phone. We had always been in close proximity to one another. At the most, we would text. I'm sure that was why the phone conversation was awkward. And then, of course, oh yeah, there was the emotional distress of the pregnancy between us.

***

Finn opted to stay the night in a hotel and not come home with the rest of the band and crew, so he could drive Hawk home the following day. The superstar called late-morning to tell us the specialist had been delayed and had only then come to examine Hawk and the images. Finn reassured me twice that everything was fine and said he would call again when they would be heading back.

I asked if there was anything I could do to help with any residual media effects of the accident. Because, of course, I had been obsessed all morning, searching online about any tidbit. Finn told me Reese had it covered. But, regardless, there wasn't much to do because there wasn't much out there. The concert site's local press praised everyone on Team Murphy for not only keeping everyone safe but making sure the show did go on. And then there were the eye-witness cell phone videos posted online. It was hard to watch how close the equipment actually got to hitting Finn, followed within seconds by Hawk's head-first fall off the stage. There were different angles of the event, but no one had video of Hawk on the ground in the first few rows of pit people. I wondered how long it took for him to get up, if he needed a stretcher, if…Lara made me stop watching. It wasn't good for either of us.

After calling and confirming that Hawk would not need surgery, Finn said the two were going to start their couple-hour commute back. But because they stopped for something to eat, filled Hawk's prescription, and dropped Hawk off at his townhome, the country singer only arrived back, via taxi, at dinner time. Lara greeted him with an extra-warm hug. Even though Finn hadn't been hurt, I knew she had been concerned and wouldn't feel one-hundred-percent better until she saw him in person.

I knew that feeling, too. While Chance and Arinn bounced at their parents' sides, I cleared the dishes and waited my turn. I hadn't heard from Hawk since the phone call the night before, and I was desperate to know.

Finn didn't need me to ask. He just spoke. "He's home. He's waiting to take the pain pills because they knock him out. He wants to see you first."

"Okay." My shoulders relaxed on the fact that Hawk was home *and* he wanted to see me. "Is it all right if I take the Range Rover?"

"Yes, Maya." Exasperated, Finn nearly cut my question off.

Lara, knowing my desperation, added, "Go!"

***

He didn't answer the door as quickly as he had the last time I had been there. And there was no warm-hug greeting. Rationally, I attributed it to his lack of mobility. He was wearing a sling on his left arm, and I was sure with a fall like he took, he wasn't ready to run a marathon. But another part of me, which I also considered rational, knew the lack of physical contact was most likely due to a different type of pain.

"Hi."

"You all right?" His health was my top priority.

"It looks worse than it is. Unless I lie on this side. And then, well, it's a toss-up—looks versus pain. Come on in."

He shut the door behind us, and we walked silently back to the same family room where I had delivered the life-altering news just days before. Despite the slightest of limps, I didn't see any external injuries. But I needed, for my own sanity, to know the extent. Part of me, after all, blamed myself for him being injured. Had he not been distracted with the baby reveal, would both he and Finn have been wound-free? Would he have gotten there sooner or not have slipped?

"Can I see?" I asked with a hint of trepidation.

Silently, he lifted the bottom of his black shirt and then the waistband of his blue sweats. A tremendous red-purplish bruise tattooed his entire side. It was possibly worse than I imagined, and the gasp that left my mouth said so.

He let the garments return to their natural place. "That's the worst. My knee is just sore. And, of course, the shoulder is broken but will heal itself. Do you want to see that?" He started going toward the strap of the sling.

"No. No! Leave the sling in place. God…."

"If you blog about this, please make sure you tie in a Superman theme."

I appreciated his effort at levity. I figured it was once again for my benefit. Because there was nothing funny about any of it.

Regardless, I tried to reciprocate. "Reese is taking care of it. Besides, you look more like the Thor type."

And then there was awkward silence. Neither of us let our eyes venture from each other's, though. The true pain in the room needed to be addressed.

"Maya…" he started.

But I knew it was on me. The entire situation was on me.

So I had to be the one to begin.

"This is…it is all my fault." By his set jaw, I could see he was set to argue my truth. But I wouldn't let him. I plowed on. "Let…let me." On his silent, if reluctant, agreement, I forged forward. "You don't know this"—I took a step back and forth and back again, unable to keep still—"but my first reaction to finding out I was pregnant was anger. I was so mad. I was told something…I was made to believe something, and it wasn't true. I went through so much heartache back then." My gaze dipped momentarily toward the hardwood floor in remembrance. "Lara told me it is a miracle." I managed to look back up at him, but I was still so anxious and sad. "I don't really believe in those, though. My life hasn't really *let* me believe in those. I called my doctor in Maryland." I was rocking my feet from left to right, whereas Hawk was soldier-still. "I haven't seen her since back then. There was no reason to, between the diagnosis and Jeff's death. You know what she told me?" I hesitated only a split second, knowing he wouldn't be able to answer. "I'm not the one who is infertile. It was Jeff." Instead of their usual squint, I noticed Hawk's eyes open slightly, and I continued speaking, needing to get the rest of the tale out. "I just hadn't listened. I had run out of the office when she told us I couldn't conceive. Jeff was going to explain everything, but I shut down. I was nearly suicidal."

That time, Hawk's eyes seemed to flash in concern, hearing the extent of my despondency back then. "Mai…"

"The more he tried to tell me, the more I shut down. He learned it was better to be quiet about it, and it was," I admitted. "I was able to get myself to be me again. I was even willing to talk about other options. And then he died, and the truth never came out. This is my fault, Hawk. I want you to understand it is my fault."

Having enough patience to let me conclude, he then took his turn. "But you believed what you told me…you couldn't conceive."

"Yes," I responded right away. "Absolutely. One hundred percent. I wouldn't do that to you." I spoke the last sentence a little slower, wanting him to know my sincerity.

"Then none of it is your fault or anybody's."

"It…" I started to deny but then realized debating fault wouldn't change the end result, anyway. "Regardless, it doesn't matter. I heard what you said yesterday…when you were talking with Finn and Lara." When his eyebrows furrowed, I clarified. "How I know how this is all going to play out and that you just haven't told me. That's just it, Hawk…you don't have to. I'll take this on. It's my responsibility." I had come to that conclusion and was just happy he was safe.

"What are you talking about?" His reply was quick. "I said, you *think* you know how this is going to play out. And I'm sorry you must have walked in just after the most important part of the conversation."

"What?" My brain and voice were both tired, preparing for the inevitable letdown.

"When Lara asked if I had told you yet, I had just said how much I love you."

My eyes seemed to be stuck on him. And my feet had somehow managed to stay still. My heart, though, was a flip-floppy mess. After a beat, my words came out in a whisper and a little bit of a hopeful plea. "You don't have to say that."

"Maya!" His voice contrasted mine and then, after an exhale, calmed slightly. "First of all, I'm not a guy who says those words very easily. And second, of course I do. I meant it when I said it on the phone when you were going into the storm cellar, I meant it yesterday, and I mean it now."

What? I had never heard… We had never said…those words.

"You said it during the storm?"

"Yeah." His eyes narrowed for a second. "I said it a couple ti— And then later? That night?" His eyes shifted around but his gaze didn't leave mine, as I relived that crazy, stormy afternoon and the calm night afterward. "I thought you felt the same. I thought…"

He was putting himself out there, and I had to reciprocate. "I didn't hear you on the phone. It kept breaking up. But Hawk, I do. Of course, I do. That's what I was going to say on your mom's porch…" *I love you.*

"Me…too," he said, ever so slowly, just like he had on that porch in Oklahoma.

Knowing then that I had been right, and we had been on the same page at the same time just a few days before brought pure happiness to my heart. But it was quickly replaced by the fact that so much had also changed since then. Him telling me he loved me made the situation actually heartbreaking because we couldn't have it all.

"But it doesn't matter now with—"

"Maya?" he interrupted. "You want the baby, right?"

"Yeah. I mean, it's a complete surprise, but yeah."

"Did you ask me what I thought?"

"Hawk…." God, why torture me?

"Ask me." His words were solid.

"I know how you feel," I said. "We've talked about it—with your ex and even your step-mom…."

"Ask me, Maya."

"I can't."

It would be the final confirmation of the end. And I wasn't ready. Denial was an easier destination to travel to.

He shook his head twice and then bent his neck, so we were more directly in line with one another. And then he answered the question I couldn't ask. "I want this baby as much as I want you. And that is more than anything in this world. I want it all. I want it with you."

"But Oaklee said…" Until it was coming out of my mouth, I hadn't realized how much her one little sentence to me in the convenience store had stuck in my soul.

"What?" He was too emotional to be mad, but I could see a bit of fury crease his face at the mention of his ex-wife's name. "What did she say?"

"She said you can't, or won't, do happily-ever-after."

"That's because…" He paused, no doubt to make sure I had his undivided attention. "It's because I never wanted it before…because it wasn't right. But you walking into my life changed all that."

Tears instantly invaded my eyes, as I listened to him say things I had refused to let myself even consider. "Please mean that."

"Maya…." With his still healthy dominant right arm, he pulled me to his chest.

I heard him wince at the obvious physical pain my body pressing against his brought. And I knew I should let go, but I couldn't. I liked feeling our hearts beating near one another's. I liked feeling secure. I liked feeling loved.

I wasn't downright sobbing, but tears were spilling across my cheeks. "I didn't mean to, though." Maybe because things were going so differently than I had scripted in my mind prior to arriving at the townhome, I still felt a need to clarify…to confirm. "I didn't mean to get—"

"Stop saying that," he commanded. "I don't think that." He kissed the top of my head. "I love you."

"The doors just opened."

"What?" Hawk asked, as he gently pulled me apart from him.

"When you walked out the other day," I explained, looking at him once again. "I was okay for a little bit. I knew it was a lot to process. But when you didn't come back and especially when I thought you were angry at Finn and Lara's? Everything was closing in. I couldn't breathe. There was no way out. Everything seemed to have plowed in so quickly. I may as well have been in that cellar or on the crowded elevator or in that car off the ravine."

"Shit."

I hadn't said that to make him to feel bad, though. "But the doors just opened, Hawk." I reiterated and wiped the last few straggler tears away.

"Stay with me," was his response.

My brain, once again, had to pause, reverse...keep up with our very active and emotional conversation. "I have Finn's car." It was the first thing that came out of my mouth.

He did a half-huffy breath. "The man has a whole fleet of them. He can spare one."

I knew that. Finn had told me that repeatedly. My answer was partially just a spontaneous reaction and partially needing that last confirmation that Hawk really did want me to stay.

"Yeah. I can stay tonight." My first legitimate smile in days spread across my face, as I touched his whiskery one. "It will reassure me that you are really all right."

"I am now." Instead of touching *my* face, his hand went to my belly and our baby-to-be. I saw the reflection of my eyes glistening in his as he said, "And I wasn't just talking about tonight. Maya, the other night, when you were here, I was going to ask you to move in with me. I couldn't believe you were going to look at places or were even going to stay a little while with Finn and Lara. I wanted you here with me. And then...well, when you told me about the baby, I didn't react well. I promise you it was just shock. It was a weird gut reaction. I'm sorry for making you doubt how I felt. I was just trying to figure out how I thought I couldn't even dream of having all of that with you and there you were saying it was actually happening. It didn't seem true. Remember what you told me the very first time I kissed you? You needed time to digest or..."

"Reflect. Appreciate," I confirmed.

"Right. I just didn't come back fast enough, like you did. That's my fault. But I wanted you to move in with me then, and I absolutely still do. I would get down on one knee if I wasn't hurting so bad and...I don't have a ring. Plus, I really want to do that right...at the right time."

Just when I thought I couldn't get more emotional, he went and laid that on me. I know my mouth was open. If I tried to shut it with a vice grip, I don't think it would have budged. I simply stared at him, and Hawk, already knowing me so well, knew to keep quiet and wait.

"Everything you just said?" I finally managed. "Yes. Yes, to tonight and moving in." My cheeks rose in a smile. "But, Hawk, the other... the..." I didn't even want to say "engagement" or "marriage," not when I wasn't convinced it was real or that it should be real. "Don't do something out of obligation or because your dad didn't. I—"

"Maya, neither could be further from the truth. I'm not my dad and that doesn't even factor in to anything. How I feel and how you feel does. Period. Got it?" He spoke with resolve.

"Yeah. I just want you to be sure. And when it is the right time?" I realized my answer would be, "yeah."

CHAPTER NINETEEN

Between Hawk's meds making him drowsy and my pregnancy and emotions tiring me out, we fell asleep pretty early that night. It wasn't a solid one on either of our parts, though. Even with medication, Hawk had the obstacle of feeling pain nearly every time he turned. And I found myself waking up periodically just to check to make sure he was okay and to confirm that everything was real. It was true…he loved me and wanted us and our baby.

I swore he might have been thinking similar thoughts when I woke for good that next morning to find him sitting up in bed and watching me with the most serene smile on his face. "It's nice waking up with you in my bed," he said.

"Our bed," I amended, feeling so refreshed. "Unless moving in meant the spare bedr—"

"I asked you to move in?" He went along with my teasing tone. "Must have been the pain meds talking. Surely, I—" When I moved my hand to smack him, he yelled out, "Uh, uh, uh, wounded soldier." When I retracted my arm and placed my lips on his, he murmured, "Mmmm-hmmm, definitely *our* bed."

"Good." I smiled. "Now, what do you think about painting the room lavender and having throw pillows scattered—"

"Oh, brother."

I laughed at his all-male response and let him off the hook. "Just kidding." In just the few silent seconds that followed, a sweep of emotions hit me, and I spoke them out loud. "I was so scared, Hawk. I could have dealt with you being mad at me for the rest of my life, but when Finn called and said what happened—"

"I'm fine," he consoled, in a solid, reassuring way.

Regardless, I wiped at a damn tear. My emotions were definitely on alert. And I wondered if it was because I felt close enough to him to let them be, especially with those three special words having been spoken, or if it was the pregnancy hormones. I suspected it was a little bit of both, and I couldn't really complain about either culprit.

"And, by the way, I was never mad at you," he continued. "Frustrated when you wouldn't talk with me? Yeah. But I left you when you'd just found out about the baby, and you thought I wasn't coming back." He paused. "I can understand how that shook you. I'm sorry."

I felt my eyes get misty all over again. But it was true. My heart had been breaking.

"But you came back, and I didn't listen. I kind of have a bad habit with doing that, I guess."

I hadn't listened to Hawk or to the doctor years before in Maryland. Both times, I should have. It would have shortened or stopped the pain altogether.

"Hmmm."

"I love you," I replied to his typical Hawk murmur and then realized it was the first time I'd actually said those words out loud to him. I had dittoed his declaration of love the night before with a "me, too" kind of response but never had used those words. God, did they feel good and right.

They must have to him, too because his non-traditional reply was, "Lavender like crazy then, sweetie."

Even though I didn't care for his current bland wall color, I was not a girly lavender gal. "No. No purples."

I looked around at his very simplistic master bedroom. Identical white lamps resided on the identical nightstands, flanking the bed that didn't even have a headboard. The only other thing in the room was a chest of drawers with a lantern on top. Was that perhaps a security measure from growing up in tornado alley?

"It wouldn't hurt, though, to have some shelves with knickknacks and some artwork or photos," I said honestly. "The rest of your place has some character. Why not in here?"

"It's just somewhere to crash," he said plainly. "No one sees it. If they do, it doesn't matter."

It brought up something we had never talked about. We had managed to know a lot about each other over the past few months. But the years after his divorce? I knew he couldn't have been celibate, but what about other women?

My curiosity must have registered on my face because I hadn't asked those questions out loud, yet he prompted me with, "You wanta know?"

"If you want to tell me."

After a piercing of his eyes, he closed his lips first and then spoke. "I've met girls. I've kissed them. I've even slept with a few or so."

I tried to kick away the jealous streams that were rushing through my body. I had no right. I had been living my life those years, too.

His next words softened, eased, and practically erased those feelings, though. "But there wasn't one—not one, Maya—until being holed up in that hotel with you, who I wanted to get to know better." He did a quick lift of his mouth and touched my healing hand.

I leaned over to kiss him and accidently rubbed against his sore, T-shirt covered side. Usually, he was a bare-chested sleeper. But I knew he didn't want me to see the injury any more than necessary—just like he tried not to let the pain of my touch show. But the strain on his cinched eyes said it all.

"Sorry," I said instead of the smooch.

"It's all right. You just don't realize how much you move until you can't even go an inch without your side screaming out at you."

"I know. I wanta help. How about if I make you some breakfast?"

"No, Mai, I'll get it."

"Hawk, am I living here or not?"

"I damn well hope so."

"Then I can get breakfast. You take it easy." I draped my legs off the side of his bed and started to get up.

"Nice shirt." He spoke of his red tee I had heisted for makeshift pajamas the night before.

It happened to be the shirt he had been wearing our first night in Louisville—our first time. Before I could comment, his phone rang and he acknowledged the caller. "It's my mom."

"Does she know?" I questioned.

"About?"

"About the baby and your accident?"

"Baby? No. Fall?" he said, and I immediately noted how his word choice minimized the severity of what happened. "Yeah. She found out somehow. She left a message yesterday, and I texted her back that I was fine. But I haven't had a chance to actually talk with her. I'll get back to her."

"Hawk! Talk to her now. If it's anything how I was feeling, she needs to hear your voice. I'm sure she's still worried."

"Okay. Okay," he partially huffed.

A little more relaxed, I asked, "Coffee?"

"Strong." His lips twitched up for a millisecond as he winked his right eye and picked up the phone.

***

There wasn't much food in the kitchen, and I wondered if it was because he had only done essential shopping since we had only gotten back from being gone for so long. But then I thought of my own house and realized how much I had learned to minimize since Jeff had died. Out of habit, those first couple of months I had continued to buy food as if there were still two of us. But then, consequently, I found myself throwing away rotting fresh produce when the sole survivor wasn't able to eat it all herself.

Hawk did have coffee, though, and half and half. So I started immediately brewing, while locating mugs and spoons. The thought of drinking coffee or eating anything strong was turning my stomach. I was quickly finding out that morning sickness was not an old wives' tale. But I was hungry, and I knew Hawk needed something in his stomach, too, especially with the meds. I found some English muffins and settled on toasting a couple of those. Then I cut up a couple bananas, and took out some cashews, chocolate chips, and honey. I would probably skip the final two but left the options open for Hawk.

Walking into the adjacent dining area, I set the food and silverware on the red and white placemats adorning the circular wood table. I had a feeling they didn't get much use and were mostly for decoration. Hawk hobbled in, still on the phone with his mother. He tilted his head upward in my direction, in an obvious way to ask if I was all right.

When I nodded, he spoke into the phone. "Hold on, Momma." Placing his cell momentarily on the table, he asked me, "Can I tell her about…?" His eyes dipped toward my stomach.

"Up to you."

He planted a sweet kiss on my forehead and picked the phone back up. "Momma, are you sitting down?" After the slightest of pauses, he said, "Well, maybe you better." I went back to pouring the coffee into his mug as he continued, "No. I said I'm fine." And then he just told her. "Maya's pregnant. We're gonna have a baby."

The ease in the way he said it—the peaceful, calm look on his face made me erase the last, tiny lingering doubt that he had any qualms about my pregnancy or our future. And that made me nearly tear up in happiness. We were complete.

I refocused on Hawk's voice as he sat down at the table and spoke with his mom. "What do you mean you knew? I...we haven't told anyone." He looked up at me as I placed the coffee in front of him and then sat across the table. "But she didn't even know then." As he paused, listening to the phone, I started putting the pieces of the conversation, and my role in it, together. "Really?" he questioned his mother and then again after a pause said, "Why didn't you say anything?"

Looking directly at him, I prompted, "She knew? About my pregnancy?"

"Your symptoms and some kind of weird mom intuition," he confirmed to me and then spoke to her again. "She is." He listened before replying. "No. Why? Whatever it is, say it." His tone with his mother had suddenly changed to agitation. "No, and I don't want you to even think that. It's not—"

He stopped speaking and looked at me. I knew he was trying to give me a reassuring look, but it didn't necessarily work. It was obvious something was disturbing him about his mother's reaction. It was concerning...not so much for me but for Hawk. I knew the level of respect he had for her. I wasn't going to touch my food until I knew what was transpiring.

"No, we didn't plan...but Momma, it doesn't matter. Maya and I can't be happier." He listened as I nodded my head, trying to reassure him. "Yes," he told her in a confirming kind of way. "Oh, you knew that, too?" With that comment, I could tell he was relaxing a little. But the question made me once again curious, and Hawk could tell. "How much I love you and the little bun," he answered my non-verbal question, and I couldn't help but internally blush. "Momma," he started back into the phone but then seemed to have been cut off. "Are you sure? I don't want you to—" After a few words from the other end, he said, "Okay," and then, once again, spoke to me. "She wants to talk with you."

I felt the rims of my eyes open. Me? Why? Feeling like I needed the support, I switched seats so I was next to, and closer to, Hawk.

"Hello?" I spoke tentatively into his phone.

"Maya, congratulations." The voice I recalled from a few days before greeted me, but I couldn't tell in her inflection where her emotions really settled.

"Thanks," I answered cautiously. "You could tell I was pregnant when we were there?"

"It was a guess. Yeah. But you didn't seem to know, and that should be something first between the man and woman."

Huh. "I didn't even know I could get pregnant," I offered. "I was told I couldn't. So it didn't even cross my mind."

"Oh, I didn't know that."

"It was a medical mix-up. My husband—"

She cut me off. "That's all right. That's your business. I apologize for what I said—the little, uh, warning—before you left here."

I practically spit. It hadn't just been my paranoia. She really had given me the momma warning. But why?

Luckily, Della continued before I had to ask. "I knew Alex was happier than I had seen him in such a long time. And if what I was guessing was right, I knew he was ready for a family. He was ready because of you. I just didn't want him deceived into it."

"Oh, Della, I would never do that," I claimed instantly.

I liked Hawk's mom more and more. She knew her son. She knew what had hurt him and didn't want it to happen again. It had been my fear, after all, with Hawk, too.

Knowing it was his turn to be curious, I rubbed the top of Hawk's hand and continued to speak with his mom. "And there is no need to apologize. You were looking out for your son. That's the kind of mom I hope to be."

"You will be, and my son will be a fantastic dad."

"He will." I softly smiled at the dad-to-be.

"So," Della offered, "you'll let me make it up to you with a real home-cooked meal sometime soon."

I recalled her words on our departure from Oklahoma. "I'm taking your word that there will be many."

"Get my son to visit more often," she said with brightness, yet sincerity, in her voice.

"Well, with my folks both gone, I'll definitely need some parenting advice and maybe some pointers on dealing with Alex." I emphasized his birth name on purpose and "Alex" shook his head.

"Good luck." His mom laughed in good humor.

"I'll give the phone back to him."

"No, that's okay," she said, surprisingly. "I got all kinds of people to call. They heard about his horrible accident."

"He's fine," I consoled the mom in her. "Just needs some ice and TLC."

"Don't let him do too much." She pegged her son. "It's just like him."

"I won't," I reassured her.

"Congratulations." She said with even stronger, legitimate enthusiasm.

"Thanks." I placed the phone on the table.

Hawk, finishing his sip of coffee, sassed, "Ice? That has your name written all over it."

My laugh was loud, partly because I hadn't thought about the ice connection and partly because it got rid of the tension I had felt initially talking with his mom. "You're right. I was kind of looking forward to the TLC part, though."

"Me, too."

***

Sitting on Hawk's doorstep was a red vase filled with red

roses and white lilies. An envelope with my name was displayed prominently right in the center. Touched by the sentiment of not only the romantic red flowers but the white ones bearing my middle name, I rang the bell, readjusted the grocery bags, and put the bouquet in my other hand. I could open up the card once inside.

But he didn't come to the door. Instead, I heard an incoming text. I placed everything back down and fished for my phone in my crossbody purse.

Open up the damn envelope, Maya. The text from Hawk read, followed quickly by, *Punch bug* ☺

I shook my head, knowing he was somewhere in the home watching me, and did what he said. Inside was a key—just a key. But I knew what it was for and all that it meant. I inserted it smoothly into Hawk's front door, gaining access to his townhome—my new home. Clutching the key and, once again, gathering the items in my hands, I shut the door behind me.

"Hey…." I managed to call out, getting a little emotional from my welcome.

"Up here." His voice traveled from the second story of the home.

I walked up the carpeted steps, put my purse and key on the kitchen counter, placed the groceries, bags and all, in the nearly empty refrigerator, and continued with my gorgeous arrangement into the bedroom. There I saw similar red rose petals beautifully decorating the white and beige bedspread. But when I went to place the flowers on top of the dresser, what I saw there made my mouth drop open…if it hadn't been already. Next to the lantern was an ornate, white, two-spot picture frame. On the left side was a selfie Hawk and I had taken mid-summer, and on the other side was a piece of paper with the words, *Future photo of Baby Brannigan.*

"Welcome home." His voice made me swirl around. Propped against the adjacent bathroom doorway, he looked more handsome than I had ever seen him, and it wasn't because of his simple attire or because of his beard that needed trimmed. It was because of him—his words, his thoughts, his heart.

I took the quick few strides over to meet him and carefully melted into his strong torso. I couldn't help the tears. The flowers alone already had me misty, but knowing he made the bedroom ours in such a meaningful, thoughtful way brought the real watershed.

"You didn't need to do all of this." I pulled slightly away and dabbed my eyes.

"I did," he said solidly. "I want you to know for sure how much I love you and want—"

"I do." I stopped him as a reassurance that he had nothing to prove—he had already done it ten thousand times over. As I leaned up and feathered a few kisses on his lips, he rested his right hand on my stomach, making me remember his left arm was in the sling. "You were supposed to be resting!" I recalled our deal. I had gone over to Finn and Lara's to gather up my limited belongings, fill the Murphys in on Hawk and me, and play with the kids for a little bit. Then I went to buy some more groceries while he was supposed to nap and take it easy.

"The florist and the hardware store are about a block away from one another," he claimed. "I already had the frame. I just didn't have anywhere to put it and nothing to put in it…until now."

He knew he had me, at least emotionally, on that one, but I still countered. "Rest, Hawk."

"Bed, Maya." His piercing eyes and slightly devilish grin emerged.

He would rest—we both would—after we made love. It was the first time since Oklahoma. It was the first time since finding out I was pregnant. It was the first time in our new home together. And what better way than surrounded by rose petals, a sentimental photo, a future photo, and, most of all, love.

CHAPTER TWENTY

"When?"

"Around May fifth," the doctor reconfirmed and then looked at Hawk, who had asked the question. "Good? Bad? What?"

"Oh, nothing," he replied with a straight face. "I just don't know how I am going to remember that day. There's nothing—"

"Cinco de Mayo?" the doctor offered.

"It's my birthday!" I exclaimed exasperated, and smacked Hawk on his good arm.

"Oh…." he jested, very well knowing.

Now that we knew when the baby was due, thanks to Lara manipulating a quick appointment with her doctor for me, a whole new sense of reality was sinking in. It was still very early in my pregnancy, but I felt like I needed to get so much in order. Even though I had officially moved in to Hawk's place, I needed to make the real move. I needed to go to Maryland and get all of my things. I needed to get Allante, who I missed so much, and I needed to get my own car, so I could return the Murphy mobile for good.

Just prior to Oklahoma, I had thought I already had everything planned out and in place. Mr. Shriver was putting the house up for sale, I was going to buy a townhome or apartment in Nashville, Juanita was going to help me drive all the contents of my Maryland abode to my new place. Best laid plans, though, right? Well, in reality, they weren't the best plans. The best plans were the Round II plans Hawk and I were creating.

The first thing that needed adjusted was what I was actually going to bring to Nashville with me. I suddenly wasn't going to need a lot of my stuff. Hawk had a fully, nicely furnished home. Nothing needed replaced, nor was there much room to add things. The only true piece of furniture I wanted to bring from my house was my brown leather writing chair that hugged, rocked, swiveled, and reclined while I wrote away. Hawk said I could put it in the guest bedroom to use as my personal writing space before we turned it into the nursery. But the chair was really it. That was all I was going to bring besides, of course, all the personal items and memorabilia. That brought up the daunting task of what to do with all the furnishings. A flea market? Goodwill? Trash?

I called my ex-in-laws to tell them of my new living arrangement. I wasn't sure how they were going to take it, but they seemed all right. It was the happy-that-I-am-happy thing. I didn't tell them the baby news yet, though—not Jeff's parents, nor Sophia. I was leery of that conversation. It was going to open up some cans of worms, and I thought it might be best to do that in person.

Luckily, Mr. Shriver, the realtor extraordinaire that he was, had a solution to my moving dilemma, though. He already had a buyer for the house. Just another swift kick to say everything was moving ahead...everything was changing. But the best part was, it was a pastor and his bride-to-be, who had little money and neither had ever lived on their own. My father-in-law was pretty sure, if I was willing, that the new owners would take and appreciate the furniture and anything else. A wash of relief flooded my body. What better solution? It would be going to someone nice...a new couple. I loved that idea. And I didn't care about making any money off it, especially since there would be so much less hassle. Within a few minutes of our conversation, Mr. Shriver called me back with the new owners' acceptance of the generous offer.

Next, I called Juanita and made sure she was still able to make the drive with me back to Tennessee. I was planning on flying up to Maryland for the week, organizing, packing, signing papers, and meeting the new owners, and then she and I were going to rent a trailer to attach to my car and drive back to Nashville. I would need the extra driver for the long trip, especially toting a trailer, which I was not used to. Juanita was more than happy to take a day or two off and help, for which I was so thankful. I was going to need the support emotionally, too.

After getting off the phone with Juanita, I ventured downstairs to find Hawk in the family room. He was stretched out and watching the hockey game. I knew it was the first game of the season. One would have to be blind and deaf not to know that, especially living in Nashville. When he caught me staring at him and the screen from the edge of the room, he grabbed the remote and flicked it off.

"You don't have to do that," I offered.

"It makes you uncomfortable. I do."

"Hawk." I chose his uninjured side to slide next to on the sofa. "You enjoy it. Go ahead." I never had to worry about hockey with Jeff—he had been a college hoops guy. "I think my dad would have liked you. He was such a genuine man. From everything I heard, he was so humble and good to his team and fans. And I know for sure he was that way with my mom and me. He would have seen that in you, too, *and* how happy you make me. I kind of like that hockey might be another thing you have in common."

He kissed me quickly and said, "Watch with me."

"No. I...I don't think I can."

He grasped my hand, looked at me a long second, and then turned the television back on. I closed my eyes and gently buried my head into his taut, dependable chest. I felt his lips rest on the top of my head.

"I love you, Maya."

I looked up at him. I looked at the TV. I looked at him again. I was loved. I loved. I was breathing.

***

The night before I was ready to set off to Maryland, Hawk and I were lying in bed. My right leg was extended and wrapped around his right leg, as that was our most comfortable position with one another. I was a side or belly sleeper, and Hawk preferred his back.

"Why aren't you sleeping?" I heard his voice from above my head.

"Huh?" I asked, wondering how he knew, since my eyes were shut and I was a quiet sleeper. "Why aren't you?" I turned the question around.

"I don't sleep until you do."

"Wha—?" I started, and then realized it was just another part of his internal need to protect.

"Mmmm," was his non-descript, if not humble, response.

"I was just thinking about how much things are going to change and yet how normal it seems."

"What?"

"This—you and me…here."

"Yeah."

"It's going to be terribly hard saying goodbye to my house and that town. All of my memories are there. But knowing I'm coming back to you? I know I can do it."

"You know I want to be there for you, but I understand and respect why you don't want me to be."

He was playing with my hair. It felt good. It felt reassuring and comforting.

We had talked at length about Hawk coming to Maryland with me and assisting in the move. I knew he wanted to and a big part of me agreed. But it just didn't seem right. So much of that week was going to be a final goodbye to Jeff and the life I had. Having the father of my child handling things in the house, or even just being there, didn't seem right.

"Besides, you can't miss your weekend away with the guys." I spoke of the annual boys weekend that Hawk went to with Finn and the band.

"It is kinda heaven—fishing, drinking, hunting." When I cringed at the last word, he soothed my hand with his. "I'm always, always careful with a firearm, Maya."

"I just don't like you putting yourself in unnecessary danger."

Dealing with guns had been part of Jeff's job. But hunting was a hobby or, at best, a sport. I ranked it right up there with the unnecessary speed of NASCAR.

"It doesn't take a gun, you know. I fell off the flipping stage, for God's sake." He joked to get me to relax.

"I know." I shook my head.

"You don't worry about me hunting, and I won't worry about you lifting or carrying things."

In addition to being super-protective, he was on top of the pregnancy thing. I adjusted myself so I could look up at his face. I ran my knuckles across the scruff of his mahogany beard and gave him a soft smile.

"What?" he insisted.

"As if." And then I added, "I love you."

He blew out an air chuckle. "If you love me, you'd go to sleep."

"You first."

"Maya…"

"Good night, Hawk." I curled back into his side.

"Good night, sweetie." He kissed the top of my head and, like magic or love, I think I actually fell asleep almost immediately.

***

The week in Maryland was, indeed, hard. It was emotional. It was listening to myself...to my past...to Jeff's family as they took in the news of a grandchild who was not going to be theirs.

It was love. It was friendship. It was letting go but not forgetting—my dad, my mom, my grandma, my husband, all the detours on the way. It was also new beginnings—for the new couple ready to inhabit their first house and for me starting afresh with a man I loved and a baby I was ready to meet.

Juanita, Allante, and I arrived in Nashville late Friday night. The irony was that Hawk had left just a couple hours before for the weekend retreat with Finn and the guys. I video-chatted with Hawk when I got back on Nashville soil to show him that my black Honda crossover and small, attached trailer were still full and that I wouldn't unpack anything heavy until he returned home. I even had Juanita jump in to our conversation to confirm.

Juanita and I had a fun day touring some of the local sights on Saturday. I hadn't had a chance to discover much of Nashville yet. So I was glad to have Juanita as my touristy excuse. We saw the Grand Ole Opry, the Ryman Theater, and Music Row, where I had originally met Reese and signed the papers that changed my life forever. That town was going to be the new fabric of my life, and I was so excited.

After taking Juanita to the airport on Sunday, I came back to the townhome and put some of the small items away. I secured photos of Jeff and me that I knew weren't going to be displayed in a fabric box inside the elongated closet of the master bathroom. Hawk had already cleared out a section for me. So I intermixed some of my clothes and things in there, too.

I did place a framed photo of my parents and me in my work-room-slash-the-future-baby's room. I know Hawk had been anxious to see photographs of my parents, and I wanted our baby to have his or her grandparents in view, too. I had been hesitant, at first, to put it out. It had always caused me sadness—a life lost. But this time, I swear it brought me peace, just like watching the hockey game with Hawk had.

It was later in the evening when Hawk texted me that he was on his way home. I sat on the carpet in the downstairs family room with Allante. Although that sweet dog had been so happy to see me when I first arrived in Maryland, he had been lethargic as I cleared out the house and then as we drove across the states to Tennessee. I was worried about him. Sophia had told me his health had deteriorated during the summer, but I had refused to believe it. After all, he wasn't crying out, and he seemed happy. He was just slow and weak...but weaker and weaker by the very minute.

"Puppy love, c'mon... Hawk's on the way. You'll like him. You'll see. He left you these cool toys and food." I brushed his light hair with my hand and thought of how thoughtful Hawk had been. I picked up the rope tug toy sitting next to the little pillow and then looked at the metal dual food and water bowl—he had not even touched it. "Allante, you gotta eat. You not only have to meet Hawk, but pretty soon there's going to be a new little friend for you." I spoke of the baby. But when I looked down, his eyes were closed against my lap. "Allante? Allante?" I feared he was sleeping too much.

The garage door opening made the dog's eyes flutter and, once I heard the truck turn off and the car door close, I called out, "Hawk!"

"Mai!" He burst more than walked into the room, obviously hearing the panic in my voice. When he saw me sitting on the floor teary-eyed with my beautiful dog in my lap and knowing Allante's status during the week, Hawk said my name again but less hurried and more solemn. "Maya." He crouched down and then sat next to me.

"Allante? This is Hawk."

The elderly dog's bloodshot eyes looked up at me and then at Hawk. His paw very weakly went out to Hawk's extended hand. It was something Jeff had taught him. He truly was the Cadillac of dogs.

"Nice to meet you, sir." Hawk spoke softly and with the kindest and sweetest of words. "You are taking such good care of my girl."

Allante's paw dropped to my stomach and his eyes went back on me before he once again brought his entire head down on my lap. I stroked his head and listened to his labored breathing. I knew it wasn't good. In fact, I knew it was bad…so bad I hadn't even considered doing anything but holding him and telling him I loved him. Hawk mirrored my actions by remaining still and silent, hugging me as I held the dog.

And then it became even more silent. And I became even more still. My next words were going to bring reality and finality, and I wanted to postpone them just for a little bit.

"He is, right?" I finally managed to say.

In response to my question, Hawk reached across me and touched Allante. His sobering eyes, even before his words, "Yeah, sweetie," confirmed the dog's death.

I sobbed openly, knowing Hawk was there and would catch me. And he did. He held me tighter and rested his lips on top of my head. He let me breathe. He let me take my time. He let me grieve.

When I was able to speak, I relayed the past few days to Hawk. "He knew," I said, looking from Allante to the rock of a man beside me. "He knew about the baby. I'm convinced. He kept sniffing at my belly and tilting his head. Then he wanted to kiss me there. He never did that before. And he just laid there, so protective. He made the whole move just to…" I couldn't say the words. "Today he was getting so still and not eating. I'm glad he got to meet you. I wasn't sure if he was going to make it until you came back."

Hawk ran his knuckle across my lips, which were wet from collecting tears. "Do you think that was it? He wanted to see your new home and make sure everything was okay? And now that he knows I am here and that everything is good, he could let go?"

"Oh, God, Hawk, do you think so?" My voice came out all nasal, as fresh tears filled my eyes.

I liked his thought. I wanted to think that, too. It would be just like my precious dog. It would have been just like how Jeff would have trained him.

"Mai, oh, sweetie…" He shrugged his loose tan cargo jacket off and let me snuggle a little more definitively into his similarly hued shirt.

Feeling his body so closely enveloped with mine brought me the comfort and courage I needed to finalize the deed. "I guess I need to call someone."

"I know a vet."

"Okay." I wiped my eyes with my fingers and then dried them on my gray tank. "He should be with Jeff," I stated. "He…yeah. We need to see about getting him to Jeff's parents."

I didn't know how or if it was even possible, but somehow, we needed to unite the dog and his rescuer. And then I thought about the fact that Allante had not only been rescued, but he had also rescued me. I thought of those months after Jeff's death and how taking care of Allante and him needing me, was one way I made it through. Did Allante know that? Maybe what Hawk suggested about his brief move to Tennessee wasn't so farfetched after all.

"Yeah, sweetie. I'll take care of it."

"Thanks," I said, and sat silently again for a little while. Eventually, I turned and touched the more-than-normal scruff of Hawk's weekend-away face. "Hi, by the way," I said, with as much of a smile as I could muster.

"Hi," he echoed.

"How was your weekend?"

"I missed you," he admitted.

"I missed you, too."

God, was I glad he was home. God, I was glad *I* was

home. And no matter the sadness that was immediately surrounding me, I was sure I had found home, and it had more to do about the arms circumferencing me than the physical structure of bricks and siding.

CHAPTER TWENTY-ONE

I was going to wait, but I couldn't. I couldn't. I tried, but I couldn't.

I don't recall the drive—the traffic lights or the other cars. I don't recall even leaving the townhome. I just needed to be with him, and I needed it to be soon. I couldn't wait.

The first thing that was a little in focus was the receptionist at the studio. I remembered him from the first and only time I had been there before. It was on the very first day I had been in Nashville. He didn't seem to recall me, though. So I explained who I was and who I was there to see. Just my word, of course, was not going to let me get through the barrier doors when a national recording artist was somewhere behind them. I wondered how many Finnatics had already tried that move.

Since I didn't have my credentials with me, I said, "I'm just going to text him. He'll—"

"If he's in the studio, he won't have his phone on."

"He's not the one recording," I tried.

"Stand over there and do it." He acted like it was Fort Knox, but I did what I was told and stood near the doorway.

I'm in the lobby. Mr. Mall Cop won't let me thru. I sent the text to Hawk and twiddled my thumbs and feet. If it took much longer, I was going to make a break for it and rush the doors. Now that I was that close, I needed him that much more.

Just as I was ready to put my plan in action, Hawk, accompanied by Finn, came through the interior doors and into the lobby where I was standing. "Hey." Hawk stopped his chat with Finn and acknowledged me.

When I looked at the receptionist-guard to make sure I could actually approach the men, he spoke. "Mr. Murphy, she didn't have any—"

"She's with us." Hawk put a kibosh to any question. "What's up?" That time his comment was directed to me. I'm sure he was more than a little curious as to my sudden, unexpected arrival.

"I'm sorry to interrupt," I said. "I know you're working. I'm sorry, Finn."

"It's fine," the crooner replied. "We just broke for a couple minutes. The sound guys are tweaking some things."

He spoke of his latest single that he was in the studio to record—one I knew nothing about because he wasn't ready for any type of promotion yet. Even Hawk was a little secretive about it. I wondered why he was even part of the recording process. But that wasn't my concern right then. There were far greater issues.

"Mai?" The way he said my name, I could tell Hawk was starting to understand that my impromptu visit wasn't an "in the neighborhood" social call. "Maya, what's wrong?"

"Is there somewhere we can go?" I side-eyeballed the receptionist, who was busy trying to look busy. "I need to talk with you alone."

"Uh…yeah." Hawk narrowed his eyes at me.

"Finn, is that okay? It won't take long."

"Yeah, Maya, of course." He nodded his head toward Hawk. "The conference room."

"Thanks," I said, as Hawk took my hand and the three of us finally headed through those doors, into the hallway, and then into the room where I had originally signed all those papers to become an official member of Team Murphy.

After Finn shut the door, giving Hawk and me privacy, I leaned right in to my sturdy man's torso. While there was still chaos reverberating through my skull, the feel of his arms around me settled it ever so slightly. His face was the first thing that was truly in focus that afternoon.

He, however, was starting to emulate my demeanor. "What's going on?" He pulled me from him so we were at least able to look at one another.

"I'm sorry I interrupted. I just needed you. I probably could have waited—"

"Maya!" he exclaimed, exasperated.

"Hawk…" I let loose a big breath, closed my eyes, and then, still trying to wrap my head around what I was going to say, slowly lifted my eyes to him. "He wants to see me."

"Who?"

I took another deep breath. Did my face look as ghostly as I felt? "The asshole who killed Jeff."

"What? Why? Maya, what are you talking about? What?" His repertoire of words sounded so similar to the ones I had used earlier, during the unexpected phone call from Maryland. "See you in person? At the prison?"

I was hearing it again that time from his mouth, and it didn't sound any better. In fact, repeating it made it seem even, somehow, more real. "Hawk…." I agonized.

"Okay." He recognized my need for a break and brought me back to his chest.

I knew, with due cause, that I was tense, but I could feel it in him then, too. After a moment, he took his hands in mine and guided me to sit in one of the many red-cushioned executive chairs. He followed suit, sitting in the one next to me and wheeling his so it was right up against mine…our knees touching, our hands holding.

"Tell me. Tell me what's going on."

I was able to get it out that time, although it certainly wasn't eloquent, coming out in choppy spurts. "He's supposedly dying…only months or so to live. So he wants to get everything off his chest. He's…" I knew Hawk was going to be upset when I revealed the next tidbit, but I had to. "He's been messaging me through the blog for a little while."

"What!" Yep, his reaction was pretty much as I'd predicted.

I nodded affirmatively as he dropped his hands. "Yeah. I've been deleting them."

"Is he even allowed to do that?"

"It was through someone else. I think a family member."

"What did the messages say?" Fury creased his forehead.

"Just that he wants to see me," I repeated plainly.

"How had I not seen that?" I managed a slight smile, appreciating that Hawk still continued to take the time to read every one of my blogs.

"I monitor it pretty close, babe. I deleted them. I didn't want anything to do with it personally, and it has nothing to do with my job. I was hoping it would go away, but now the warden just called with a more formal request. That was when I found out he is dying."

"But you're not considering it, are you? There's no way. He killed your husband."

"I know," I said, probably louder than I should have.

The stress of the request and hiding the initial correspondence was getting to me. It wasn't that I didn't trust Hawk. The truth was, I wanted to pretend it wasn't real. I wanted to pretend it wasn't happening. The magic delete button had helped…until that phone call.

"I know." I spoke a tad bit softer but almost immediately revved back up again. "In cold blood. He was high and had nothing else better to do than shoot down a cop. No. No, I don't want to. But—"

"But? But what?" He tilted his head even closer to mine, his hazel eyes boring in to me.

"There is a part of me—" The stillness and simplicity of the words chilled me to the core.

"Wh—?"

"The warden said he wants to sit down with me and explain before he dies. He's found God. He's remorseful," I continued.

"You don't believe that, do you?"

My response was immediate and blunt. "No. I don't."

"I don't want you going through something like that. You don't owe him anything." He pierced those damn mesmerizing eyes at me. "Anything," he reiterated. "Don't even dignify the request with a response."

"But maybe…" I said slowly because everything was a mumbled "maybe" in my manic brain. "Maybe I should, you know, go. If anything, it would be the last time I would ever have to hear or see him again. Let him talk, and I could let him know what pain I've gone through."

"Maya, he doesn't care. He's using you to clear his own conscience. You're only going to get hurt all over again." He placed his large hands on my knees. "He could never say anything that would make it all right."

"I don't know." My mind was such a muddled mess.

"Ignore it. And pull the blog for a while. Take it down. Don't write. He won't have an outlet to contact you. I'll talk with Finn for you. I'll—"

"No." I got up from my chair. "First of all, I can talk with Finn about my job all by myself, *if* I need to."

"Ah, Maya, don't go there." He stood up to meet me, surely catching the fact that I was referring to the time in summer when he'd tried to defend my job to Finn.

I ignored the comment. "No, I'm not giving up blogging. And I don't know… I think seeing him might—"

"Maya, you don't want me to put myself in danger going away for a fun weekend, for God's sake, and yet here you are walking right into—" There was no denying it—he was clearly upset.

"He's in prison. Besides, he can't hurt me any more than he already has." Truth.

"No. No. You can't do this."

I hadn't made up my mind. I had actually been far from it. But the direct dictation from Hawk irked me.

"I just wanted to talk to someone. I needed someone to listen—for you to just listen, not yell at me." Already an emotional mess and not needing any more, I pivoted on my foot, walked to the door, and turned the knob.

"I'm not," he said, but the volume in his voice said otherwise. "Maya…shit. C'mon…."

"I shouldn't have interrupted your job." I realized I had done exactly what I asked him not to do, even though I knew he didn't care if I did. "I'll see you later."

"I'll come with you."

"No," I said, adamantly. "I need my alone time. Let me be."

"Mai…"

But I didn't give him any more opportunity. I strolled silently past Finn in the hall and then by the paunchy guard at the desk. And then I made my way out to the gray, foreboding skies of the late Tennessee afternoon.

***

I think the stress of the whole situation must have exhausted me. Or maybe I just couldn't handle thinking for one more minute about the decision I had to make or the fact that Hawk and I had argued. I pulled the comforter off the bed, dragged it to the living room sofa, and curled myself deeply under its warmth and support.

When I woke, it was to a virtual botanical garden. Resting on the floor in front of me, there was literally a barrel full of flowers in all types and color variations. I rubbed my eyes and looked across the room to where the obvious flower-giver was located. Sitting in one of the dinette's chairs, Hawk put down his tablet and looked at me.

"First of all," he said as I slowly got into a seated position myself, "I thought we established from the start that neither of us sleeps on the sofa."

I tried not to smile at his recollection of our first night together. I wanted to maintain my stance on how I felt when I had left the recording studio. But it was hard. It was hard because it was him, and, if I was honest, I knew I was being extra-sensitive.

"Second," he continued, but yet did not move, "and more importantly, I'm sorry." When I continued to stare at my ruggedly handsome man, he spoke beseechingly. "C'mon, you gotta give me a break. I just love you."

A fresh wave of emotion washed over me. As if the pregnancy hormones weren't already going to wreak havoc over me, the potential prison meeting was bound to put me over the edge. And then to add Hawk's love and thoughtfulness to the mix?

"I'm sorry, too." I sat up a little straighter. "I know you just don't want me hurt. I think I'm more trouble than I'm worth."

He stood up and came to join me on the sofa. "That's exactly what I was sitting there thinking." His lightheartedness was short-lived as he realized how serious I was. "Maya…" He sighed.

"Hawk, you always have to put up with this…with me…all the…messes. The elevator, the storm shelter, the baby, the move, Allante, and now—"

"Maya." He calmly, but with conviction, interrupted me. "Our baby is not a mess."

"No," I agreed, and, after a breath, started to say what *was* the truth. "But I—"

"Hold on."

When he got up and left the room, it shocked me. But at least he returned quickly. Once again sitting on the sofa, he put down a small stack of blank copier paper. He took the first sheet, folded it in half, reopened it, and drew a line along the fold to create two even sides. He wrote an "M" on the top of one side and an "H" on the top of the other.

Under the "H," he drew a vertical line and said, "elevator." Then he drew another same-sized line right next to it and said, "storm shelter—which I put you in, by the way." A third line warranted the comment, "the move—highly debatable." He was reciting my list back to me but omitting the baby. When he said, "Allante," he drew a fourth line and lifted his lips in a sad smile before continuing. "That motherfucker in prison." He slashed a line across the other four.

I got it. They were tally marks. And I had pretty much guessed from the start that the letters represented our names. All the more proving my point, I wanted to say. But before I could verbalize that, he started drawing multiple groups of five tally marks in rapid succession under my "M."

"What?" Confusion covered my face just as the tally marks did all over the paper.

He put the pencil down and dipped his head ever so slightly so we were directly eye to eye. "Every time I see you...think of you...knowing how much happier I am because of you...there's not enough paper in the world to show what *you* do for *me*." While my mouth hung open in awe of his words and chart, he continued. "I *want* you to come to me at the studio, in the elevator, when you're sad, upset, scared. That's part of loving you." When I brought my tented hands up to my mouth, he glanced down and breathed. Hawk was a hand-holder and protector, but he wasn't a wordsmith. And, yet, he was speaking openly and freely, just as he had when we had finally gotten everything out about the baby. I knew he meant every part of it and wouldn't take it back but, nevertheless, he still reserved his machoism. "Don't ever debate that with me again."

Wanting to soak up all that was Hawk and all that was, somehow, wonderful in my life, I crawled onto his lap. As his arm found its natural security wrap around my body, I caressed kisses onto his lips and then laid my head on his shoulder. I looked at the beyond beautiful flower arrangement. Decisions about people states away would have to wait. His arms and our love were my only priority.

***

"So, I'm dying to know, those flowers…they aren't decorations for this little party, are they?" Vanessa prompted.

"No. Not exactly." I admired the barrel full of flowers from the night before that were tucked as much as they could be into the corner of the living room.

I looked across the room to Hawk, who was busy clinking beer bottles with Finn, Carter, and a couple of the band brothers. We had planned the little Halloween gathering a couple weeks before, and a prisoner wanting a one-on-one wasn't going to derail it. Hawk and I both agreed to table that discussion for the day and chose instead to celebrate the holiday and friendship.

It wasn't exactly working, though. It was constantly on my mind. I knew Hawk could tell. I knew because it was mirrored on his face most of the time, too.

Lara nibbled on a mini-sandwich while monitoring Chance and Arinn at the table as they ate their pizza, fruit, and cheese. They knew the real prize was the cupcake, though, when they finished. Hawk had teased about my menu of appetizers and desserts, referencing the "chick thing" theme, but everyone seemed to like it.

"What did Hawk do to get so far in the doghouse that he had to buy all of those?" Lara astutely assessed.

To which Vanessa added, "Did he click a dislike on your blog?"

As I picked up a chocolate-covered treat and prepared to answer, Carter chimed in, obviously listening to our conversation. "He is so whipped," which promptly got him a smack in the arm from the flower-giver.

"He didn't need to do it. I was as much to blame." I looked my man in the eyes as he approached me.

"I'm just setting the standard for when *she* does something wrong." He kissed my temple as a punctuation mark.

"God, I'll owe you, like, personalized floor mats for the truck."

"Hmmm…" His eyebrows lifted in a dreamy way.

"Or some fancy-schmancy fishing rod," I tacked on.

"She knows you," Zeke, one of the guitarists, agreed.

"Mai?" Hawk said, a little softer and more personally, into my ear. "Your phone was just buzzing." He handed it to me.

I looked at the screen and saw that it had been Jeff's parents. Everything and everyone around me seemed to drown out momentarily as the issue of Percy Kellerman, dying cop killer, came front and center again in my mind. I had called the Shrivers earlier in the morning because I knew I needed to tell them what was going on. The warden had informed me that Percy only asked to see me. But I wanted their input and thoughts on the matter. Unfortunately, I had only gotten their voicemail. So I had left a generic message for them to call me back. There was no way I was going to tell them what I knew on a voicemail.

"Go ahead." Hawk encouraged me to call them back. Even though we had agreed to no evil-prison-dwellers talk, he knew how important it was for me to tell my ex-in-laws.

I squeezed his hand in appreciation and excused myself to return the call in the privacy of our bedroom. I didn't talk long. For one thing, the story raced out of my mouth…sort of like food-poison vomit. And, for another, the Shrivers were in a state of shock. They needed time to comprehend what I was telling them.

When I returned back to our little gathering, the kids were getting the final touches on their Halloween costumes. Chance was decked out as a bad biker dude and Arinn was Wonder Woman. It at least brought a momentary curve to my lips.

Hawk, seeing my smile fade and, most likely, my eyes vacate, mouthed the word "patio" to me. I nodded my head in agreement and watched as he walked down the stairs. I adjusted Chance's black leather vest and complimented him on his fake tattoos before telling Lara I would be right back.

When I made my way to the back patio, I simply and silently adhered to Hawk's chest. The crisp end-of-October air was brisk enough for a jacket among costumes, but it was still not enough to let me breathe quite correctly. The beating of Hawk's heart and the embrace of his arms helped, though.

"Okay." The last breath was actually quite cleansing. I smiled softly in appreciation and started to go back in to the townhouse.

"Okay?" He grabbed at my hand so I would turn and see his shocked expression.

"Yep." I put on a brave face.

"Maya, we can talk about it. What did the Shrivers—"

"No. We decided not to today. And I really think that is a good idea. They were pretty neutral, anyway."

And their reaction only confused me more. I actually wanted someone to tell me what to do. I wanted a clear-cut answer, and I knew I wasn't going to get one. Well, Hawk had given me one, but he was biased.

"Neut—?"

I cut him off, knowing I didn't want my emotions to go into overload. I truly did want to put it off for the day. "It's time to go trick-or-treating, anyway."

Lara, Vanessa, and I were taking the kids trick-or-treating in our neighborhood because the Murphy's ranch was beyond isolated and did not align itself to any neighbor-type traditions. The guys, of course, had other plans. Alcohol and video games, I believed, topped the list.

Hawk, thank goodness, was very good at letting things go—at least externally—when he knew it was what I needed. "Have fun with that," he said, in his most mocking tone.

I shook my head but knew I legitimately would. Collecting sweet treats with two of my favorite kids was the part of the holiday I could appreciate. Because, God knew, I already had enough evil and scary things to last a lifetime.

CHAPTER TWENTY-TWO

I wasn't sure what woke me, but I found Hawk sitting on the edge of the foot of the bed. A glance at the clock told me it was almost half past two a.m. My rest hadn't been solid because I had, on occasion, heard the sounds of the guys in the downstairs family room, cheering at either their own video game or a televised one. And also, while not dreaming, I knew my mind was fitful with memories and decisions.

"Hey…" I scooted up a little. When he didn't turn to face me, I asked, "Everybody gone?"

I knew Vanessa, Lara, and the kids had left shortly after we returned from trick-or-treating. But the guys had planned on staying for a while. When Hawk turned, his gaze pierced mine and not in an amorous way. I knew he had to be a little drunk, but there was definitely something more.

"What's the matter?" I tried.

"When I just came up here, I kissed you."

"Well, that doesn't sound wrong. That sounds right." I reached my hand out to rub his back. "Maybe you should try it again now that I am awake."

His words came out plain and almost taunting. "You said Jeff's name."

I was awake then for sure. My hand dropped. "I did?"

With not even a blink from him, I continued. "Sorry. It's just probably because he's been on my mind with this whole Percy mess."

"I can't compete with a dead hero, Maya." His comment nearly tore my heart in two.

"Hawk…" That time I laid my hand on top of his. "You don't have to compete. There is no competition."

I had never seen Hawk jealous, even with the vast amount of men around us that summer. And they were, by nature, a flirtatious bunch. Was it because he knew them? Or was it because saying 'I love you,' a baby, and living together was a whole new emotional playing field? Regardless, he didn't need to worry, and I wanted to reassure him of that.

I took a moment to look at him, trying to make an on-sight assessment, not only of his emotional state but of how sober he was. Luckily, I believed he was just slightly under par with both. And that was workable.

"What we have is so different than what I had with Jeff."

"Because of the baby." He was mellow but obviously agitated and hurt.

"No," I objected right away. "I said 'we'—you and me."

I applied a little more pressure—more love—to our hand connection. And I paused. I not only wanted those words to sink in, but I also wanted to make sure I got the next ones right. I wanted to tell him so much of what I felt and, yet, didn't want to degrade the relationship and love I had with Jeff. But it *was* different. There were no comparisons.

"Did I ever tell you that the first time Jeff asked me out, I turned him down?"

His eyes found mine, and I knew I had his full attention. He wanted to know. He, in a way, needed to know.

"I thought he was a playboy," I continued my story about Jeff. "But he persisted. And I found out he wasn't. He was a good guy. But I still, you know…it took me a while. In fact, I almost didn't go on a second date with him.

It wasn't this instant thing with me. Our love grew, and we had a good marriage, and I thought it would be that way forever." Breath. "You, though?" I felt my face burn and then flush in slight embarrassment, even after all the months that had passed and the intimate talks and love between us. "The kiss in the hotel in the Keys? I knew I had to go back and find you. I…yeah. I knew. And then once I got home? Every day, I thought of you."

His nose twitched slightly and his eyes seemed to brighten a bit, too. "Hmmm," he murmured, in a way I suspected he had had a similar experience as mine.

"Different. You and me. See what I mean?" I continued. "And as far as Jeff being a hero? No doubt he was. But not so much the day he was killed. He should have waited for backup. He should have thought of me before going rogue and charging in all tough-guy." I purposefully slowed down my dialogue then. "You don't have to compete. I love you."

This time, I almost got a smile. "I will always think of you, Maya."

"I know. I know. I have tally marks to prove it." I glanced in the direction of the romantic paper lying on top of the dresser, awaiting a frame.

"Not enough paper," he claimed, and I could sense him once again becoming the Hawk I knew.

"Me…too." Just like "punch bug," those words were our words of love. "How about Alex?"

"Huh?"

"When you kiss me…if I said 'Alex'?"

His abs rolled in silent laughter. "No."

"Hawk…" I said it to confirm the only name of the person I ever wanted to kiss me and as a plea to make sure we were all right. When he kissed me then, I reiterated my feelings. "I love you."

***

We had ended our evening the right way. But,

unfortunately, the next day did not follow suit. We were arguing almost from the start. And it was my fault. It was because of my decision.

It wasn't that I *wanted* to see him. It was that I felt like I *needed* to see him. Closure was a word I didn't believe in. I didn't think there could be anything that would ever say everything was over and done with and put in the past. But I couldn't live with the turmoil that, with a couple messages and a call from Maryland, had me spinning and scarcely thinking of anything else. It wasn't good for me. It wasn't good for our unborn child. And it wasn't good for my relationship with Hawk. The honest name mistake in the middle of the night was proof. It was the only thing I could do—face the demon, Percy, and move on…move on to the life I deserved and loved and treasured so much.

Hawk hated it. He was adamant that I should not go to the prison and was barely listening to my reasoning. I knew his side. I heard his side. I even understood his side. But it was still something I felt like I needed to do.

He found me sitting on the low steps leading from the slightly raised patio out to the yard. My legs were bent, and I was rocking slightly. I knew he was there even though he approached from behind and didn't say a word. Carefully, he joined me on the wooden surface. We sat in silence for a moment or two, staring at nothing but a couple of potted plants, trees, and grass. I wiped an unexpected tear and turned to him.

He dropped his left hand to my right knee. "Mai, I hate seeing you hurt. But, sweetie, I'm just trying to keep you from more pain."

I exhaled. We were going round and round. Again.

"I know. But I can't concentrate on anything. You've seen it. I want my focus back on here, on you, on us. I just feel like I have to do this. I need it…both for me and for you."

"No! Not for me."

I closed my eyes at his insistent demeanor. "I don't know

what else to say." I tried looking at him again. "Yes, I wanted you on board with this, but you aren't. And I guess I understand. But I have to. I have—"

"Maya!"

"Hawk, please." My voice actually broke that time. "I don't want to argue. Please. This is all so much without the two of us...feeling like you..."

His mouth opened like he was about to say something. But he didn't. It gave us both another moment to breathe.

Finally, I broke the silence and changed the subject. "I'm supposed to be at the bridal shower." Standing up, I straightened the ruffles of my polka dot high-low dress.

"You don't have to go to that." He stood up to meet me. "Or you can be late."

I was already late. And Vanessa didn't have many friends in town. The shower was being thrown by Carter's family. The main one had already taken place in New York, where she lived and still worked. Lara said Vanessa was superstitious, as she was not quitting her job and moving until the ring was on her finger. But none of us had any doubt. She and Carter already acted like they were married...the honeymoon variety.

In contrast, Hawk and I were acting like an old married couple. "I said I would go to support Vanessa, and, right now, it might be for the best."

He didn't sigh, but he might as well have. "We'll be gone by the time the shower is over." He and Finn were taking a short trip to Manhattan so Finn could do interviews before the CMA Awards.

"I know." I hoped Hawk could tell in those two little words how sad it made me that A: he was leaving, and B: we hadn't come to a resolve.

"Mai..." It was much more of a legitimate sigh that time. And then, "All right. Okay. We'll figure it out when I get back."

Relieved by the pause in topic, I gently brought my lips to his. "I need you to know how much I love you."

He nodded his head affirmatively. "I love you, too."

***

"Hey, in between gigs and was hoping to catch you. Can't wait to do this city with you. If I don't get a chance to call again, see you tomorrow. Punch bug." I listened to his voicemail message an hour or so after he had left it, since I had been mid-flight.

The guilt over not telling Hawk where I was overwhelmed me after hearing his genuine, loving words. Sure, he knew I had been digging in about following through with the prison meeting, but he hadn't expected me to do it immediately. And I'm sure he thought he could change my mind once he returned home. But I was convinced that facing the cop-killing bastard and showing him I had survived his reign of terror was the right thing to do. And, ultimately, it was my past and my decision to make.

I tossed around the idea of calling my protective man back and letting him know where I was. But that would either worry him or set him on fire. And I didn't want either of those outcomes. It would do neither of us any good. He would find out soon enough when he got back to Nashville the next evening and saw the handwritten note with a couple of the flowers he had given me propped beside it.

As my taxi pulled up to my ex-in-laws' that evening, I, instead, texted Hawk back, hoping he would forgive me. *I miss & love U.*

***

I slept in spurts that night in the Shriver guest room—the same room my nephews shared when staying over at Grammy and Grampy's. It was almost as if something was physically jabbing me awake. But I knew it was a mental poke in the side, not a physical one. It was being surrounded by memories of Jeff in his parents' home. Those both comforted and saddened me.

And it was knowing I still had a whole other day to wait before completing my mission. Visitors were only allowed on certain days, and the warden was already making an exception for me.

The Shrivers, thankfully, kept me busy that next day. We had a heart wrenching, yet peaceful, conversation about my decision to meet with Percy Kellerman. They supported me and were willing to go to the prison the following day, even if they would not go inside. It meant the world to me. Then we met Sophia for lunch at one of my favorite restaurants. I was, admittedly, distracted at that point because Hawk had neither returned my text nor called me. I assumed he would have at least called from the airport before they left to return to Nashville. But he hadn't. And I knew his itinerary meant that boarding the plane was about to take place.

The last part of the day, I chose to do solo. I think everyone understood. I borrowed the Shrivers' car and drove to the cemetery. I had been there during the week of the move, and it had been emotional because of the finality of everything. But this was equally as hard.

First squatting and then sitting in front of the smooth, curved, raised headstone of my late husband, I thought of how Allante's ashes were with Jeff...partially scattered on the hard, cold ground I was sitting on. I sat for a long time in the still, silent setting that only a cemetery creates. Memories of our life together, that final day, the hospital, and the trial raced and raced through my head.

I wondered what Jeff would have wanted me to do. Would he have wanted me to stay away from the whole situation and let everything be? Or would he have wanted me to confront his killer...give him hell for cutting his life way too short? Or would he have wanted me to forgive Percy Kellerman, especially since he was dying? Jeff had the heart and upbringing of parents who always wanted to see the best in people. It was what had made him a good cop. It was also what had put him at risk, especially the night he was murdered. But as the distance of his death grew greater, it was getting harder and harder to envision his mannerisms, his idiosyncrasies, and his voice. And that made me sad.

I pressed my lips up to his marker, closed my eyes, and whispered, "Thanks for keeping me on track."

***

There was a truck in the Shrivers' driveway. Since it was blocking my passage into the garage, I had to park in front of their house. I dreaded going back into the home only to have to put up with a guest who I either didn't know or, maybe even worse, someone I did. I really didn't feel like making conversation. I felt like being in the internal state I was already in. As I passed the truck on my way to the front door, I noted its similarity to Hawk's, making me think he was probably at that same exact moment just entering our Nashville townhome and seeing my note. As I opened the front door, I closed my eyes, imagining Hawk swearing, swiping at the paper...

But he wasn't. At least not at that exact moment. Because he wasn't in Nashville at all. He was right there in the Shriver living room.

I'm not sure if my mouth dropped open or if the vocalization of his name came first, but they both definitely happened. "Hawk."

All three of them stopped whatever they were doing and were standing there looking at me. Mrs. Shriver had a sad kind of smile on her face, while her husband looked like he was trying to stand as tall as his new guest. Hawk, though, looked more worn than I had ever seen him. Sporting a dark blue, plaid pattern, his button-down hung loose and wrinkled over his black jeans, and his hazel eyes were mixed with the type of red only tiredness or worry created. And I guessed his was a mixture of the two.

"Maya," he said plainly, while pinning me with those eyes.

"What…? How did you…?" I couldn't formulate any complete sentences.

"We caught an earlier flight back to Nashville," he explained as Mrs. Shriver closed the front door behind me. "Got in this morning."

"And? Oh, my God. That *is* your truck." Everything was starting to register. I asked the question but I already, unfortunately, knew the answer. "Tell me you didn't. Tell me you didn't drive here."

"There really wasn't another option."

"By yourself?" My eyes felt like they were the size of the tires on his truck.

I had driven it. But it had been with Juanita, and we had taken our time. There was no way if he gotten off a plane earlier in the morning, he should have been in Maryland that quick. Oh, my God.

"Maya…" Even if he was upset, he knew my issue with driving tired. So he pacified me. "It's okay. I'm okay." He paused for the slightest of seconds. "But I could use a hug."

I blinked more than closed my eyes and then, at first, tentatively wrapped my arms around him. I was trying to determine his temperament. But the safe, familiar feel of his body entwined with mine made me put that aside and, instead, just treasure the touch I had missed over those past couple of days.

"Don't ever do that again," he whispered firmly in my ear.

I released our bodies and looked up at him. There was tension, but I could also see the relaxing of some of his facial muscles. His eyes were becoming a little less squinty…his jaw line a little less rigid.

"How did you find—?" I knew my note had said I would be at Jeff's parents, but I had not given an address or their phone number and he, most certainly, hadn't called me.

"We have Sophia's information listed for the backstage passes." He spoke of our summer stop in Baltimore. "I called once I got near town."

Oh. "What about the CMAs? You're supposed to be—
"

"We'll talk about it later," was his abrupt end to my query about the major awards show. He was supposed to be working it as part of Finn's team.

"I didn't mean for you to come up here. I—"

"Clearly." There was a *definite* minimizing of the eyes that time.

Thank goodness for Jeff's dad, who could sense the bit of tension between Hawk and me. "You sure we can't get you anything? To eat? Drink?" He was looking at Hawk.

"No, sir. I'm fine. Thanks so much."

"How about you, Maya?"

"I'm good." I turned to my kindhearted ex-father-in-law.

I couldn't help but think how incredibly hard it was for him and his wife to see their son's widow with another man—a man who'd driven miles and miles to be with her. And, also, to witness our embrace and have the new knowledge that there was a baby between us. I knew what an adjustment it had been for Sophia. And even though I had spoken of Hawk with Jeff's parents and they had given me their blessing, I was sure this scene, on top of what was going on with the prison, had to be painful.

"Everything all right at the cemetery?" Mrs. Shriver asked.

I automatically glanced at the photo of Jeff on the mantel. I had been the photographer of that one. He was holding a beer and hugging Allante. There was a genuine smile on his face and a large tongue-pant on Allante's.

"Yeah."

"The flag still there?" she asked.

"It is. There are so many little things people still leave…" My voice faded as I then looked at Hawk.

It had to be incredibly hard for him, too. He was surrounded by everything "Jeff." There were the photos, his family… But we had that talk. Did he still trust what I had said about not comparing? As if reading my mind, Hawk took my hand in his and gave me a quick, little squeeze. It made both me and my ex-mother-in-law smile slightly.

"Are we sure we can't talk you into staying?" Jeff's dad questioned the broad man by my side.

"No, sir." Hawk's manners, which I had determined were a fantastic mix of both Della and John, shined through. "Already got the hotel. Thanks, though." He then looked at me. "But Mai, if you're ready, I wouldn't mind heading out. I am a little tired."

Even though I was sure he added that last little line on purpose, I didn't let it show. Now that Hawk was there, I wanted to be with him. I wanted to talk and hopefully not argue. "I'll go get my bag. It's in the—"

"I already have it in my truck," he said and took a couple steps toward the back of the sofa, where he picked up his forest green hoodie. "Sir. Ma'am." He extended his hand to each of the Shrivers.

"We'll see you before you both leave." Her words were a mix of question and hopeful statement.

Before I could answer, Hawk did for us. "You got it." His response made me think he was staying for a couple days. But could he? And did that mean he was on board with what I was doing?

"I'll call you tomorrow after I…" I looked at Hawk. I looked back at Jeff's parents. Not needing to say anything more—everyone knew what the "after" was—I just simply said, "Yeah."

Hawk shook Mr. Shriver's hand once more as we left my ex in-laws in the entryway of their home. When Hawk tossed me his car keys, I truly knew how tired he was. He, who drove everywhere, was relinquishing the task to me. I had done that to him. He was that tired because of me. I breathed in as best I could and started the truck as he gave me the name of the hotel and leaned to the side window to go to sleep.

CHAPTER TWENTY-THREE

Hawk managed to snooze on the approximate twenty-minute ride to the hotel but immediately became macho-man again upon our arrival. He carried both of our bags to the front desk and confirmed our ground-floor reservation. Even in his haste and probable fury, he had been thinking of me and my fear of crowded elevators.

We walked in silence to and into our room. When he laid the bags on the sofa, I stayed back. "What?" he asked, noting my distance away from him.

"I know a lot of that before was just for my in-laws' benefit." I spoke of the handshakes and kind words. "How mad are you at me?"

His exhale was loud and partially included my name. "Maya…."

"Hawk, tell me," I encouraged. "We need to be strong enough to yell or tell each other—"

His voice raised like I had asked and expected it to, but it did make me flinch slightly. "I was pissed, okay? Talk about telling each other? What were you thinking, taking off like that and not letting me know?"

I didn't cry. There were so many emotions coming from every single solitary angle of my life they almost counterbalanced each other. I was so sad, distraught, and worried that I couldn't even cry. In a way, it helped, though. I was able to speak clearly and say exactly what I felt instead of losing it altogether…which I knew was somewhere right around the corner. "I was just trying to respect how you feel. You were against it, and I understand why. And when I thought about it, I realized this didn't need to concern you, anyway. It's about me. It's about my past and my—"

"Of course, it has to do with me." At first, his voice was just as raised as before but then became a little softer…yet just as adamant. "If it has to do with you, then it has to do with me. If it's you…it's me." He let his statement register in my brain for a few seconds before taking a couple steps toward me. "Maya, don't you know I wouldn't let you go through this alone? I know I was—I am—against it. But that doesn't mean I'm not going to be beside you."

My whole body instantly relaxed. He wasn't fighting me any more about it. He was just there to support me.

"Beside me and protecting me." I took the remaining couple of steps to him.

"Well, I want to. You need to let me. I'm in love with you, Maya. And the thought of you and little bun in danger? Even if you push my buttons, I want to be there."

"I'm sorry." God, was I. "Thank you." When he shook his head in the way that said he couldn't believe what I had put him through but was calming down, I flashed to where he should be. "But what about the CMAs tomorrow?"

"It's fine," he said with simple authority.

"Hawk, what about Finn?" Once again, I felt like I was putting Hawk's job in jeopardy. I didn't have to worry about mine—Reese had anything with the CMAs covered.

"He has plenty of people. Plus, he's not presenting or up for anything this year."

"But he is performing. So you should—" I cut off my own sentence, realizing Hawk was suddenly on his phone.

There were a bunch of "yeahs" in between a few pauses, as he listened to the other person on the line. And then,

"You tell her." And Hawk handed me his phone.

When I looked at the screen to identify the person Hawk was speaking to, I saw Finn's name. My eyes opened as my mouth tightened. I shook my head "no" at my personal protector. But he just shook his head, too, and took a few steps back.

"Finn?" I spoke into the phone, knowing Hawk was basically forcing me to. "I'm sorry. Hawk"—I emphasized his name while glaring at him—"shouldn't have come here. He should be—"

The crooner himself cut me off then, too. "Maya, Hawk is exactly where he needs to be and who he needs to be with. Let him be there for you. He wants to. I think he even needs to." My glare softened as I listened to Finn describe the sensitive side of one of his best friends. "And you do, too. Lara and I are thinking of you, okay? We have your back if you need anything. But I think you have it more than covered with the guy next to you."

"Yeah." Agreed. "Finn? You're not premiering the new single tomorrow, are you?"

"Nope, waiting for a better time," he said about the mysterious song.

"It's not 'Dark and Dusty' the sequel, is it?" I managed to joke.

He laughed. "No. This one has a lot more heart."

I said goodbye and handed the phone to Hawk who promptly hung it up and placed it on the dresser. "It was almost like you had that call planned," I semi-teased.

"Well, you are pretty predictable with some things," he admitted. "Hightailing it up here, though, threw me a bit."

"I'm sorry." I knew I had already apologized, but it seemed like I, personally, couldn't do it enough. I really did feel bad, especially witnessing his physical and emotional state. "I can't believe you drove up here like that."

"I did out of pure adrenaline, worry, and, yes, a little bit of anger…and I'm exhausted." He saw my cringe—it wasn't well disguised. "Come here," he soothed me. "I love you."

My voice was partly muffled, being suctioned onto his chest. "So, which one?"

"Which one what?"

"The customized floor mats or the fishing rod?"

I expected him to laugh, but he didn't. Instead, he pulled me arm's length away. "You want to get me either of those, great, but Christmas is fine. We're both going to do things, Maya, but hopefully we'll learn from them."

"I'll still take a flower or two every so often." I smiled.

"You got it." His partial chuckle was followed by a sweet kiss, which started to turn into so much more.

"I thought you were tired," I said but slid my hands under his shirt.

"I am. Rock me to sleep." He pulled me as tight as he could up against his body, and I lifted my legs so he could take us to the bed.

Our lovemaking was a mix of extremes. We were both emotional and had missed one another. But it also felt like Hawk wanted to keep me as protected as he could by covering his massive body on top of mine. His kisses were soft. Yet I could also feel a little of his self-proclaimed anger and fear letting go as his body met mine.

"You okay?" he asked after, while still breathing a little heavy.

"Yeah." I touched the scruff of his beard. "I'm sorry for worrying you when you got home."

He was able to hold my eyes but only for a millisecond, and then he brought my head swiftly to his chest. I could feel him bring his arm up to shield his eyes, but I didn't look. I knew he didn't want me to. I had never seen tears from that strong and sturdy man, but I was pretty sure they were threatening then. I pressed my lips onto his torso to show my love and appreciation for all he was.

"I love you...so much," he mumbled above my head.

"Me...too."

***

Hawk was not pacing, or on his phone, or reading, or sleeping, or anything else. He was looking straight ahead, just like he had been when I had turned away from him earlier and had walked into the prison. I imagined he had stood there the entire time just like that, propped against his truck, looking at the institution's door as if he were an additional guard.

When he saw me, he took swift, sturdy steps in my direction. My steps were lighter and faster. I had just confronted a killer. I felt sick. I felt dirty. I needed it erased.

Once again, his arms were like magic. They transported me to a safer, happier world. He let me be…just like that. He didn't speak. He just held on tight.

Eventually, I lifted my face away from the soft cashmere of his sweater and looked up at him. But I didn't dare take even one step away. I breathed in. And again. It was like I was coming down from one of my claustrophobic episodes.

"Tell me. You got to tell me what to do. What do you want me to do?" he asked, and, for the first time ever, I could tell he was at a loss for how to help and protect me.

"Just take me away from here, okay?"

He took my hand and led me to the truck. Once we were both in and the engine started, Hawk's right hand immediately claimed my left. It felt so good. It felt so reassuring. It felt so right.

While we drove away from that horrific place, he took some side glances at me. I knew he was worried. I wished there was some way or some thing I could do or say to reassure him that I was fine. But I still needed a few minutes to debrief internally.

"Do you want to go see Jeff's parents?"

I knew I should, but I definitely wasn't ready for that. They would be emotional, and I would feel a need to comfort them. But I couldn't do that just yet. Selfishly, I was the one who needed comforted. "No. I…no. I just need you and me for a moment."

"Yeah." He squeezed my hand. "You got it."

The silence continued in the car. My window was down despite it being cold, and Hawk didn't make a snarky remark about it. He was being very patient and allowing me to dictate how things were going to go. I knew he was heading back to the hotel. It was really the only place he knew in the area, and it was our home base. But then, en route, another destination came into sight.

"Pull over here," my voice whispered.

"Really?"

When I didn't respond, he did as I asked. I got out and he followed. It was a park. There were some teens playing…hockey. For a change, it made me feel safe and at home. I sat down on the bench and stared at the players. They seemed good. Maybe one day one of them would be the future Noah Collins.

Hawk, sitting next to me, prompted, "Sweetie?"

"I feel free…so free. I…honestly? It was one of the scariest things I have ever had to do. But it was so…it was such a release. I feel like I can put it away. I thought I had before, but I…I didn't…not completely. I don't care what happens to him. I said what I needed to. And he did, too. And it's not like I forgive him, and I'll never forget. But I'm free. It was the one last tiny puzzle piece that had fallen out, and it didn't seem like it mattered. You know, it was on the frame and was solid and didn't affect the image, but it completed everything." It was my turn to put his hands in mine. "Thank you for being here. Because if you hadn't…truly, I think I would have walked away. My legs were shaking so bad. But then I thought about you being right outside, and I knew nothing could hurt me."

"Oh, God, Maya. The whole time you were in there, I think I aged ten years. I nearly had a stroke, thinking of what he was saying to you and how he was making you feel."

I positioned my head against his. "All I could feel was your love and protection."

"A given."

***

We did end up going then to see the Shrivers, who also seemed at peace with what happened at the prison. And then after meeting up with Juanita and her boyfriend for dinner, we went back to the hotel room to watch the CMAs on TV. Hawk covered my mouth with his hand when I made the comment about how he should have been there. But when I kissed it, he let go.

"Well, the plan was for you to be there, too." As Hawk's guest.

"I know," I lamented as I snuggled against his side on the bed. "Maybe if you still like me, I could get invited to the next one," I teased.

"Maybe," he said in just his Hawk way, and did the slightest of smiles along with the piercing of his eyes.

***

Instead of driving straight back to Nashville that next day, we were going to make a stopover in Louisville. It wasn't a direct route, but Finn and Lara had invited us to Arinn's second birthday party at his mom's house. And, of course, I wanted to go—not only to celebrate their little girl but to thank the Murphys for their support. And, oh, it was Louisville.

Set to leave Maryland really early that morning, Hawk asked if I would mind making one short stop first. I was surprised by his request. He wanted to see where my parents were buried. I hadn't visited their graves during that trip. For one thing, my focus had been on Jeff. And, for another, I just didn't often. But especially not knowing when I might be back in the area again, I agreed.

Hawk cut the engine and helped me out of his truck. My parents were not in the same cemetery as Jeff. Theirs was a little farther out of town, back near where the three of us used to live when we were a happy, little family. Of course, their resting place had been a debate from the beginning—one that I had been too little to have known about at the time. My dad's parents had wanted my father buried in Canada. My mother insisted he lived and planned on living in Maryland for the rest of his life and, sadly, that was true. She also wanted to be buried with him—no matter what…no matter where her life would take her after his untimely death.

I knelt down next to my parents' grave. It was taller than my late husband's, partly because there were two of them buried there, but really because of my father's celebrity status. It was a simple marker, though. Taking up most of the stone, in the center and top, were a bunch of engraved trilliums—Ontario's flower. "Collins" was etched on the center bottom with their first names and dates just below. Next to my dad's was an engraved small hockey stick and next to my mom's was a camera.

"What's with the camera?" Kneeling next to me, Hawk's hushed tone was respectful of the setting.

"She was a photographer…artist. That's how they met. From what I was told, it was pretty much love at first click."

"I would have liked to have known them."

"I would have liked that, too."

He was staring straight ahead at the grave as if he were actually talking to them. "I'd tell them how much I love you and will always take care of you."

I took his hand and he helped us stand, united. Leaning in to his side and resting my head on his shoulder, I wanted to think they already knew that. After all, I sure did.

***

Hawk clasped my hand tightly as we boarded the glass elevator in the same Louisville hotel we had stayed at our first night together. It was, once again, fairly packed. But I didn't feel quite as apprehensive as I had that time in July.

Hawk talked me through it just as he had before, apologizing all along that our room was up so high again.

As it turned out, it wasn't only just as many floors up. It was the same exact room! I shook my head.

"That had to take some finagling."

"I know people who know people." He smiled.

"I wanta shower before I change…at least rinse off." I had already washed my hair that morning. "I feel kinda grimy after being in the car all day." We had left early in the morning so we could make it for the dinnertime birthday party. I thought it was kind of late, but Arinn was a road baby, so both she and Chance were used to the odd and late hours.

"Fine, sweetie, I got stuff to do." He gave me a gentle kiss and swatted me into the bathroom.

When I reemerged into the connecting dressing area in just a towel, lip gloss, and mascara, Hawk was standing there. His eyes scanned my body as he handed me my long, red dress with a slit up one side and a dipping V neckline. We had, at the last minute, picked it out together in Maryland, since I certainly hadn't thought to pack something so fancy on my spontaneous trip up there. He also handed me my lacy black bra and panty set.

"Oh, uh, thanks."

I was both a little taken back from his action *and* the way he looked. Standing in front of me, he was completely, handsomely clothed. He had on a black shirt with matching tie, a light gray vest, and coordinating pants. It was all form-fitting and so damn fine. Breathtakingly so.

"You look—crap—handsome."

It was a breath more than a laugh. "Crap handsome? Is that a compliment?"

"You look like I may need to check the lines on that suit."

Even his smile was sexy as he raised his eyebrows in a suggestive way. "You're very welcome to."

I pursed my lips a couple times, knowing I needed to

resist. We would be late. Instead, "Are you sure this isn't too dressy? It's a two-year-old's birthday party!"

"I think it might be a little too casual, but if you want to stick with the towel…" he teased, and I was glad things were so much more relaxed with us since sitting on that bench, watching the hockey game. We seemed better than ever, in fact.

"All right!" I laughed.

When I started to slip on my undergarments, Hawk just stood there against the doorframe, staring. He had never done that before. I was a little shy but mostly turned on. The way his hands were in his pant pockets suggested to me he might have been, too.

After I got the dress on, he stood a little straighter and said, "Go check the bucket in the living area. See if we need some ice."

"Really?" I thought of the irony.

"Yeah. We might want a drink later."

"You're not just ready to get rid of me for a while?" I teased.

"Nope." He squinted his eyes quickly yet mesmerizingly. "Actually, I'm hoping everything we need is in there."

Hawk followed me as I went into the other room. I grabbed the hotel's ice bucket from the mini-bar, hoping it was already filled. But I could tell by the weight and temperature alone that it wasn't. Regardless, I opened it up, envisioning myself tromping down the hallway in my eveningwear, looking for the nearest machine.

But I didn't move an inch. I would be surprised if my lungs had even moved. Was I breathing? The bucket was, indeed, empty…all except for one thing at the bottom. There was an open black box with a stunning, gleaming, diamond ring centered in its cushion.

"Not the ice you were looking for?"

I managed to look up and at him, my mouth as open as the box and bucket. "Better," I practically whispered.

When I didn't say or do anything more, Hawk took

another step toward me. "Do you want me to take it out?"

My head nodded up and down like a slow-mo bobble-head. This was happening. It…it was …Oh, my God.

Without letting his gaze drift from mine, he took the box out and then the ring itself. "Mai—"

"I love you."

"Good. That makes the answer I want much more likely." He seemed calm which helped regulate me a little back down from the shock. "We talked about this—wanting it to be the right time. And I think after listening to what you said in Maryland, this is it. I know it is for me. It's not about either of our pasts or because of circumstances. This is about us. This is about how much I love you." He bent his one knee and lowered his magnificent body down to the floor. "Maya, will you please marry me?"

I didn't hesitate. I didn't wait. I practically exclaimed, "Yes. Yes!"

When he stood up and slipped the ring onto my finger, a happy tear slid from my eye. I looked down at the beautiful ring. It was so perfect. There was a magnificent center cushion-cut diamond encircled by two rows of additional smaller diamonds. And the band was made up of a bunch of mini-diamonds, too. I felt like a princess.

"It's gorgeous. When? When did you get it?"

"Picked it up in New York. Finn had set me up with his jeweler. That's really the reason I went."

"Oh…I'm sorry."

"Yeah," he said, just a tad mellow. "I wasn't sure exactly how or when, but, you know, Mai, I think it worked out—"

"Perfectly," I said at the same time he did. "It's perfect. All of…all of this. I love you."

"I love you, too."

As we started kissing, I began to, indeed, check the seam of his pants. "You think the birthday party can wait?" I suggested.

"Maybe even until tomorrow."

I started to say that I didn't want to miss the party but then realized there had been a certain inflection in his voice. "Wait. What? What does that mean?"

"The party is tomorrow and jeans and a casual shirt are fine." I shook my head as he laughed. "The two of us do have dinner reservations, but there's time for me to slip you out and back into this dress again." The eyebrows, those eyes…that smile.

The last time we had been in that room together, we had been two single souls traveling the roadie life and connecting for the first time. Now we were on a different road…together. And I couldn't wait to experience every mile and memory.

CONTINUE MAYA'S JOURNEY
IN
EVERY DAY YOU & ME

Maya Collins has lived through more than her share of heartbreak—losing both her parents as a child and then her husband tragically years later. It shattered everything she believed in about happiness. But now, with Hawk by her side and a miracle baby on the way, the social media assistant has come to trust in second chances.

When a sudden death rocks the Brannigans, Maya feels the tug of past grief and its lingering pain. Amid the family mourning, a dangerous situation causes an immediate and long-term threat to the beautiful future she is building. Maya must ignore the feeling of the walls closing in and the pleas of those around her in order to protect all she holds dear—even if it means risking her own life.

Set against the backdrop of the country music world, *Every Day You & Me* is the powerful continuation of Maya and Hawk's emotional journey in the bestselling novel *Every*

Mile a Memory. Poignant and realistic, it is a story of resilience, healing, and familial love … and a reminder that you should fight for what matters but understand you aren't always in charge of where life takes you.

CHAPTER ONE

"I like that it's a secret," I whispered while looping my arm through Hawk's and leaning in closer to him.

Placing his finger to his mouth in the universal quiet sign, he nodded. "But first, we need to get through this."

An abundance of greenery, pillar candles, and the white-cloth chairs we were sitting in created an elegant and romantic setting for Carter and Vanessa's nuptials. Carrying white hydrangeas, Vanessa wore a similarly colored, fluffy dress with a long train, and Carter was in a black suit with white shirt minus any kind of tie—he was too hip for such traditional attire. As best man, Finn stood beside his good friend/drummer, while Lara did the same as matron-of-honor for Vanessa. Rounding out those standing up for the couple on their special day were Carter's younger brother and sister.

Since both the ceremony and reception were taking place in the same Nashville venue, the staff needed to quickly transform the main area. The soaring room with exposed beams would go from rows of chairs and an aisle to one of food and linen-covered tables. To expedite the transition, the wedding party took pictures out front while the guests were asked to go to the temperature-controlled patio for cocktails.

Hawk and I, however, did not. *We* retreated to a secluded spot in the intimate, upper-level mezzanine. We had only made the decision to do so the day before and, luckily, Tennessee's laws were bountiful. We could. So, we were. It was our turn for the exchanging of words … minus all the hoopla.

Both of us had that type of wedding before—his ending in divorce and mine leaving me a widow. This time around, we didn't want everyone making a fuss with parties, hugs, food, and … everything. We simply needed us … and the minister, of course. It was our secret.

Because of that, I didn't walk down steps or an aisle like Vanessa had. I didn't wear white. Although, my beaded dress was a soft cream hue. I also didn't have my father give me away, but I swear I could feel him with me. There was *no* family with me for that matter. And that would have been the truth even if we weren't saying our vows covertly.

Hawk was my family. He and the precious baby growing inside me were my life and my future. Since it was the last weekend of November, our "little bun's" actual arrival was still many months away. However, I counted him or her as our wedding witness, even though the state did not require one.

Adorning the darkest of blue suits, which coordinated with his tie and my eyes, Hawk gazed lovingly at me as the minister performed the wedding ceremony. While it was basic and quick, we did make sure to include some personal touches, too. I wore my late grandmother's necklace and had a trillium in my hair to honor the other side of my family's Canadian roots. In turn, Hawk wore his father's gold watch—one he rarely took out of the box—in memory of him. And we exchanged a few of our own words.

Accompanied by instrumental music playing below us in the historic building, I was the one who spoke first. "I was up most of last night trying to think of the perfect thing to say to you today."

"That's what all the shifting around and kicking me in bed has been about?" Hawk mock grumbled.

I shook my head. There was definitely something else on my mind disturbing my sleep, but I wasn't going to let it spoil our day. "You'd think it would be easy," I forged on. "I blog for a living. I use words constantly. But what do you write—say—to the most important person in your life on a day which means everything? I can't find the perfect words. I can't. I keep internally editing. I think it's because I will always want to add more. I don't want to just say them today. I want to say them for a lifetime." I was going completely rogue and off the cuff, which wasn't like me. "We both know that lifetimes, though …" I swallowed and cut myself off. I didn't need to say it. We both knew. "So, what I want to make sure to say today is, I am so thankful for"—I squeezed his hands—"you working for Finn, for me taking a girls' trip … for a bucket of ice." I paused as we both smiled at our first unforgettable meeting in the Keys. "It could have ended there. Thankfully, though, we both took chances—you with a kiss and me with a job—and we've had friends to help us along the way. It is that wonderfully complex. But it is also as beautifully simple as I love you." I tilted my head up and he dipped his so our lips could meet.

In contrast to my lengthy monologue, Hawk's vows were suited for those social media sites that have character count limitations. Yet, his words were beyond meaningful. "Every mile traveled, every memory made, every day lived … I want them to be you and me." He winked and added, "Me, too, Maya."

I recognized, of course, those final two words before my name as our *I love you*. "How'd you do that?" I whispered my exasperation and appreciation. "It was perfect."

"I've been thinking of and replaying them in my mind from the moment you accepted this ring." He encircled the engagement rock on my finger—the only symbol we would have of our union for a while since we decided to get married so spontaneously and had only gotten engaged a few weeks prior.

I shook my head. I'd met a number of macho men in my life, and Hawk was definitely a top contender. He didn't let a lot of people see the internal, soft, emotional side of him. When he showed it to me, though, I could not be in more awe or love.

It was weird how different I felt after those couple minutes of words and the minister's proclamation of my new status as Mrs. Brannigan. I knew paper didn't make the commitment. The two people involved did. Somehow, though, formalizing our bond provided me a sense of calm and rejuvenation. It was like mystical doors had opened and I was breathing more completely than I, perhaps, ever had.

When we rejoined the formal wedding festivities out on the patio, my internal happiness must have shown right through. Smiling brightly, I was taking a selfie with my new secret husband when Finn and Lara approached us. Drinks in their hands, they were obviously done with *their* photo obligations.

"You're acting like *you* are the bride and groom," Lara noted my demeanor. "I mean, pretty soon, though, right? Did you pick a date?"

Finn must have noticed my look at Hawk because he hardly let his wife finish her question before proposing one himself. "Shit, you already did, didn't you?"

"What? Did what?" Lara looked at her husband.

"That's why you wanted to make sure you two could take off for a bit." Finn Murphy wasn't just Hawk's long-time employer. He was mine, too, although I had only joined the country music star's team six or so months prior.

While I looked at Hawk again—curious about Finn's time-off comment—Lara started putting the pieces together. "They did what ... got married?"

I poked Hawk on his side. "Are we going somewhere?"

He rolled his eyes at Finn. "Thanks, man."

"What? Maya doesn't know? Rule number one: no omissions from your wife."

"True," Lara seemed to give a particularly knowing look at her husband. "But is it also true that you are already married?"

When Lara opened her eyes wide at me, I looked at my husband. My husband! His shrug encouraged me to give up the guise, which was pretty much already over. "Yeah," I admitted. "Actually, a few minutes ago." I felt Hawk's hand affectionately playing around with mine. "We went upstairs and had the minister perform—"

"Oh my God! Congratulations!"

Lara's interruption and hug attack caused my hand to separate from Hawk's. I was laughing lightly and looking at him from behind Lara's embrace as he accepted Finn's congratulatory handshake. The men were much more than workmates. They were truly good friends.

"Oh." Lara suddenly pulled me away from her. "But I wanted to throw you a—"

"No. No. No. No." I declined any party or shower or whatever Lara had in mind. "We don't want all that." I reclaimed Hawk's hand. "Please. Okay? And wait to tell anyone. We don't want to take away from Vanessa and Carter's day."

"It was kind of last minute," Hawk added.

"But perfect." Then I got back to the question unanswered. "We're going somewhere?"

"Yeah, with those two." Hawk nodded toward the corner of the room where Carter and Vanessa stood.

"Oh." I hoped my one word came out without the sound of the disappointment I felt.

Finn had gifted his drummer a trip to Monte Carlo so the newlyweds could gamble and go on wine tours. It was perfect for the flashy couple, who loved that life and didn't want kids. Although I got along with both of them, it was far from my style and not where a pregnant me wanted to spend her honeymoon.

"Maya ..." Hawk shook his head and, boy, was I relieved when he said, "Do you think I'm crazy? No. How about the Keys?" Although it was asked as a question, I was pretty confident he had already booked it. And then he confirmed. "Tomorrow."

That destination couldn't have made me happier. "Really?"

"I think we might have to be holed up in that room

again." Even though he was referring to an extremely frightening experience, it was also what had propelled him and me to first meet and start our story.

As I curled myself onto Hawk's side, I replied the way he did when feeling free and easy. "Mayyybe."

Glancing at the spot on the patio that hosted a mic, stool, and guitar, Finn announced, "Looks like they're ready for me."

"You're not singing the next single, are you?"

As the "real" bride and groom entered the patio area, Finn answered his right-hand man. "It couldn't be a more perfect time … especially now." He swung his finger at Hawk and me.

"God, Finn," I exclaimed. "What is the song about? I want to promote."

My job for team Murphy was to assist his publicist, Reese. I was mostly in charge of a day-in-the-life blog, updating social media, and looking for anything with Finn's name on it. Yes, Reese would handle the releases and contacts, but I was always informed … except for that song, which seemed to be coated in complete secrecy.

"Hope you like it, Maya," Finn spoke to me and then to his wife, "You too, Beauty." He gave Lara a kiss, handed her his glass, and then started walking toward the mic.

"You haven't heard it?" I was shocked the singer's own wife wasn't privy to the new song.

"No. I'm in the dark as much as you. Though, in the past, if I don't know about a particular song, it's something extra special."

"Maybe you and I should be jealous," I jested to Lara. "Hawk seems to know all about it. What exactly happens at these boys' weekends?" The only thing I knew about the song was that the lyrics were composed during their last getaway.

"Supposed to just be hunting and fishing," Hawk grumbled. "Give me his bourbon." He reached his hand out to Lara. "He owes me that much."

As Hawk took a swig, I commented, "You're making it seem like the song is awful."

"It's …" He shook his head, alongside a second sip. "No. You'll see."

Not needing an introduction, especially with the crowd of friends and friends-of-friends, Finn spoke into the mic, setting up the song. "For the newlyweds and for all them girls. This is called 'Boys' Weekend.' I hope you like it." And so started the vocals …

> *It's the weekend we look forward to every year*
> *An escape to the woods for good times and some beer*
>
> *It's bro code, man cave, tunes, and some fishing*
> *It's gambling and hunting and not doing dishes*
> *There's no worries, no honeys, no fast-paced worlds*
> *But why, oh, why, do we keep talking 'bout them girls …"*

From the opening lines and chorus alone, I knew the latest Finn Murphy song was definitely not a sad, depressing tune like his "Dark and Dusty." As big of a hit and as beautifully done as that one was, I turned it off every time. It made me go back to a dark place of my own—losing my husband, Jeff. "Boys' Weekend" seemed to have the beat and tone of a classic country song but with a lighthearted, fun twist. It was a little unusual for Finn, but I could already see how it would be a hit.

The multi-award-winning country music artist looked directly at his wife as he started singing the next lines.

> *"I admit it, I started with pics of the kids*
> *And vids of what both of them did*
> *But after a few brewskis or two,*
> *The stories came out about me and you*
> *I explained to the guys—my bros in the band*
> *What makes you the most beautiful"*—he nodded at Lara—
> *"one in the land"*

It was obvious then that it was really a song about them—his wife and their kids, who were with Finn's mom during the adults-only wedding festivities. The lyrics were, indeed, going to be special like Lara had predicted. She wasn't one for the spotlight, and the family kept their private life pretty much that. It didn't mean, though, that it wasn't one robust with love. Finn and Lara Murphy were the ultimate relationship goals in my eyes. While being on Finn's concert tour all summer, I had personally been witness to their devotion to each other and their two children— Chance, age four, and Arinn, freshly minted age two. And since then, the family had truly become very good friends of mine.

Finn was right. I did like "Boys' Weekend." Not only was it sweet, but it would also be easy to promote. Fans loved songs that connected directly to the artist themselves. I was already beginning to think of hashtags for social media. First, though, I needed to refocus on the next round of lyrics.

"A long time ago we were nothing but friends
Our life now, though, has a happily ever after end
Strawberry blonde with eyes like the sea,
God, girl, what you do to a man like me

"It's bro code, man cave, tunes, and some fishing
It's gambling and hunting and not doing dishes
There's no worries, no honeys, no fast-paced worlds
But why, oh, why do we keep talking 'bout them girls …"

Hawk took another gulp of Finn's bourbon, and I looked at him with curiosity. He truly was acting a little bizarre, and I knew it had to be about the song. But why?

"The drummer was next after a few hands of cards"

On the lyrical proclamation of Carter's profession, the

groom raised both his hands in the air, as if the party gathered didn't already know he was the drummer. In contrast to Lara, Carter wasn't shy. He was a happy-go-lucky, talk-straight kind of guy. And his new bride had a similar personality.

Smiling and shaking his head, Finn continued singing.

"He easily concurred that he had fell hard
So in love with her dark eyes and matching hair
Long, loose waves of curls everywhere"

Oh, that was why Finn said it was the perfect time to premiere the song. I got it. It was a song about marriage. And Vanessa could not have been more thrilled, as her dark waves bounced with delight upon hearing the lyrics.

"Awww, this is perfect for their wedding." I nudged Hawk, who put his finger up to his mouth, urging me to listen.

"A casual fling was all they were s'posed to be"

Finn's lyrics made Vanessa shrug at her parents.

"But that all changed when he got down on one knee
Now forgoing his playboy ways
The two have made it to their wedding day"

"Woo-hoo!" Carter exclaimed midst lyric.
Finn chuckled a bit as he began his next line.

"God, he said, what that girl can do to a man like me

It's bro code, man cave, tunes, and some fishing
It's gambling and hunting and not doing dishes"

"I think I have the chorus down already," I proclaimed, starting the next couple words.

"Maya ..." Hawk shook his head.

There's no worries, no honeys, no fast-paced worlds
But why, oh, why do we keep talking 'bout them girls...

I didn't expect it. He's a man of little words,
But whiskey made him spill about his girl
Sun-kissed hair brushing her shoulders and eyes,
They met by chance on a search for some ice"

Oh ... my ... God. I know my mouth dropped open, but I couldn't actually feel it. I was in such complete astonishment. Finn was singing about Hawk and me. The country music star's focus became solely on us, and I could tell Lara's was, too. But I was turning to my other side and looking at Hawk. Even though his mouth was perfectly straight, his hazel eyes were blinking and looking at me. I couldn't determine what his exact thoughts were, and I couldn't spend the time thinking about it. I had to listen ...

"Each letting go of things from their pasts
To find a new love that'll forever last
Now there's a baby due sometime in May
And he loves it and its momma in every which way"

And then after the last round of the chorus, Finn ended the song with words that were more spoken than sung, "*I'm coming home, baby.*"

In the midst of the sound of applause, the singer replaced the mic to the stand. Some of the wedding guests gathered around Vanessa and Carter. Others were talking with Finn.

My focus, though, was solely on one person and one person only. "Hawk ..."

His response to my awe was to lift the corners of his mouth ever so slightly and take a final gulp of the bourbon. "What?"

It was true what the lyrics had said—Hawk was a man of few words. In that way, we were opposite, for sure. But, as he had proved in our vows, a lot of times it was quality, not quantity that mattered.

Right then, though, I needed more. "What? What? Hawk … God, that was … You … That was beautiful." Even if it was Finn who was singing it, I knew Hawk had some part in the song. "If we weren't already married, I would be down on my knee asking you."

"Well, I'm glad you said *yes* before hearing some silly song."

I ignored his attempt at being nonchalant. "It wasn't silly. It's how you feel."

That time his response was more truthfully heartfelt. "Yeah, but you already know that."

"I do." I stroked his cheeks and close-cut, dark-auburn beard. "And the people in our lives know, too. But still, it … it was special." I started putting the pieces together. "No wonder the song was such a secret."

AVAILABLE WHERE BOOKS ARE SOLD

HAVE YOU READ LARA AND FINN'S STORY?

CHECK OUT *COUNTRY ROADS*

A young woman content with her solitary life.

A rising country music star.

They were friends once …until their lives took them down separate roads.

Now, years later, when a child volunteers his uncle to sing for a fundraiser, LARA FAULKNER realizes it is none other than her college pal, FINN MURPHY. As the two get a chance to reconnect, Lara reveals to a compassionate Finn details of her shocking past and the traumatic decision she had to make.

Through trust and love, the bond between Finn and Lara deepens as the country singer manages to get an emotionally scarred Lara to let down her self-proclaimed walls. But will secrets, lies, and tragedy cause a bumpy detour on their road to complete happiness?

Emotional, dramatic, heartwarming… fall in love with *COUNTRY ROADS* – the first in a continuing

series by author Grea Warner.

CHAPTER ONE

Back where I grew up, the roads went from cement to gravel to dirt and back again with no rhyme or reason. They twisted and turned. They intersected weedy railroad tracks and climbed hills with no guardrail to guide. These roads were surrounded by pine covered woods filled with Mother Nature's creatures who, only part of the time, knew their forest-like boundaries. People gave directions not by street names but by landmarks like a country inn or a local market. It was on these roads that I found my freedom…that I learned to escape. I could go miles without seeing a soul and get lost in the simplicity of nothingness.

It's funny how similar the city is. The subway's darkness burrows underground and leads you directly into a hub encompassed by the pure chaos of millions. Everyone walks fast among the buzzing noise and brilliant lights, not daring to make eye contact. Again, I have nowhere particular to go. There are masses around me, but I am still alone. I feel that sense of solitary freedom, and that is all that is important.

The truth is, it doesn't matter what your surroundings— be it the big city, suburbia, or a quaint country town—your heart and your memory follow you wherever you go. There is no escaping what lies deep down in your innermost self. And while there are things that you might want to forget, there are also those precious few keystones that you wish you could not just conjure up but bring back to life with a click of your heels. That only happens in fairy tales, though. And, every once in a while, when the cities and the towns become that cliché small world rolled into one, it happens in schools too.

***

"My uncle can sing!" first grader Wyatt blurted out in the computer club I was in charge of toward the end of each school day.

"Oh, okay. Well, that's a good idea. But maybe instead of your uncle, we can have a talent show and some kids can sing." I didn't want to totally douse his idea. "Your uncle can come and watch us perform, Wyatt. In fact, I'm sure he would like that better than singing himself."

The brown-haired child's offer had been in response to a sad topic we had been asked to talk about with the club classes. One of the students had been diagnosed with cardiomyopathy. The principal and school counselor wanted to develop a plan for helping the family. Because of the numerous hospital visits, they were trying to find ways to raise money to assist with some of the costs. And they also wanted the students to be aware, empathize, and help if they could with fundraising ideas. There were reasonable suggestions like selling popcorn or cookies, having a car wash, and making artwork to sell. But having a family member sing was surely not one of them.

"But he's good, Miss Faulkner."

"I'm sure he is, Wyatt. I wrote it down." I added his idea to the paper but had no real intention of having it actually make the official list I would give to Principal Lennock. Uncle "Joe Shmoe" could thank me later for the save, I smirked internally.

Available Now- in Ebook and Print

ABOUT THE AUTHOR

There really wasn't any other path. Grea Warner knew from a young age that she wanted to write. She was born to write. First it was in diaries with little metal keys and in written tales that she slipped to friends in study hall. School newspapers, a college television drama, and the soap opera world were next. After producing and writing a local show, she decided to delve into the world of the novelist. When her fingers aren't tapping out her latest book filled with angst and romance, Grea can be found hiking the trails or jamming to her favorite country artists on the radio.

Website: http://greawarner.com/
Facebook: https://www.facebook.com/Grea-Warner
Twitter:@grea_warner
GoodReads:
https://www.goodreads.com/author/show/17230140.Grea_Warner
BookBub: https://www.bookbub.com/authors/grea-warner